Totally Bound Publishing books by Sara Ohlin

Graciella

Handling the Rancher

Seducing the Dragonfly

Flirting with Forever

Rescue Me

Salvaging Love

Igniting Love

Promising Love

Rescue Me

PROMISING LOVE

SARA OHLIN

Promising Love
ISBN # 978-1-83943-753-3

Interior text design by Claire Siemaszkiewicz
Totally Bound Publishing

Published in 2021 by Totally Bound Publishing, United Kingdom.

Totally Bound Publishing is an imprint of Totally Entwined Group Limited.

PROMISING LOVE

Dedication

To my beautiful sister-in-law Tricia and my sister Megan, and all the fun we used to have at Spa La La. Maybe we'll find another gem like it someday. Cheers!

Chapter One

"Lachlan MacGregory, are you ever going to kiss me?" Ruby whispered. Leaving the key in the lock, she turned so they fit flush together, front to front. *What's a successful, sexy woman supposed to do anyway?*

She'd been waiting for an eternity, it seemed, for Lachlan MacGregory to make a move, or accept her move. Okay, so it had only been a year and a half, but everyone knew time could be its own demon or goddess when love was concerned. Either way there was magic involved when sashaying around her feelings for Lachlan. It definitely felt more demon than goddess-inspired to her. Time she'd spent watching him casually date other women, while she herself had occasionally casually dated other men. They'd circled each other. And yet the forces had never aligned in their favor. Either that or neither one of them had been brave enough to step up.

Until now. Now she was going to ask for what she'd dreamed of. "I want you to kiss me."

Aside from the deep burn in his gorgeous eyes, Lachlan's face was stone and his entire body was rock-hard. Large and sexy, but most definitely a fortress at the moment. Or most moments, she'd found, during all the months she'd been drooling over him. She almost spun away from the freeze.

Maybe he's not interested? It didn't seem so, standing this close to him—even though he held himself like granite, his eyes gave him away. Using that courage, she searched into those golden-brown depths of his. *Swirling pools of secrets or desire, or maybe both.* They had a mind of their own and she'd caught him many a time sneaking glances her way. There were a few occasions when she'd almost made him laugh, and she'd taken them as wins. *Stoic statue of a man. Does he even know how to laugh?*

She hadn't actually ever gotten a laugh from him, but she had gotten a different, more subtle and—in her mind—no less cute reaction. His mouth sometimes quirked up on one side while his left eyebrow did this little curve as if to say, "*Give it your best, woman. You can't break me. But it's damn amusing to watch.*" The man tried so hard not to show emotion, not to ask her out, not to kiss her. So, right this perfect minute when he was walking her upstairs to her apartment above his pub, when neither one of them was dating someone else, when the tango had put them smack-dab together, she'd decided to take matters into her own hands, and words and mouth. *That's what a confident woman does.*

Or was it the hot-and-bothered woman in her? Because his body was so supremely close to hers, whisking all rational thought away from her. She'd tried flirting with him, and she'd tried ignoring him. It was time to ask for what she wanted, and hope, *hope* he felt the same. She leaned against him. He was a wall propping her up by her apartment door. She couldn't take it one second longer. Pressing closer, she reached up and placed her hands on his shoulders. His hands immediately went to her waist. *Oh, the warmth.*

"You're drunk," Lachlan said. He looked down at his hands on her almost as if he couldn't believe how they'd gotten there. One twitched and he gripped her, steadying her or himself—she wasn't sure. But he didn't pull away. When he began to move his thumb on her waist, searching little circles, exploring the tiniest bit of her, he watched, lost in her. *Goody, goody, goody*!

Lachlan's fingers seared a brand on Ruby's skin and almost took her legs out from under her. *Nothing casual about our connection at all.* She'd known it. And maybe that gave her the power to push her luck.

"Not drunk." She pouted and got to see that almost-smile with the eyebrow betraying his attempt to remain stoic. *Okay, maybe a teeny bit drunk,* which did not dull the fact that she desired him.

"The gin and tonics were flowing to your table tonight, Ruby. And you ladies came in tipsy. I know Ellie wasn't drinking them."

This time there was no subtle eyebrow-lift, but both eyes—sparkly brown orbs that seemed to have a novel written in them, and boy she longed to read that story—lifted, his tone and his expression reprimanding. His voice was deeper. Perhaps because his eyes were both serious and searching, that reprimand went straight to her core. *I wonder if he'd reprimand me in the bedroom?*

She smiled, a full-on smile, because she, Ruby Naylor, had no problems showing her emotions, and leaned into his powerful muscles. "No, it wasn't Ellie, although the ginger seltzer concoctions you made specially for her with the cute umbrella-cherry garnish were a huge hit and calmed her stomach. You thoughtful, thoughtful man." Ruby gave his shoulders a gentle squeeze. *My God, the man even has sexy shoulders, powerful, firm.* She'd love to get her hands all over him, massage all his muscles, investigate each and every one.

"Besides, I'm tipsy from talking about love, dear man. I only had a few of your spectacular drinks. Ellie sipped her ginger drink while swooning over her life with Jackson and the new baby coming, and Natalie drinks like a sailor. But I'm not asking you to kiss Ellie or Nat, Lachlan MacGregory. I'm asking you to kiss me. Don't you like me? It's hard to tell some days," Ruby purred. She was not above using all the tactics in her arsenal to seduce him. The man was a vault and she aimed to crash through, so he'd never know what hit him. Watching and waiting on the sidelines had gotten her nowhere, except a lot of great dreams. Now, Ruby sought the reality.

He'd offered to help her drunk butt upstairs, and even though she could have made it to her apartment above his bar perfectly fine, she wasn't stupid. And whoosh, did it feel good to be so close to him. Finally. She *was* tipsy. Tipsy on Lachlan contact. It was a real thing, she could say, now that he was touching her.

His one hand clenched and unclenched at her side, then he slid it around to her back bringing them into a nice snug fit. *What is happening? Maybe I am dreaming?* His other one braced against the door behind her, almost as if he needed to balance himself, to hold on. And, holy smokes, he was looking at her now. Looking was too calm a word. His eyes had woken from their stoic slumber and were piercing and hot. And to have Lachlan MacGregory holding her, finally giving her the full direct force of his gaze? Oh, she could melt into a puddle. It was all too powerful.

"I like you." His voice was deep and quiet, with a sharpened edge to it.

"I like you, too." She watched those eyes of his, a page flipped over, or perhaps opened to her. "I've liked you for so long." He blinked. But he didn't focus on her eyes—he concentrated on her lips. A battle waged in his expression. To stay through the storm or run away to safety…which would he choose?

"Please," she whispered. *Please don't run.*

He tightened his grip on her, his fingers molding her through her jeans. "When I kiss you, I want you to remember it in the morning," he rasped out. He was standing up taller now, all traces of casual disappeared into the night. He was intent.

Yay! He does want to kiss me! Ruby almost jumped up and down in cheers, but she settled for putting her hand on his cheek, unprepared for the sigh that wove through his body at her touch, how it sang through her nerves, but also gave her joy and strength. "I promise, Lachlan. I'll remember. Will you?"

"Yes, beautiful, I'll remember," Lachlan said. He lifted her gently against the door and ghosted his lips over hers, sending shivers through her as he moved those amazing lips of his over her cheek and down her neck. Ruby's head fell against the door, while the rest of her body tried so hard to stay molded to his. He stopped right beneath her ear. "I'll remember how soft your skin is right here."

Oh, my! It was a good thing that he held her up or she might have blown away from lack of oxygen. The man hadn't even kissed her yet, and he'd stolen the breath from within her. And she could shoot herself for wearing a coat and her blouse tucked in when she craved the man's hands all over her bare skin, not just the tiny patch where he'd snaked his fingers underneath the fabric to reach her waist. Although it might cause her to combust. She welcomed that combustion.

"I'll remember how you smell, that fucking sexy, musky perfume you command."

Huh. I was wrong, I am drunk. The man has skills. Command? Does he realize he's going to brand me with his words?

Keeping her close, Lachlan took one hand away to unlock her door and walked her through the opening. Ruby had had no idea such intense concentration could be so fucking sexy. Lachlan's heady gaze on hers, while walking them to her kitchen island, without a sound, added to the feeling that she was floating. A whimper escaped her mouth and she gripped his arms to hold on. This was not the time to close her eyes—this was her chance, warm in his embrace, to see his beauty up close. *A man on a mission.* And his mission was her. No distractions allowed. The power of that type of gaze mixed with his words went right to her head and her heart and other parts of her body. All those other parts that wanted his skin, his lips on her.

"The way you feel in my arms, Christ, Ruby, you have no idea."

I do! I so do. I feel it too.

Now he'd kiss her. *Yes, please!* Lachlan lifted her onto her counter and, keeping his hands braced on her hips, held himself at the tiniest bit of distance. She had been waiting for forever for this. She'd beg. *I wonder what other talents he keeps close to his belt?* She reached to pull him closer.

"Ruby." He'd nearly lost his voice, raw, edgy need feeding out of him with one word. *My name.* Jesus, he was going to undo her.

"Promise?" he asked. No, he was going to break her heart open with one request. If she was this turned on and whimpering with the touch of his lips soft on her neck, whispering gorgeous words to her, his kiss would probably brand her. *Stake your claim, Lachlan. I'm here waiting for you.*

She nodded. "I won't forget. I promise, Lachlan."

He gave it to her then, not the kiss she was desperate for, but the smile, his true smile. It changed his face from broody stone to brilliant, handsome man one hundred percent zeroed in on her. His eyes caught the fire and a shade lifted from those dark mysteries, like he'd been searching for light and he'd discovered it in her, finally. *Holy cow!*

And he strode from her apartment with one final announcement. "Goodnight then."

What? Wait! What the heck is happening? "Goodnight?" She slid down from the counter and tried to anchor her feet on the floor because her legs were wobbly noodles and her heart was trying to beat out of her chest. Lust raced through her blood and she gripped the countertop for support.

He paused in the doorway, his hands on the frame, facing away from her, gathering himself.

No! Don't gather your wits – come here. Throw your wits out of the window with mine.

And when he faced her, he blew her world into a million pieces of stardust. "I'm going to kiss you all night, kiss you into the morning, make you remember every single caress I place on your skin because I've imagined kissing you since the day you filled out the lease and teased me about lacking any sort of smile.

When I nearly fell over at your beauty, the shimmer in your gorgeous eyes, that glow you spread out to everyone in your path. You have no idea." Lachlan shook his head, lost in his thoughts. *Or a memory?* "I've wanted to kiss you since…since you altered my world."

"Lachlan," she whispered and took a shaky step toward him. Her body pulled her to his. They were connected now and the path to him was the only one for her. It was the feeling she'd had when she first met him too, and it had only grown stronger over the months. His words validated her romantic heart that existed in a world with so many people who didn't believe, who walked their gray path and were fine with mediocrity.

He held up his hand to stop her. "Now that I know we're here in the same space." He made a circle in the air with his hands. "Now that I get to taste you, there's no way I'm going to rush it. I'm going to savor every damn second."

The man knew how to seduce, wielding anticipation like a gift, not a weapon. But she enjoyed rushing too. She *loved* rushing. *Rush me into bed with your kisses now, you wonderful man, you!*

"See you tomorrow," he said. Then the handsome, frustrating-as-hell man smiled and strode out, closing the door behind him.

Lost in the laser hit of that smile for a minute, Ruby swayed on her feet as if she were truly drunk. Then his words filtered through her loopy state, wove themselves into her heart and set her on fire. "Oh, my beautiful goodness!"

Well, she hadn't gotten a kiss. Any other man, any other spectacular moment and she might be pouting. Instead, her world had been spun in gold. She gently pressed her fingertips to her heart to feel the flip-flops it was doing. Drop-dead gorgeous, kind, sexy Lachlan MacGregory had zapped lightning through her with merely the promise of a kiss. Yet so much more than a kiss—he had *noticed* her. He did want her. Ruby held tight to the special moment, closed her eyes and cherished the luminous glow bursting in her dreams, in her heart at the promise tomorrow would bring.

Chapter Two

Damn slow Sunday night. It had only been raining solidly for a day, pouring, like the sky had been ripped open and buckets tipped over to drench the world below, but it might as well have been months. It was a cold rain that had changed the sultry, warm fall they'd been enjoying into a chilly wet mess. Business was often slower and more casual on Sundays anyway and with treacherous driving and some flooded-out roads, the pub had almost been a ghost town. He was thankful for the neighbors within walking distance who patronized his business at the best and worst of times. But tonight, Lachlan MacGregory had a smile on his face that no monsoon or slow business could affect.

He ducked inside his pub, shook the rainwater out of his hair and headed behind the bar. He allowed his smile to widen at the night that lay ahead of him. A night that involved promises and kisses and new beginnings. Ruby Naylor liked him. *Shit.* He laughed at himself. *Giddy, ridiculous.* A fucking kid at the carnival with a bucketful of tickets to spend on whatever games he desired. Better, the gods and goddesses themselves were shining down on him.

Regal and super smart, she was as pretty as a star and constantly spreading an infinite amount of goodness and beauty over the world. Her confidence and kindness were two of the things he appreciated most about her. Her loopy, sincere come-on last night had been the last straw, the point at which he'd decided to say fuck it and quit avoiding all attempts at a relationship with her. Because he wanted so much with her. Because he knew, one kiss from her would mark him forever.

He hadn't seen her all day, to his intense frustration—it had taken a million times longer than he'd planned to fix his mom's kitchen plumbing. *Old houses.* People loved them, but they were more often the devil himself. Especially discovering the "updates" others had done over the years. When he'd renovated the pub, he'd intentionally gutted the entire place so he could build up new without having to puzzle and shift around any surprises.

He'd wanted to kiss Ruby last night, every time he was near her or thought of her. Restraint was a code he lived by. It had served him well and gotten him where he was today, successful, healthy, clear-minded. Restraint and the discipline that came with routine, hard work, solid workouts and a few good mentors in his past.

But Ruby Naylor asking him to kiss her, saying she'd wanted it for a long time, putting it all out there, open and honest for him, while she pressed her warm, soft curves up against him? Suddenly restraint was a flimsy fucker. If she hadn't been tipsy, he might have allowed himself to break, but he would never take advantage of a woman, especially Ruby. So the thread hadn't snapped. *At least for now.* He'd meant his words, that he intended to savor each second. Lachlan wanted more than a superficial fling with Ms. Naylor. He wanted *everything* with her. And restraint meant not blurting that out too early.

But now that she'd given him the go-ahead, he was gearing up to be all in. He'd start slow and intentional. Tonight, he'd bring her the fancy, pretty cookies he'd picked up at the macaron shop near his mom's. Sophisticated and stylish beyond belief, Ruby also had a sweet tooth she embraced with an intense devotion. There had been many a night when she'd come to the pub for dinner and started with dessert.

"Life should be lived dessert-first, don't you think?" She'd practically cooed over his cakes and puddings.

He grinned again, picturing her gorgeous face opening the door to him. For some men it didn't take much to put a smile on their faces, but Lachlan wasn't a smiler. It took something amazing. It took something special. His grandma and his mom, his bar.

And Ruby Naylor. He'd had a crush on her since he was twelve years old. *You nearly blurted that bit out too last night, idiot.* Lachlan would never forget the first time he'd been struck by her shining smile and eyes that glittered with joy. He'd been a kid and Isaac Naylor, Ruby's dad, had been his Big Brother for six months. They'd just finished playing basketball at the YMCA. Lachlan had been in the lobby, hood up, trying to become invisible to the eighth-grade gang that picked on the younger kids—he hadn't known how to fight at that age.

"Daddy!" she'd yelled and Lachlan had glanced up in time to see her launch herself into Mr. Naylor's arms.

"My beautiful girl," the man had replied. Pure joy had washed over Mr. Naylor's face and he'd walked out, hand in hand with his girl.

Honestly, at that moment, Lachlan had been more jealous of Ruby for having a good man and a stellar basketball player as a dad.

It hadn't taken long for him to become infatuated with Ruby. She had come to swim Tuesdays and Thursdays, the same days Lachlan had gotten to hang out with Mr. Naylor. Sometimes when basketball had finished and he'd had to wait for his mom, he'd sit up in the bleachers in the natatorium, hidden behind a cement pillar, and watch Ruby swim. She had been more graceful than a dolphin. She'd flown through the water as though she belonged there. It had awed him, struck him in the chest not only because of how graceful and sleek she was in the water but because he had never belonged anywhere.

He hadn't forgotten the time he'd passed her in the hallway to the locker rooms. It was the one time she hadn't been surrounded by friends or kids clamoring to be her friend. Her face and hair had still been wet, and she'd nearly slipped on the tiles when he'd held out a hand to steady her. *"Thank you,"* she'd said and trilled out a goofy laugh. *"I could have landed flat on my bottom, if it weren't for you saving me. You're a secret prince."*

That night her mom had picked Ruby and Mr. Naylor up. The three had walked out of the YMCA smiling, belonging. Ruby Naylor was the kind of girl who'd had it all. He'd stumbled and bumped into the wall before he'd realized he'd been blindly following them out. It was the last time he'd seen her. He and his mom had left town a week later.

He'd carried the image of her face with him, dark hair slicked over her shoulders, smooth skin, glowing from the water, round cheeks damp and a bit rosy from swimming, her huge dark-greenish-blue eyes laughing and sparkling, all aimed at him. It nearly blinded him. *Pure beauty.*

When she'd shown up to lease the apartment above his bar a year and a half ago, his heart had stopped. Ruby Naylor all grown up, seriously grown up, with curves a man would be stupid not to love and cherish. And those eyes of hers still sparkling through life in pure celebration, a celebration one should enjoy every day.

She'd flirted, but she hadn't remembered him. To be fair, he'd never been in her orbit. *Not even close.* They'd only met as kids that one time when he'd saved her from slipping. Even while making excuses for her, valid ones at that, it had still stung that she hadn't recognized him. But only for a moment. Then he'd kicked himself for acting so ridiculously.

Of course she hadn't known him.

She wanted to know him now. That was the important fact.

Lachlan stuck a bottle of cider under his arm, grabbed the box of macarons and headed upstairs to Ruby's apartment. Last night seemed like a hallucination, too good to be true. Except her words, her desire for him had imprinted onto his skin so that it might as well have been a tattoo, a claiming. That was not his imagination. Seeing the smile on her face right before he'd said goodnight had nearly had him walking her right into her bed and exploring every last inch of her.

He'd been trying so hard not to make a move on her from the minute she'd walked up last year and stopped his heart. He was her landlord. That was the excuse he gave for why he got cold feet in her presence. *Not to mention she's always dating some random yahoo.* But damn, he'd been tempted. When she'd come on to him last night in the hallway, when she'd brushed his cheek with her hand, he'd felt his heart start again, or maybe simply start, like he'd been a walking dead man his entire life until Ruby Naylor had touched him.

Tonight, maybe he'd get to feel that sensation again. Tonight, he was going to make damn good on his promise. It was going to be a kiss neither one of them would forget. Once at her door he was about to knock when he heard voices.

Ruby's laughter sounded out first.

"God, that's amazing," a man moaned. "Damn, girl, you are the best." A pause then, "*Jesus*, Ruby." The same deep voice. And one long grunt of pleasure…

Silence reigned for a minute. A coiling, tightening moment of silence before the tornado came, when the sky turned that eerie greenish-gray and even the trees stopped swaying. One instant, before destruction thundered down upon the land. A bloated silence in which Lachlan's chest took a beating.

Then her soft voice came. "Feel good?"

"Yeah, love. Could you be more incredible?"

Lachlan stepped backward. His heart wasn't tripping over itself to get to her now. It was screaming at him to get the fuck out.

"You two hungry?" Another deep voice sounded through the door and beat at his head.

"Starving! Absolutely oh-my-goodness starving." Ruby's voice, full of the passion she always infused it with, was aimed at someone else. *Two* someone *elses*.

He'd been wrong, so fucking wrong. She hadn't intended to start something special with him. Any man would do. Apparently two men would do. He stumbled down the stairs in a rush to get out. He busted out through the back door and toward the dumpster, where he tossed in the cookies. The cider slipped from his arm and shattered on the pavement.

"Fuck me." *I should have known.* He'd watched her flirt and date her way through a chorus of men. No one in particular was special. It was her style. The men were all castles, falling at her feet. And he was a loner. There was no reason for her to be with him. *Fuck!*

Lachlan punched the dumpster. It wasn't the first time he'd made a rookie mistake and hit something his hand would feel the bruise from for days. It didn't matter. Nothing hurt as much as his chest did. Standing in the dark, taking deep breaths, he let the damp ground and garbage reel his senses in. The rain had stopped and humid air smothered him. Minutes, an hour later—who knew—he tried to shake off the pain and anger. He *was* angry, as he went inside for the broom and dustpan.

He was cleaning up the broken glass bottle when two men exited the back door his bar shared with Ruby's back staircase, and made their way to a car, oblivious to him. He'd seen them in the bar before with Ruby. Friends of hers. *Fucking great friends, apparently.*

"God, I love her. She's my goddess."

The other man laughed and patted his friend on the shoulder. "She's good for you." The sound of the laughter left an empty hollow in Lachlan's stomach as they climbed into a truck and drove away.

"Christ!" He swore one last time and slammed the dumpster closed, the sound ringing through his head. *She's always been surrounded by guys. There's no way in hell she's the kind of woman who'd settle for me and me alone.* After he tossed the glass in the dumpster, he locked up and headed home alone. *Again.* This time beneath a starless sky. This time without anticipating tomorrow. This time with a hole burning through him.

Chapter Three

Christ! Lachlan parked and stared at the man standing on his front steps. As soon as he saw Lachlan, he sat, like he was settling in for a nice long visit. Lachlan had zero fucks left to give tonight. He wanted to be *anywhere* else, avoid this confrontation. He didn't have the mental or physical capacity to deal with his dad right this moment. He exited his truck and approached. At least he was bigger now, no longer a puny child without the knowledge of how to deal with an addict. Who was he kidding? Did a son ever really figure out how to handle their parent who loved alcohol and gambling more than family, more than life?

Everything about this man, their entire relationship, made him feel, if he were honest, confused and angry and mostly shitty. Age hadn't made Lachlan smarter, just capable of erecting barriers. One of the barriers he'd put up was not giving his dad his address. Somehow Denny had discovered it.

"What do you want?" He stopped several feet away, habit making him wary, trying to gage his dad's mood, the kid inside him ever vigilant. Lachlan had a few loving, warm memories of his dad, early ones from when he was five or six. Maybe that was why they stayed cemented in his brain.

As he'd grown, things had darkened. He'd learned to determine if Denny was going to be high and happy, in a goofy things-are-going-swell mood, or so drunk and down that he pissed his emotions out all over anyone who was nearby. Memories battled inside his head. Lachlan walked a tightrope of helping his dad out without letting him get too close. Meanwhile he'd been grieving the kind of father he'd always longed for, even while his dad was still alive. It was fucking exhausting.

"What makes you think I want anything?" Denny sucked the life out of his cigarette and tossed the butt onto Lachlan's walkway. "Can't a father visit his boy?" *Jovial, sing-songy voice.* He'd had some alcohol, but wasn't too far gone to stumble over his words yet.

"Haven't been a boy in a long time. And the only time I see you, since I moved home, is when you're looking to gain something. So, again, what is it?"

"Jesus, I go out of my way to see my own child and this is how you treat me. A man sits down to enjoy a meal with his son, talk life and business, and he gets shoved aside." *Offended, indignant.*

A man?

Maybe he'd had more to drink than Lachlan had realized. Or maybe a deal had gone wrong. Maybe Denny had played the wrong card, literally and figuratively. Denny fumbled in his shirt pocket, hand shaking, for his pack of cigarettes and his lighter. One light after the other. One addiction after another.

He looks…small. For the first time in his life, his father's physical appearance matched the person he was inside. His face was pale and gaunt, shadows haunting his sunken eyes. The wrinkles and dry, weathered skin added on the years. He'd lost more weight since the last time Lachlan had seen him, this past summer, when his bartender Pepper had called a cab while Lachlan had escorted Denny MacGregory out through the door. It had been the first and last time his father had set foot inside the pub.

"First you toss me out of your bar—now you're too good to have me in your life—kicking me out of that, too, huh?"

You took yourself out of my life. "I escort out anyone who's had too much to drink and acts like an asshole." His dad had been drunk and belligerent, singing a tune about going into business with Lachlan. *When hell freezes over.*

"Ha," his dad scoffed. "A man can't drink a few at a pub, it ain't no kind of pub in my book."

"Great. Then find a better one. Goodnight." Lachlan brushed past him. He wished he were the kind of man who could shut out his father completely. It was what his counselor had suggested years ago. *Easier fucking said than done.*

"I only need a little bit," Denny MacGregory pleaded. Lachlan paused. He was no longer impressed with how his dad could change his tone, his temper, so quickly. From happy and manic, to indignant, then to needy and pleading, with barely a breath in between. Once Lachlan had seen the whole picture, past the addictions, to the manipulation with a good dose of immaturity, most of his fears *and* hopes had faded away. It was too bad his guilt hadn't. *And why the hell do I feel guilty for what my dad has done to his own sorry life?* Lachlan hadn't pissed it away. Denny had done it all on his own.

"A couple of hundred. So I can eat. I haven't eaten a proper meal in days. You don't want me to starve, do you?" Lachlan had heard this one before, too. He often wondered if this was the real Denny MacGregory, under all the fake layers. The fuck of it was he didn't want the man to starve, even though Lachlan knew Denny would choose booze or gambling first before he entertained the idea of a healthy meal plan.

"I don't...I don't have anyone."

You and me both, asshole. The animosity bit at him, quickly overshadowed by a hollow feeling. *Was* he destined to be like his father—alone?

Lachlan pulled out his wallet and gave his dad the cash inside, without even counting it. "Here." He leaned down and put it in his dad's hands. "It's all I've got." There was guilt here too, that he couldn't do more for his dad, take away the man's love of booze and betting, obsessions that had twisted Denny's soul dark, cost the man his wife and outweighed his love for his son. He'd gone to unlock his door when he heard Denny grumbling as he walked away.

"All you've got, my ass. You've got a thriving pub. Making money all over the place. Could really get me out of the predicament I'm in, if you cared enough. You think you're the lucky one. Maybe your luck's about to run out."

Fuck! Lachlan thrummed his head against the door. What had the man gotten himself into now?

His dad's need for one more hit, one more scheme, one more bet to go in his favor... Denny the drunk was moody and annoying, but Denny the gambler was a shady, motherfucking unpredictable character.

His father disappeared before he could comment, which was for the best, because the last thing Lachlan needed tonight was to unleash his temper on the man.

Lachlan prided himself on maintaining control of his temper. What would it say about him if he lost it now on a small, pathetic old man?

He slammed the door of his condo, grabbed his mail and followed the small light he left on in the kitchen. He opened the fridge in search of a beer, unsuccessfully, when Baby twined through his legs and purred.

He shut the fridge and picked up his kitten, a gift from his mother. The silly thing made the softest vibration against his chest as Lachlan stroked her head. "Hey, girl." She was warm and silky and yet still too skinny. Her tiny heart thudded into his hand. The runt of the litter, she'd been neglected until she was nearly dead. "I bet you're hungry."

Baby leapt out of his arms and pranced around her bowl. *Dumb question.* The sprite was always hungry. He couldn't blame her. She'd had to struggle to stay alive since birth. She might always have that hungry belly. But after one circle, she darted toward the back door and mewed at Lachlan. Normally hush quiet, she definitely had something to say. After he'd filled her bowl, he followed her. She sat swishing her tail, trying to communicate some secret to him.

When Lachlan reached for the door handle, she ran to her food and dove in. Her mission accomplished. Lachlan smiled at his smart feline until he opened the door without having to unlock it. His back door was unlocked, and, having lived in all kinds of neighborhoods in his life, Lachlan MacGregory had learned never to leave his doors unlocked. It didn't pay to be stupid.

Huh? He stepped out onto the small deck he rarely used. It was similar to everything else in the condo, small and efficient. His pub came first. A home would come later. Two cigarette butts had been left in the grass by the bottom step.

Anger seethed inside him. So, his dad had already been here and helped himself inside. God knew how long Denny had spent going through the place before Lachlan had gotten home. Lachlan cleaned up the butts then did a sweep of his house. There wasn't much to take, no cash, and even the fridge was mostly empty.

Denny must have been pissed that his own son's home, a home he'd broken into, didn't have anything for him to steal. The patheticness of it was Lachlan would have, *had* given his dad what he'd asked for. The man hadn't had to break in to take it.

Moving back to Opal, especially opening a pub in the small neighborhood of Corvallis, had always included the risk of interacting with his dad. He'd returned anyway, hoping age and maturity would guide him. But the only thing he knew for sure was his dad's presence prodded at Lachlan's worst emotions and the singular, age-old wound that he'd never been good enough for his father. Just because it fucking embarrassed him to admit it didn't make it any less true.

Christ. What a night. Another sharp jab. He didn't know whether to be livid or relieved. Clarity was a fucking bitch sometimes, but it reminded him that he also wasn't *enough* for someone like Ruby Naylor.

Lachlan walked upstairs to bed with a furball humming in his arms. *Maybe I'm not meant to take risks.* Tomorrow he'd get an early start at the gym and if he couldn't find a partner to spar with, he'd beat the hell out of the punching bag, and realign his focus on the thing that wouldn't let him down—his pub.

Chapter Four

Ruby set the blow dryer down and spun the salon chair for her client to see the back of her hair. It was a gorgeous Monday. She knew many people hated Mondays, but since she'd opened her salon, she'd swooned over them. It was such a treat to unlock the doors and walk into her own fabulous business, Spa La La. She'd done it every week for almost two years now, and it never got old. Her eyes caught on a streak. Out through the large picture window at the front of her salon, she saw Sasha's dog racing down the sidewalk and making a weird high-pitched bark. He was in a frenzy, running so fast his hind legs were nearly faster than his front.

"Goodness, I'll be right back," she said to her client.

Ruby raced outside and ran right into Sasha. The woman was a mess and crying out for her dog. "What happened, Sasha?" Ruby steadied her. Sasha had a cut on her cheek and her knee was all scraped up.

Sasha pushed away, so out of breath she could hardly talk. "Braveheart took off… I can't catch him. I don't know what happened..." She bent over and took some deep breaths. Pounding feet startled them both.

"Are you okay?" Lachlan asked Sasha. He'd run across the street to get to them. He was here and Ruby couldn't help her smile, the warmth that filtered through her.

"Hey," she said, letting him see how happy she was to see him. She'd been so hopeful all day yesterday, but he hadn't come up, at least not when she'd been home. She'd told herself he'd probably dropped by when she'd been running errands, that she'd missed him. She'd even snuck down to the pub to see if he was there after Noah and Ford had left, but she'd found it closed and empty.

The chill she'd felt when she'd walked back upstairs in the darkness, after finding no one there, especially not Lachlan, had been difficult to shake. She'd tried to convince herself it was from the cold rain and not from Lachlan forgetting his promise. It had been harder to shake when she wondered why he hadn't even called her. For a moment she'd wondered if she'd imagined the entire almost-kiss and promise from Saturday.

"I saw your Boxer hightailing it up the street." Lachlan drew Ruby's attention to the situation. *Right, Sasha. Something's wrong.* Although she still noticed every detail of Lachlan, he spoke softly to Sasha and didn't get too close. It was remarkable how intuitive he was of other people, and how careful he was with them, how kind. One more thing to adore about him. She was truly gaga.

"There was a bang and he went loopy, a high-pitched bark-whine and he pulled me down on the sidewalk. Tore away from me. Shot off like a fire was chasing him."

"Something spooked him." Sasha's dog had been saved by Ellie when he arrived at her clinic so badly beaten Ellie hadn't been sure he would survive. His past matched Sasha's in so many ways.

Sasha, anguish bleeding through her expression, nodded. "Yes, maybe. I don't... I can't..." She bent over again, and Lachlan was there to catch her before she fell.

"I'll find him. You stay here with her." Lachlan jerked his head in Ruby's direction. "Call Ellie, too. We might need her." Lachlan held out his hand. For a moment Sasha hesitated. Then she glanced at Ruby, took a deep breath and placed the leash in his hand.

"Okay," Sasha whispered. And Lachlan took off running.

Both women stood there watching him until he rounded the corner and was out of sight, but Ruby suspected they watched for different reasons and with different emotions. Sasha most likely with hope, and Ruby with confusion. Because not only had Lachlan completely ignored her, he hadn't been able to even *bring himself* to say her name and had avoided everything to do with her. Which was so very black and white, from how he'd been on Saturday evening.

"He's all I have...I can't lose him." Sasha was panting. She gripped Ruby's arm tight enough to hurt. It was the first time Sasha had willingly touched her. And Ruby noticed because she and her friends, all of them, were an affectionate group. Hugs and pats and cheek kisses were nothing out of the ordinary for any of them, except Sasha.

"Come inside and sit here by the window." Ruby tossed off her own selfish, worried thoughts about Lachlan and led Sasha into her salon. "I'm going to get you some water and something to clean your scrapes with, okay?" She patted Sasha's hand and pried it off her wrist.

Sasha startled and pulled away. "I'm so sorry...I didn't mean..."

"No, honey, I'm okay. You're okay. I'm here to help, however I can. How about some water?"

Sasha nodded and kept her face toward the window. "Thank you."

"I'll be right back. Amelia's here." Ruby gestured to her pedicurist. "I'm going to call Ellie too."

* * * *

Ruby loved the face of her salon, the enormous paned windows, new but made to appear old. She'd arranged her velvet chairs and a small loveseat in front of one of the south-facing windows, making a soft, lovely place for customers to wait. Pale pink dupioni curtains trailed to the floor, but were held open with floral iron hooks she'd had specially made. The light flooded in and gave the entire salon exactly the feel she'd always dreamed of, open, opulent and shimmery. Today that spot was crowded with people too.

Ellie had come down the street with Natalie and Natalie's two daughters. The young girls adored Sasha and seemed to put her at ease more than any adult could. Ellie had promptly called her husband, Jackson, also Sasha's brother. He and Connor Duggan were working a few blocks up the hill on a new house project. The men had jogged down to check on Sasha and had headed back out to help Lachlan find her dog.

Then Ellie had checked out Sasha's scrapes and assured her they were minor. Amelia, magical woman that she was, had somehow convinced Sasha that a warm hand massage with a nice essential oil would soothe her nerves. And shocking to all of them, Sasha had let her, as long as she could sit in the chair and face the window.

Ruby had always intended her salon and spa to be both a luxurious space to be in as well as a healing one. She'd never imagined it happening in exactly this manner, however. But it made her smile more than any pampering service she provided. Her friends here in Corvallis had become the best kind of family. And they were trying to convince Sasha that she was a part of that, that she was safe and loved with these people.

"Oh!" Sasha jumped up and darted outside with everyone following. Lachlan carried Sasha's Boxer in his arms. He slowly knelt and set the dog on the ground, cooing to it with his deep voice. "It's okay, buddy. You're going to be fine. Your mama is right here." *Kind, strong, gentle man.* Ruby had seen these qualities over and over again in Lachlan, had tucked each one into a special place inside her.

"I leashed him, but he sort of collapsed so I carried him. I think he burned out all that energy."

Sasha threw herself on her dog. "Thank you," she cried. "Thank you. Thank you. He's all I have. I don't know what I would have done if he…if you hadn't found him. God I'm a mess, throwing a fit over a dog… I… He…"

Lachlan flashed Sasha his easy smile and stroked a hand over the dog's fur. "He's a good boy. Sometimes our pets mean more to us than humans do, don't they? We can trust *them.*"

His smile slipped, something passing through him and all traces of warmth disappearing from his face. A shiver ran through Ruby at the change.

"Hey." Ellie knelt by Sasha. "Let's take him down to the clinic and check him out, honey?" Braveheart slathered kisses all over Sasha and Ellie, whining like a baby. "Yeah, you big buffoon," Ellie said. "You scared us, scared your mom."

Jackson and Connor jogged up, both out of breath. "Christ! Is he okay?" Jackson asked.

"I think so." Ellie gave Jackson her bright smile and held out her hand. He helped her up.

"Are *you* okay?" Connor asked Sasha. Sasha barely glanced at the man who, Ruby realized at that moment, had his heart open and ready for Sasha Kincaid. *Well, these men are just full of emotions.*

"We're going to walk down to the clinic and have a little visit," Ellie said. Jackson helped his sister up next. She held the leash, but she hardly needed it at this moment as Braveheart plastered himself to her side. And one by one they all walked away. Ellie, Sasha and Braveheart with Jackson and Connor following them. Natalie gave Ruby a smooch on the cheek and headed in the same direction with her girls. Amelia entered the salon.

And Ruby stood alone on the sidewalk under a blue sky, and watched the hero of the day, Lachlan MacGregory turn his back, walk across the street and into his pub. Just like that. Without speaking to her, looking at her, acknowledging her at all. Not even a smirk. Nothing. And even with the bright, full sun, Ruby felt the chill of being absolutely ignored, tear through her.

"Good crowd for a Monday." Ruby's dad, Detective Isaac Naylor, took a stool at the bar.

Jesus, this day. First, he'd had to endure Ruby's presence with the dog fiasco and now her father was at his pub. Was this some sort of twisted karma coming to bite him in the ass?

"Who am I kidding?" Isaac chuckled. "You've always got a good crowd."

"Yep, been busy since lunch." Lachlan manned up and faced his friend and old mentor, instead of exiting out through the kitchen as fast as he could.

Detective Naylor was a force in the neighborhood. Powerful, intelligent and the hardest-working man Lachlan had ever met. He was a good man too, kind and loved his family. He'd advised Lachlan on how to set up the neighborhood watch organization, and kept Lachlan informed about the anti-gang task force. They'd been discussing a plan to sponsor kids at the gym who couldn't afford sports but were interested in learning boxing, martial arts and even yoga and meditating. Basketball had been great for Lachlan as a kid, but he was intent on providing more choices to the kids here.

It had been one more bonus in coming back to Corvallis, meeting up with his old Big Brother and striking up a friendship again. Lachlan wasn't great at making friends, maybe because he didn't put much effort into it. He'd moved so often as a kid that it had become easier not to try. *Don't try. Don't get disappointed.* That had changed somewhat since opening his pub. Whether he'd chosen it or not, he'd been woven into a group of friends. And now he'd have to figure out what to do about that. They were Ruby's friends too and he needed to stay away from her if he was going to get over this shit.

Detective or not, in this moment, all Lachlan could see, all he could think about was that this man sitting before him, smiling, chatting him up, was Ruby's father. And all the painful emotions from last night still simmered in Lachlan's gut.

"You meeting Ruby?" *Please let him not be meeting his daughter for dinner like they did often at the pub.* It was only four—maybe Lachlan would get lucky and Ruby would still be working. He didn't know if he was capable of putting on his fake kindness if she sat next to her dad right now, and he was the only one working out front as his employees were between shifts.

"No. I have a quick break before I have to get back to work. Missed lunch. Can I get one of your famous blue cheese and bacon burgers?"

"Sure thing." Lachlan turned away and let out a sigh of relief, although it didn't make him feel any better. He punched in the order and grabbed a silverware set.

"Busy across the street too. Her spa is thriving. Couldn't be prouder of both of you. Smart, dedicated, hardworking. You're both doing something you love and you've both shaped the changes in this neighborhood."

"Mmm." Lachlan gave a non-answer as he filled a few pints for a group at the other end of the bar. It only took him a few minutes to wipe down some tables then Isaac's order was ready. He set Isaac's burger down.

"I worry about her though." Isaac gazed toward Ruby's spa. "Worry that I haven't been a good example since Skye died, Ruby's mother. Work was the only thing I could concentrate on after..." He took a sip of his water. "Being able to lose myself in work got me through, but I didn't set a good example for her. I want Ruby to see there's more to life than a job."

Oh, I'm sure she's got that down. Shut up, asshole. Lachlan paused and built his cool restraint brick by brick. He could be upset with Ruby without acting like a jerk. But, Christ, he could not be having this conversation, or any conversation about Ruby with Isaac.

"There's family, there's love. You could take a lesson here too, son." Isaac gave Lachlan a cold assessing expression. Then he broke out into a huge smile and held up his lunch. "But most importantly, there's Mac's famous bacon blue to be enjoyed by me, right this moment."

Lachlan let him eat and closed out a few tabs. There was a lull, and he sure hoped it wouldn't last long. Good example or not, Lachlan was going to take a play out of Isaac's book and lose himself in work. *And there's your insensitive jerk coming out again.* Ruby not choosing Lachlan in no way compared to a good man losing the love of his life to cancer.

Isaac got out his wallet. "I'm going to stop in and see Ruby on my way out. Got any fabulous desserts I could surprise her with?"

"Nope," Lachlan lied. Icebox Cake with Whipped Cream frosting—one of Ruby's favorites—was in the kitchen freezer. In fact, there was an entire cake left. She could have the whole thing. Apparently being a jerk came easy to him. But damn, he didn't want to know her favorites or picture her enjoying them. He didn't want to know anything about her anymore. And there was another lie that burned through his insides.

"My loss. Your business is *too* good," Isaac chuckled. "I'll see you at the meeting on Thursday?"

"Yep." Lachlan nodded as the man left and jogged across the street. He couldn't help the pull that had him watching Isaac open the door to Ruby's spa and step inside. From where he watched, Lachlan could see her lean into her father's arms for a hug. And here he stood, on the outside of their connection. *On the outside once again.*

Well, he'd gotten what he wished for. She hadn't come to join her father for a meal. What was the word he'd used? *Lucky.* Lachlan didn't feel one bit lucky at all.

Chapter Five

"Lachlan's helping Jackson fix the fence, so Chewie won't get stuck underneath it again, poor puppy. He doesn't realize he's closer to eighty pounds, not eight anymore. They should finish it tonight. Lachlan's done so much work. I think they're also forming a friendship and it makes me so happy, because that's exactly what Jackson needs, more good friends in his life. He's been alone for so long."

Ruby finished wiping down the front counter and iPad at her salon while Ellie gushed about her fiancé. Ellie was in love and it made Ruby so happy, even while her own heart curled inward to soothe the bruises that a certain bar owner had left over the last two weeks. And how on earth could someone leave bruises by not doing a thing? Apparently, Mr. MacGregory was quite talented in the *I'm going to mess with your emotions by withholding myself.* The old, *abstinence will keep you safe* promotors would be flush to know the truth. *Not* doing a thing could harm.

"Lachlan brought all his own tools and table saw, thank goodness, because I'm not sure Jackson even owns a hammer. Ahh," Ellie sighed. "They were two cute boys teasing and ribbing each other. I actually heard Jackson laugh. It was nice of Lachlan to help, considering how busy he is."

Lachlan, Lachlan, Lachlan. The man and his good deeds were everywhere. *Neighborhood golden boy.* Right before Ruby had opened her salon, he'd refurbished his pub in this neighborhood before it was the hot place to be and staffed it with men and women coming out of prison. He made sure to call and pay for cabs if he suspected people drank too much. There'd been many times he'd shoveled the sidewalks in front of the bakery for the Heelys when it was icy. He might have been silent and surly on the outside, but she'd thought, after observing him and getting to know him from a distance and through their mutual friends, that, scowl or not, on the inside he was a good man.

And yet, after blasting open her world, after promising her all her heart's wishes, he'd ghosted her. For some reason, a reason she couldn't name because he wouldn't talk to her, he'd changed his mind. He might be the neighborhood's hero, but he didn't want to be hers. One minute, one special late evening, he'd finally seen her. Now it was like she'd never even existed. Being ignored was worse than a lot of things Ruby could think of, especially when he'd promised to cherish, to remember her. He'd *promised.* She'd had thirteen days to simmer with his unfulfilled promise and it had felt like a decade.

"Oh, Jackson texted. He's fixing me dinner. Ruby, I'm so lucky. How did I get to be with someone so thoughtful?"

Tell me all about Jackson, because I'm so over hearing how wonderful Mr. MacGregory is.

"I'm thrilled you're happy, Ellie, my love. You deserve it. It makes you shine even brighter than you did before. Engaged, pregnant, in love...you're absolutely glorious. You know Jackson thinks he's the fortunate one." *Ahh, to have a man believe that about me.* It was essential in a relationship and, she was learning, near impossible for her to find.

Ellie gave her a huge hug and sailed out, glowing with the flush of happiness.

Ruby locked up and tried to enjoy the lovely evening as she walked across the street to her apartment. An orange, autumn sky lit the horizon and provided the perfect stage for the sun to sink beneath the few clouds. There was a touch of heat in the air, clinging to the evening, warm but not too humid. The torrential rains had ended and the planters along the sidewalk still bloomed full and lush, reaching out for the last rays of sun before hibernation came.

Normally it was the type of weather Ruby would bask in. But she'd been riding the rollercoaster of hope to confusion to anger for too many days now. Her emotions prevented her from simply relishing the moment. It was a rare experience for her, and she didn't like it one bit.

Why had Lachlan been so amazing to her, tipped her world upside down, then treated her so crappily? *We in middle school or what?* What had happened between the best almost-kiss of her life, the '*When I kiss you, I want you to remember it in the morning.*' And the very next day? Something had to have changed and Ruby wanted the facts. Pretty difficult when Lachlan avoided her at all costs. She walked to the back entrance of the pub when her cell rang with her dad's number.

"Hi, Dad."

"My beautiful girl. How was your day?"

"Busy. Yours?"

Lachlan drove up and parked his enormous silver pickup in his space behind the pub.

"Christ, busy here at the station too. Got off early. Have dinner with your old man?"

"I..." Lachlan was on his phone too as he neared her. She covered hers with her hand and spoke to the man in front of her. "Hey."

Lachlan looked at her—no, correction—he looked *through* her, gave a quick nod and entered the pub without giving her one single ounce of anything else. As if she were a statue, a stranger. As if that life-changing Saturday encounter hadn't happened. It was infinitely worse than the disappearing act, or the going out of his way to ignore her that he'd perfected for the last two weeks.

"Ruby, everything okay?"

"Yeah, Dad." Ruby sat on the bench outside the pub. It was surrounded by an enormous bougainvillea. It was overcome with deep pink, almost red blooms and brightened up this side of the pub as well as the patio, making it all so much more inviting. "Or, maybe no. I guess."

"Anything I can help with?"

She shook her head, having trouble getting the words out. "No, it's only...I thought I met someone." Ruby's sigh shuddered out of her. "*I like you.*" Lachlan's heated admission shuddered through her. Had he been lying? Had an alien taken over his body?

"Someone worthy of you?"

Ruby took a deep breath. Her dad believed she deserved the moon, her own bright love. And she did. Boy, did it sting when she'd thought, *finally,* that she'd found her moon, but then he'd changed his mind. *Why? Fickle man.* "Yeah, but it turns out he's not interested after all."

"I'm sorry, honey. His loss. He must be an idiot."

Seems like. Too bad idiots can still cause damage.

"Can I get a raincheck on dinner? I think I'll just go home." Home was the last place she wanted to be. Her apartment above the bar was so close to Lachlan, while he pretended she didn't exist. But she was in no mood for dinner and conversation with anyone either, even her dad whom she adored more than anyone on the planet.

"Anytime, honey."

"Breakfast tomorrow?"

"Good idea. We can drown our sorrows in pancakes."

"Sounds good, Dad. Love you."

"Love you too. Don't let it get you down too much. There's a great man out there for you. It'll be a privilege to meet him some day. Say hello to Lachlan for me."

Ruby shook her head at the phone after her dad had hung up. Even Isaac Naylor was a fan of the charming owner of everyone's favorite downtown pub. "If you only knew, Dad," she whispered.

Ruby walked inside the back door of the pub that led to her stairs, replaying that epic night, sifting through the words, the emotions, and the emptiness that had followed. Good Lord, she'd done nothing but replay it all for days now.

"The way you feel in my arms, Christ, Ruby, you have no idea." That memory alone made her shiver with desire.

Unfortunately, it now also made her ache. She'd felt the connection between them even before he'd carried her into her apartment and declared his feelings, when she'd first met him, and he'd glanced at her with that impassive gaze. She'd seen through his stony façade all those months ago. How could she have been so, so wrong?

That next day, after his promise of beauty, he'd been gone. *No biggie.* She'd initially reasoned away her worry, until he'd ignored her during the fiasco with Sasha's dog. Then poof! He'd disappeared into the universe. Or at least from anywhere in her orbit. His bartender Shae had said something about him taking some vacation days. That had been Ruby's first clue that something was definitely wrong. Lachlan MacGregory never took time off. Shae hadn't been telling the truth. When Ruby had seen him, he'd pretended to be busy and ignored her every single time.

Tonight had been the worst, when he'd barely acknowledged her.

If it were any other man, she'd probably let it go. She'd encountered her fair share of immature boys who might be in their twenties and thirties but did not have a clue how to treat a woman, a relationship, a promise. And that was okay, because she didn't belong with someone who couldn't see how precious she was, how precious it was to be in a healthy relationship, how to care for it. *I thought he knew how to care for things.* Ruby closed her eyes and tried to locate the truth of it all.

It went both ways. She'd be thrilled to treat the man in her life like he was a beloved gift, as her parents had treated each other. Lachlan wasn't anywhere close to those other guys. *Had* she completely imagined it all? Had he really only been indulging her tipsiness? *No, no, no.* If that had been the case, he would have seen her inside and disappeared without a word, without a promise. *Such a beautiful promise.* And he wouldn't be acting so weird and evasive now.

Lachlan was in his office with the door open speaking to someone on the phone. *That deep voice made of gravel and sin.*

She started up the stairs. The memory of his body pressed against hers, his lips on her neck washed over her. She stopped and gripped the handrail before she made a fool out of herself and tripped.

"I've wanted to kiss you since the day you filled out the lease and teased me about lacking any sort of smile, when I nearly fell over at your beauty... Since...since that day so long ago when you altered my world."

The last words had been said with such meaning, like he'd been aching for her for eons, not merely the year and a half she'd been living above his pub. She could still feel his lips whispering over her skin, his hands on her waist, how braced he'd been and all the words and declarations he made before he'd bade her goodnight.

Lachlan MacGregory, wonder-boy, town hero, had broken his promise. *Liar, liar pants on fire.* The old children's song stung with its appropriateness. His voice echoed up the stairwell as he said goodbye to whomever he'd been speaking to. A moment later, an old Johnny Cash song drifted toward her. Ruby braced herself, took a deep breath and made a decision. Turning, she aimed herself toward his office. She, Ruby Naylor, deserved to know what had happened to change his mind. And cornering him in his office might be the best chance she'd get. She and Mr. MacGregory needed to have a conversation, whether he wished it or not.

Chapter Six

"Got a minute?" Ruby pushed his door all the way open and strode into his office with all the confidence of a model commanding the runway. Dazzling, haughty, determined and so fucking stunning it pierced his heart each time she appeared. Why the hell did her beauty have to take up every inch of breathable space? Why did her presence promise to slay him? Had he done enough bad things in life to warrant this kind of punishment?

He'd nearly pivoted and gotten right back in his truck when he'd seen her outside a few minutes ago, as she'd stood there, framed in the bright pink bougainvillea he'd planted with her in mind, glamorous in her body-hugging white dress that showed off her slightly freckled skin. Skin he now knew was smooth as silk and beckoned all the world's delights. She'd straightened her hair and added a teal color to the tips. A matching blue flower tucked behind her ear showed off the long column of her neck. *Flaunting her sexy legs in those sky-high heels.*

But he was no coward. He'd have to get used to seeing her and remaining unaffected. She lived above his bar, he reminded himself daily. They shared friends. Her business was right across the street. They were bound to run into each other now and then. So, he'd nodded and walked by and choked down all his emotions. *Rational, polite, problem solved.*

Who was he kidding? Coward was exactly what he was. He'd been avoiding her for weeks, for exactly this reason, because her beauty, her scent, her presence overwhelmed him, nearly brought him to his knees. And seeing her after she'd unknowingly hurt him, well, it stung. *Every fucking time.* Ruby Naylor, the girl of his dreams, who'd grown into the woman of his dreams, had then shattered them all in one moment.

He *was* a damn coward and an idiot, thinking he could erase all his feelings for her because she didn't feel the same. All this time he'd kept his shit together near her, never letting on how she affected him…until that single moment he'd had her in his arms. One thing he hadn't realized in his dreams was how fucking amazing it would feel to hold her, touch her, breathe in her scent, not simply in passing, but as though it was made for him and he deserved to be enveloped by her aura. *Fuck.* He should have stuck with his imagination.

Now she was here in his crowded, messy office. The walls pressed in on him. He gripped the desk as her fragrance enveloped him. "I'm a bit busy, actually," he said, avoiding her gaze. He rifled through some folders on his desk. He barely recognized them, and couldn't read what they said. She made him blind and dumb.

"Hey, Lachlan..." His friend Jill stepped into the office. "Oh, sorry, didn't mean to interrupt. Your bartender sent me back. You ready to go? Hi, Ruby. Great shoes."

Ruby stared at Jill, her mouth open. It was quick but Lachlan caught the hurt flash over her face.

"Yeah, Jill. Give me a minute. I'll meet you up front."

"Busy, huh?" Ruby asked. "Busy dating Jill again?" She faltered for a split second. She took one step away and braced herself against the wall. "So..." Ruby swallowed, screwed up her face as if he were a pile of stinking garbage. "So all those promises you made to me, the careful way you handled me, those lovely words...you didn't..." She swallowed and gestured between them. "You didn't mean any of them?" The confused expression on her face spoke volumes, only he didn't understand what those volumes said. *She* was the one with someone else. *Two someone elses.*

"Let's not do this," Lachlan said, his jaw tight. He had no intention of reliving what had made him attempt to wipe her memory from his mind, his heart, his...everywhere. *Fuck, is that what I really want?*

"Let's not do what? Explain why you're ignoring me after that precious, magical moment, after you...strongly indicated... I thought we were starting something, Lachlan? At the least...*the least,* I...we were friends."

He'd never seen her stumble through her words like this.

But yeah, he'd absolutely thought they were starting something too. How could she call it precious and magical, words that sang to his cold heart, with that deep, rich voice of hers, when it had meant nothing of the sort to her? This witchy combination was lethal. He did not need to be more twisted up over her than he already was. *Keep it together, man, keep your shit together and she'll walk away, and everything will return to normal.*

"Trust me. It's better if we stay landlord and tenant." He tried to keep his gaze averted, but a quick glance and he saw past the flush on her cheeks to… *Is that hurt again?* The skin on her chest was all flushed too, with the same heat that crept up her neck. He'd seen her react the same, once before in the pub, when some jackass had insulted her father with disgusting racial slurs. *Oh fuck, she's upset.*

"I did trust you. You could have left that night without saying anything. Without making any promises. I—"

"I made a mistake," he clipped. The only mistake he'd made was thinking she was available, that their feelings for each other were mutual. *Hope.* That was his mistake. He hadn't gone down that fucking rabbit hole in a long time. Hope was for dreamers and people who were good at emotions, not for someone like him. Only hard work, routine and more hard work. Building his business and keeping it thriving was his goal and he needed to stick with it.

"A mistake?" she demanded, her voice husky and angry. "Which parts? Your hands on me, the whispered, cherishing words, telling me you'd wanted to kiss me since that day I altered your world? Or were…were they *all* errors on your part?"

Jesus, she sounded how he felt. Someone was bleeding him out, taking his very last breath against his will. Something pricked at his brain, a warning, but he ignored it. It was probably the headache he'd had since she'd gutted him.

"Please tell me. I…I felt…what we shared felt special. And now you're going out with Jill. Again. I thought you two were over. Why would you say those meaningful things to me if you were with Jill?"

He and Jill weren't dating. They'd hadn't ever. They were just friends. But he didn't need to explain that to Ruby. She was the one who'd smashed everything precious to pieces. "My love life is no business of yours. Just like yours is no business of mine. At least let's agree on that."

"Don't tell me what to agree on. And you, *you* sound annoyed. At *me*. What the hell is going on? I'm so confused."

"Look, Ruby." Lachlan ran his hands through his hair, desperate to reach out and grab her, pull her into his arms and never let her go, to feel that warmth he'd had in his arms for a few minutes all those days ago. *Talk about precious.* It felt like eons and seconds at the same time, now that he wouldn't get to hold her again. Time was a cruel demon. "Let's drop it. I'm trying to be a gentleman and let it go."

She huffed. "We spell what you're being A.S.S.H.O.L.E."

His body locked. He crossed his arms over his chest and tried to sink into his rigid state. "Ruby." It was a warning. He *really* wished she'd drop it. He did not want to have this conversation with her.

"I believed your words." Her whispered admission caught him off guard. Her confidence had plummeted, leaving in its place a vulnerable, confused, wounded woman. What right did she have to play the victim? "I believed you."

It took all he had not to fling her own words in her face. *I believed you, Ruby.*

"You made me a promise, Lachlan."

Fuck, would she quit saying his name? The way she gave it pause, gave it reverence, like it was special to her, like *he* was special to her. She was torturing him. Lachlan grabbed his keys and phone. He had to get the hell out of here before he lost it. No matter what, he couldn't take his anger out on her.

"But you broke that promise. Worse, you acted as if it never happened, ignored me. What happened between then and now? You hurt me. Why?" Her voice wobbled. *"You hurt me."* She said it with such vulnerability, as if she meant it. As if she had no idea.

He stiffened. *Broken promises?* Too late—his temper boiled. They stared at each other, a fire lit between them, a connection, one that sizzled and caught. It stung all right. Maybe he'd be better off burning it to the ground. He could barely stand to be in the same room with her knowing he wasn't good enough.

"Lachlan," she demanded.

"I did," he bit out. He met her gaze, did his best to try to ignore the emotions simmering in their gorgeous green depths, and soldiered on. "I did come up the next evening, Sunday, but you were busy with your…threesome." He gritted the words out, wishing they'd never had to exist.

All the color drained from her face, all the light and joy. Christ, he should have stuck with ignoring her.

"What?"

Why was she pretending not to know what the hell he was talking about?

"The two men, dammit, Ruby, in your apartment, that Sunday night. I heard you and them, doing…" He threw his hands out. He did *not* need the image of them plaguing him. "Whatever it is you three do together.

'Damn, girl, you are the best.' and 'Harder, Ruby.' I watched them leave a few minutes later gushing about how much they love you. Christ...seriously."

He took a deep breath and tried to shake out his simmering emotions. "You date a lot. Do what suits you. I'm not judging your sex life, but I don't share and I'm not into threesomes. I made a huge mistake in thinking you wanted to start something with only me. I'm not the only one who broke a promise..."

She reared as if he'd slapped her. Fuck, he didn't enjoy causing her pain, even if what he'd said was the truth. He needed to end this and get out of here. "Ruby, I'm sorry—"

"Not judging? You patronizing, ignorant asshole, with your assumptions and cowardice. How dare you! Go to hell!" Then she ran from his office, taking every last beautiful thing from the room.

Chapter Seven

"Thanks for meeting me, Dad."

"Glad you asked me to come. Wow, Ruby." He crossed his arms over his chest and scanned the house with his quiet, intense study. "She's a beauty."

"Isn't she." Ruby knew she was ridiculous swooning over a house, but it wasn't *any* house. It was a small two-story Italianate built in eighteen-sixty-seven. The gorgeous front porch was decorated with tons of swirly ornamentation, but the brick façade had been painted an odd shade of ivory at one point, giving it a sallow appearance. It was a good thing Ruby could see past the ugly duckling to the swan beneath. A black iron fence surrounded the property, which included a long backyard and patio. She'd already been to view the place three times this week, falling deeper in love after each visit. Some girls dreamed of diamonds and babies. Ruby Naylor craved her own house, her own historic house.

"Tell me the bad news first," her father said.

Ruby grinned and clapped her hands together. "From what my realtor and I can tell before inspection, there isn't much. She knows the current owner. All the wiring and plumbing were updated a few years ago. The foundation is in great shape. It needs a new roof, and I'm going to paint the exterior and fix up the porch, but wait until you see the inside."

She couldn't keep the excitement from her voice. She'd been hoping to buy in the neighborhood ever since she'd opened her salon, but she hadn't fallen in love until now. And she was not settling for a house she didn't love. *No way. Fine motto for life too.* At least the house couldn't toss her aside and ignore her.

Ruby shoved the pain of Lachlan MacGregory away and focused.

Her house was going to be similar to a perfectly curated wardrobe one selected over time that had character from many different places, the perfect pieces, or in this case rooms. More than that, it had to be full of passion. And this beauty before her, this was the one. It spoke to her. Grand, royal, lush, maybe a tiny bit haunted, full of history and waiting for her to color it alive with her flair.

The house stood empty, so her realtor had given her the key code. And like every time so far, as soon as Ruby opened the door and stepped into the entryway, a sigh of pleasure left her lips. Sunlight flickered in through the tall windows, casting gorgeous light across the regal staircase. One could see down the long hall to the kitchen at the back of the house. place wasn't huge, but it was enormous in charm and possibility. It was perfect.

"Unbelievable how good of condition these old features are." The awe in her dad's voice made her want to sing. She'd thought the exact same thing, but her dad's opinion meant the world to her.

"Please tell me you're not going to knock down all the walls and make it all open concept and lose this history?" He stroked the curved banister with reverence.

"Never." Ruby shuddered. "This is not the house for that. I love each room as its own and I cannot wait to dress them up. A previous owner made some horrible carpet and wallpaper choices not fitting with the style of the house at all, but I'll have a blast making her shine again."

She showed him the upstairs, which was the only place she might take a wall down to create a master bedroom and bath. But she could have a few modern touches and still keep all the charm. They didn't spend long in the kitchen. The tall windows were the kitchen's only good features. Ruby would need to buy all new cabinets, countertops and appliances to bring the room into the current century. A lazy sun graced them with her warmth as they stepped onto the patio.

"You picked a gem, love." Her dad had his arm around her shoulder. They stood side by side, taking in the house. She was already mentally designing a lush garden out here, full of climbing roses and vines and every rich-scented darling she could find. *A wrought-iron patio table and chairs with cushions I'll cover in some deep teal peacock fabric. Tiny lights overhead. A perfect place for me to host outdoor dinners with friends.* "Shall we go talk about it over breakfast?"

"I'd love to," Ruby said, basking in the pride her dad had in her.

* * * *

She and her dad spent an hour going over all the house facts. Ruby took specific notes. Even though an inspector would do his or her job, there was no way Isaac Naylor would let his beloved daughter buy a house that was unsafe. He might not be able to do all the work required, but he knew what issues to investigate, and which were most expensive. Because she'd dragged him out of bed extra early, she'd offered to treat him to Grizzly's, only the best breakfast diner in the world. *Possibly the oldest too.* Grizzly's appearance said it had lived through many centuries and wore the scars from adventures on the high seas. It was not a pretty diner, in any sense of the word, but nobody cared when they ate the food. The pancakes were to die for.

"Tell me about this guy who's got you down?" He was smooth. She'd give him that. No way he hadn't picked up on her mood the other night, and probably this morning, though she'd tried to shove all thoughts of the jerk away from the good aura of her house. Hmm, she was already imagining it as hers.

"Oh, you know, someone I believed might be worth it." *Someone I really hoped might be worth it.* Ruby was absolutely not going to tell her father it was Lachlan. He respected Lachlan as a business owner and her dad loved the pub. She wouldn't ruin that for either man. "No one special, apparently," she said.

"What did he do?"

Oh. At that she choked out a laugh, because the thought of explaining to her dad what Lachlan imagined he'd overheard in her apartment would embarrass her and Lachlan, and there was no way in hell she could even begin to explain that…situation to her father, Mr. Conservative Detective Naylor. Nope.

No way. Picturing it almost made it seem funny, *almost* took away how much she ached.

"Nothing," Ruby said, which was the truth too, in its own way. Lachlan had done nothing. He hadn't been kind or patient or intuitive, the way he was with everyone else. He hadn't asked her about what he'd overheard. He hadn't given her a chance to fall into giggles, then explain how wrong his imagination was. He'd excommunicated her from his life.

It cut. It still cut. She didn't appreciate being treated badly. No one did. And because she'd had such a huge crush on the man, because she saw such amazingness in him and wanted him to shine that glow on her, *thought* he felt the same. But when the dust settled and he'd been content to ghost her then accuse her, well…there was an open sore on her heart she hoped would disappear someday. "He didn't measure up."

"I'm sorry, honey."

"You and Mom were so…" Ruby twirled her hand. "In love. I'm searching for what you had. Your relationship is a hard act to follow, how much you loved each other. Even with all you sacrificed, you always made each other feel special and you made it look so easy."

"Ha!" Her dad barked out a laugh and covered his pancakes with the fluffy butter they piped on top. "When you find the right person, there are parts of the relationship that are easy. I'll give you that. Being in the same space with someone you get on so many levels, who gets you. It's like puzzle pieces sliding into place. But not every moment is easy. You still have to put in a lot of effort, have patience, communicate, be willing to learn, give each other grace. And you"—he pointed his fork at her—"were never a sacrifice. Not for me, and not for your mother."

"I know, Dad. You never made me feel that way. I mean, getting married so young, becoming a husband and dad at the same time. That's a lot for anyone. I meant it when I said you were a good role model. You and Mom were always communicating and supporting each other. I want to have that ease and rarity with someone *and* put forth the effort because it will be worth it. Because I've seen it with my own eyes."

He passed her the syrup. "We didn't start out that way. Your mom couldn't stand me when we first met."

"No way?" Ruby slathered her own pancakes with butter and syrup, making a well in the center of the stack like she'd done as a child to let the syrup pool up then flood over the side.

Her dad chuckled and gazed out of the window for a moment, both love and grief in his expression. It would be nine years since her mom's death and there were moments that the pain felt as fresh as yesterday. She could only imagine how it must feel for her dad, for *anyone* to lose the love of a lifetime. After he'd cleared his throat and taken a sip of coffee he said, "She thought I was an egotistical jerk who couldn't bother to give her the time of day or speak in her presence."

Sounds like someone else I know.

"No!" Ruby said and laughed. "I don't believe it."

"It's true. I'll admit. It was damn hard to speak in her presence. She was so beautiful and vibrant. She took my breath away. Always surrounded by friends and people coming to her for help. People itching to be in her space. And I didn't have a chance of competing with that."

"What happened?"

Her dad's grin was warm and held a memory he must have loved. "I knocked her down at the grocery store one day. I was too flustered to keep my mouth shut because I felt like an idiot and hoped she wasn't injured. I kept apologizing and asking if she was all right and she gave me her killer smile and said in her soft voice, 'Well, Isaac Naylor, I was wondering what it was going to take for you to talk to me. Help me up?' I was a goner from that moment on. Didn't care if I fit in with her crowd or not. All I could see was her. I went for it."

Ruby laughed. "I can't believe I haven't heard this story. I thought you met at college."

"Officially, we did, but like I said. I was too tongue-tied to form a complete sentence. Outside the student union. It was winter. We'd gotten snow and there she was in her group. A soft gray hat on her head and bundled under this enormous puffy jacket, gifting her smile to everyone. She and her friends were laughing and throwing snowballs. The sun was bouncing off the snow, making it almost too bright to see without sunglasses, but her smile was what blinded me."

"I've heard this part," Ruby said.

Her dad nodded. "I was introduced to her that night, but I was pitiful. It felt easier to walk the other way rather than embarrass myself by trying to speak to her. Then for a while I didn't see her."

"Because she'd gotten pregnant with me and quit school."

"Yep. I didn't know any of that, of course. I simply thought I'd lost my chance. Couldn't get her image out of my head. Once I saw her again, I decided to be brave. As I got to know her, I could still see her brilliance, but it wasn't inaccessible to me. She liked me too. We were equals. Her being a single mom, already having you, didn't deter me. I wanted you both."

"Well." Ruby stuffed her mouth with a pancake to stop the tears that threatened all of a sudden at a memory of her mom laughing under the snowy lights. Skye Naylor had always had a glow about her, even when she'd been on her deathbed. The three of them had been such a tight family. Blood might not have connected Ruby and Isaac, but he was her dad in every other way. She couldn't imagine a better one. "I will settle for nothing short of that beauty and commitment."

She needed to change the subject or she was going to drown her breakfast in tears, some from the sorrow of missing her mom, and more from not being enough for Lachlan MacGregory. "In the meantime, what do you think of my dream house?"

Her dad studied her and took a sip of his coffee. "I think you should put in an offer."

"Fabulous!" Ruby squealed. "I already have some numbers in mind." Her dream man didn't want her, but that wouldn't stop Ruby from reaching for the rest of her dreams all by herself.

Chapter Eight

Three months later

"Are you ever going to tell him, Ruby?" Noah clinked his beer to hers and Ford's. Lachlan's pub was packed. It was Thursday night and low lights flittered over the handsome dark bar. A hip band with a mix of alternative and bluegrass jammed on the tiny stage, and bodies hummed in every square inch. Not even the freezing, bitter temps and blah of January could keep people away from Lachlan's pub. Winter actually drew people in to its ultra-dark chic meets cozy atmosphere, delicious food and great music. It was community and friendship and belonging all rolled into one. She'd missed it.

"What?" Ruby brought her focus to the table and took a long sip of her stout. Lachlan was in his element behind the busy bar tonight with two other bartenders, filling drink orders and chatting customers up with his stoic good looks and deep-set eyes. She'd incorrectly labeled him as silent and closed off, but when he was surrounded by his patrons who adored his pub… *I guess his silence is only for me.* It still hurt to observe him, even months after his rejection. But she was a glutton. Sometimes self-torture was all a woman had.

"You keep sneaking glances at him, although I'd hardly call you good at it. Captain Obvious is more like it."

Ruby flushed and swallowed her embarrassment. It was easy to get lost in her old wishes when the pub was crowded and no one could—at least, the man himself couldn't—tell she was spying, her heart still full of longing. She rubbed at her chest. *Will it ever go away?*

"He's much better at it, but even he's not aces," Ford, Noah's fiancé, said.

"Seriously," Noah agreed. "Every time she turns away, Lachlan's laser eyes find her and get all broody, or *more* broody. Like he wants to wring someone's neck."

"Or kiss the heck out of someone," Ford added and started chuckling with Noah.

"Let's not be ridiculous, shall we. He wants nothing of the sort." Ruby eyed her menu and tried to read the specials. She loved food, but absolutely nothing sounded good tonight, not even the chocolate raspberry melting cake. She'd been too tired to vote for a different restaurant this evening. Plus, she was thrilled to treat Ford and Noah to a dinner to celebrate their wedding weekend. Only, she hadn't thought for one second they'd pick Lachlan's. Or that they'd tease her with their heart-shaped vision about her own lack of love life. "What are we eating tonight to kick off this super fantabulous weekend wedding of two of my favorite people in the world? Why did you pick this place anyway? You two are usually more fine dining." Ruby infused her words with all the haughty control she could muster.

Ford flattened her menu. He didn't hide his offense or his eye roll at all. "First of all, we adore this place. Secondly, the food's as good if not better than most of the restaurants in town. And thirdly, duh, we came to see this little dance you two do."

Noah nodded. "It tugs on your heartstrings, a perfect romance movie. Why don't they make more of those anyway, all the angst and sex and happily ever afters? Goldmine, if you ask me."

"All could be set right if you told him the truth, Rube." Ford took her hand between his. "Why didn't you tell him? It's been months and you're still hurting. Want me to go punch him out for you?"

That garnered a laugh from her. They weren't teasing in a mean way, but even though Ford Downs and Lachlan MacGregory were the same height, Lachlan had at least sixty pounds of muscle on her lovely, but skinny and extremely uncoordinated friend.

"No punching anyone two days before our wedding, love," Noah said and gave Ford a kiss on his cheek.

"*You* could do it, and not even break a sweat," Ford said. Which was probably true. Two hundred and fifty pounds of muscle, and three inches taller than MacGregory, Noah Bridges looked the part. Inside he was all fluffy teddy bear. Ruby wondered if he even knew *how* to punch someone. And why was she even weighing the options? Noah was right. There'd be no punching anyone.

"True." Noah took a sip of his beer. "But I'm not sure he's worth it."

"He made an honest mistake," Ford said.

"A mistake that hurt," Ruby whispered glancing down at her menu. "Still does."

"Ruby, beautiful," Noah hushed.

"You know…" She blinked away her tears. "I love you two. I appreciate your interest in my silly soap opera, even though it ended months ago, but we've had this conversation before. He was an ass who basically called me a slut, when he could have asked me about what he heard."

"I know, honey." Ford stole a glance at Lachlan. "And I would fight him for you, but I feel like there's more to your story with him. He's had a crush on you for forever, no matter how well he's tried to hide it. Don't you want to give him one more chance to be loved by you, his soulmate?"

Ruby couldn't stop her watery eyes that time. She had spectacular friends. Maybe she wasn't meant to have spectacular love too. Was it all too much to ask for?

"He's not my soulmate," she said. Ruby took a deep breath and tried to calm her emotions.

"I think he is," Ford whispered.

"It's my favorite clients!" Katie Walsh, soon to be Katie Treversini, stopped at their table with her drink in hand and gave hugs to everyone. Geesh, Ruby was surrounded by the happy and engaged. "I can't wait for you guys to taste your food on Saturday. It's the most fun I've had with a menu in ages. I…Ruby? Oh my gosh, are you okay?" Katie slid into the booth next to Ruby and squeezed her hand. "What happened?"

Ruby sucked in her woes and dabbed at her mascara with a tissue, donning her confident smile for all the world to see. "Nothing."

"We're talking about the long-fated love story between her and MacGregory," Noah whispered, as if anyone in the rest of the crowded noisy pub could hear him.

"There's no fated love anything," Ruby hissed and raised her eyebrows at the men, hoping they would get a clue and zip their lips.

"Oh, sure, if you call Lachlan nearly kissing her, declaring his love, promising her all kinds of goodness, *finally*, then acting like a complete and utter jerk when he incorrectly thought Ruby was involved in an elicit threesome with Noah and me 'nothing', then you're right, Ruby darling."

"What?" Katie whispered, shining her wide eyes on Ruby, who was trying to hide from the embarrassment of the entire world by holding her hands over her head. She wasn't even wearing anything stylish tonight. And there was no way she would die of embarrassment in old jeans and last season's sweater with the supposed to be chic but actually were a bit annoying shoulder cut outs. The only thing she liked about it was the hint of pretty green bra strap it showed off. Had she worn it hoping it would annoy the hell out of Lachlan? Maybe. She, like every woman, was entitled to a few ogle-inducing fashion secrets to be used as weapons.

"I knew none of this. Tell me what happened. Wait." Katie put her hand up. "We need all the girls for this. Let me call them."

"No, no, no." Ruby gently took Katie's phone from her hand and set it down. She did not need her best girlfriends hearing about her most humiliating moment on the planet. "Not tonight. Or any time this weekend. It's celebration time for these two." She gestured toward her best guy friends, gushing with love for each other.

"You're right. It's just that we've all been wondering when the hell he was going to get that tick out of his ass and make a move. It's too juicy to wait. Give me a few nuggets of goodness."

"*He* didn't make a move. I did."

"Ahhh," Katie squealed.

"Then he fumbled big-time. I mean we're talking rookie move, wobbly hands, first-class jerk fumble," Noah added. "To be honest, I never suspected he had that in him. I mean the man is calm, focused, hardworking."

"Intense. Mmm-hmm," Ford agreed.

She should have known her friends would completely ignore her wishes.

"Dumb," Ford added, and they all burst out laughing. It was the bit of relief Ruby needed.

"Ruby, why didn't you tell us. I mean your friendship with me is newer, but Natalie and Ellie would definitely have supported you. Sasha too—she's a great listener."

A bit of shame washed over her. Katie was right. "I felt humiliated, honestly, by the way it all went down. I'd made a huge deal out of my feelings for a man, only for him to toss them aside so easily. I…I didn't enjoy thinking of myself that way, weak, ridiculous."

"You are not weak," all three voices chimed in adamantly at the same time. And it melted the grip on her heart.

"Just ridiculous?" she joked.

"Ridiculously gorgeous, generous, smart, talented, fierce, yes," Ford said. "Everything that man"—he pointed to Lachlan—"is dying to have."

"He isn't." Ruby shook her head. It still left her lungs breathless to face that truth.

"I can't believe you've been suffering with this. I can give him the stink eye anytime you need me to. Foolish man." Katie shot a glare Lachlan's way, then grasped Ruby's hand.

Staying away from the pub had been necessary at first, after he'd struck her with his sword in the office that evening. Then she'd dived into her busiest holiday season at her spa and told herself she didn't have time to frequent the pub like she used to. Subconsciously she'd shied away from several get-togethers with her friends where he'd been invited as well. All that had done was add to her sadness. She had fabulous friends, and she needed to surround herself with them again, not push them away. She'd missed all of this. The close-knit neighborhood, the music, running into people she loved, great food and drinks, celebrating with loved ones. This was her community too and she was done hiding from it.

"I love you all, and, Katie, I'll fill you and the girls in later, but now I want to talk about rehearsal dinner and wedding stuff." Ruby clapped her hands together. "That's why we're here tonight." She raised her glass again. "Cheers to Noah and Ford, to true love and to the beginning of your happily ever after."

She might still be searching for her happy ending, but Ruby had so many blessings. "Let's talk clothes. Katie, what did you decide on, the black off-the-shoulder number or the drop-dead, blinding silver dress with the slit up to your thigh?"

Katie wiggled her eyes and stole a glance at Leo who was sitting at the bar smiling at her. "The silver."

"Oh, you are so in love with your hottie, Katie. That glow is fabulous on you," Ford said.

Katie beamed and stood. "Yeah, I better get back to him before he comes over here, tosses me over his shoulder and drags me home."

"Maybe you should let him," Noah whispered.

They laughed again and Ruby fed on the joy. "Get out of here, my beautiful friend." Ruby gave her a gentle shove. "We'll see you at the wedding on Saturday."

Katie sighed, gave them air kisses and sashayed to her man.

Ruby was surrounded by love, even if she didn't have her own. When she took her gaze off Katie, Ruby caught Lachlan's heated, fierce eyes on her. Ruby returned the glare, tossed her hair out of her eyes, then looked away from the pulsing, angry energy between them.

Deep in her heart of hearts, she longed to give him one more chance, but he'd been such a jerk. He'd made stupid assumptions and hurt her. She'd been surprised at the strength of that pain. Instead of fighting back, she'd secluded herself and licked her wounds. She didn't know if she could withstand the fallout if it all spoiled again. The memory of him looking right through her, *that shattered me.*

She might project to the world a confident, sassy woman. Most days she felt like it. But, as she'd discovered the hard way, when it came to Lachlan MacGregory, her confidence hid a vulnerable beating heart. One that was capable of being bruised. One that still ached.

Chapter Nine

Well, doing Jill a favor and coming to a wedding for people he didn't know as her plus one had ended up being not in *his* favor at all. Fuck, his heart still felt smashed. How could the torment last so long? Lachlan propped himself against a wall, beer in hand, and watched Ruby dance with a crowd of wedding guests. He hadn't seen her much since that hellish encounter in his office. He still had the feeling he'd been the one in the wrong, but now, after seeing her friends get married, he was also fucking confused.

Just because she'd avoided him didn't mean she wasn't every-fucking-where. Her musky perfume lingered on the stairs from her apartment long after she'd left in the mornings. It was the first thing that smacked him the face every day he arrived at the pub, until she'd avoided the back stairs completely and started using the ones from the front that went directly up to her apartment. He'd done that, shoved her away, so she didn't even enjoy inhabiting the same space as him.

One evening as she'd canoodled with Ellie in front of the pub, her full deep laughter had punched him in the lungs and stolen his breath. Even Jackson had asked him where Ruby was at the last few get-togethers at their house, as if it was his business because she lived above his bar. It didn't help that he met weekly with her father, Detective Naylor, regarding the amped-up crime in the neighborhood.

They'd been able to link a few crimes with the remnants of the Lucciano crew, a gang which had mostly scattered when Anthony Lucciano had been killed last summer. The stragglers had been making a play this winter and it was not pretty. Trying to concentrate on the serious shit, like gangs with vendettas, while Ruby's wounded expression hammered in his head was a cold and bitter job. Lachlan felt guilty for even being in her dad's presence.

She'd seemed devastated when she'd slammed out of his office that evening. *Why?* Had she honestly thought he'd keep a promise to her when she had a string of men? The fact that he was in the right hadn't helped him feel one bit better.

The worst was this past Thursday night at the bar when he'd caught a glimpse of her in the corner booth with her men. Weeks, *months* she'd barely entered his pub save for super crowded music nights or knit nights when the place was either too packed to pick her out—although he could always pick her out—or when she'd find some guy and flirt her ass off. Thursday had been busy, but there'd been space enough for them to catch each other's eyes across the pub. She'd dared him with her clear, angry glare that scolded, "*Go to hell!*" He should have felt fine holding his own, but even while she was flaunting her threesome in his space, he still ached for her.

Never believe things can't get worse.

Tonight smashed Thursday night to smithereens. The *worst* was right this fucking minute. On the dance floor, she shimmered light from all the stars in the galaxy in the shortest gold dress he'd ever seen. Long, see-through sleeves, studded with large gold sequins that glittered beneath the lights and lit up against her glowing skin. The neckline took a deep dive almost to her navel, and a flared short skirt showed off her sexy, strong legs, highlighted by simple skyscraper-high black heels with a shimmer of gold across the delicate strap.

He wanted to peel off those shoes and worship those legs of hers. She outshone everyone in the room. A flower held her hair tucked on one side and even from here he could tell she'd gone with glamorous makeup. *Smoke and gold.* Some ripe plum lipstick graced her full lips that smiled wide while she danced and laughed with Katie Walsh's youngest, Cece. From his spot in the corner, he tortured himself watching her.

"Lachlan, this is my friend Noah, the groom," Jill said, startling him from behind. "Or, one of the grooms."

Great. This night keeps getting better and better.

He'd come tonight with Jill who'd said she couldn't handle arriving single to one more of her friends' nuptials. He had no idea, until the festivities had begun, that the wedding was for Ruby's two men. He found himself wondering, or fuming over, how the hell it worked. The men were married now, so were they done with Ruby? Had their arrangement run its course, or were they all three still involved? If they were, did it mean Ruby never got to have her own dream wedding? *Jesus.* He tried to clear his head. Why in the hell was he worried about her getting married?

"He's the accountant slash financial planner guru extraordinaire I told you about. You'd mentioned searching for advice with your accounting since your pub has gotten so busy. Now you two chat while I disappear onto the dance floor and enjoy myself."

"Lachlan MacGregory." Lachlan held out his hand, difficult as it was. Having pretended for years that nothing affected him had its advantages.

Noah smirked, and smacked him once on the shoulder. "I know who you are." He studied the dancers. "Isn't Ruby wonderful? I'm lucky to have her for a friend. Not everybody is as open with their kindness and generosity."

Lachlan braced, wished he'd go deaf suddenly, so he didn't have to listen to all the ways this man thought Ruby was wonderful.

"Not everyone is okay with gay men, but with Ruby, I could always be myself. Now, if I was bi or straight, you can bet your bar I would be down on one knee begging for her love, worshiping her the way she deserves."

"What?" Lachlan set his beer down and faced the man. "I thought..." He cleared his throat. *How the fuck is this conversation supposed to go?* "No offense, I mean...you three..."

The smug look that took over Noah's face sent warning signals through Lachlan's head. "Yeah, Ruby told us all about what you *thought*. We had a damn good laugh over the ridiculousness of it all."

Lachlan rubbed a fist over his chest. *Ridiculousness? What the fuck?*

"Until Ruby started crying. Fucking heartbroken. You crushed her."

"She..." Lachlan shook his head. "I saw you..." He clenched his jaw and swallowed the bile that rose in his throat. That warning signal in his head now screamed, *"Oh, fuck! Oh, fuck!"*

"Yeah, she does massage on me. Since I was in a car accident last year. Not sure I'd be upright if it weren't for her. You didn't know she was a massage therapist too? Well, it's mostly in her past, but thank goodness she still sees me as a client. My husband—damn, it feels great to finally call him that—Ford cooks for her at her apartment and she takes care of my back. Once or twice a month. Best trade ever. It's a win-win for all of us. Except you, I guess." Noah's tone lost any sense of casual.

As that night swirled in his brain, Lachlan's balance shifted and his world rattled. He stood outside the moment, gazing in at the destruction after an earthquake—destruction he'd caused by one incorrect assumption. One horribly wrong choice he'd made. The aftershocks rumbled beneath him.

"You seem like a good man, Lachlan. I love your pub. You've done great things for the Corvallis neighborhood. But you messed up big-time with her. You made our gem cry tears of pain. Takes a lot to make that happen. Haven't seen her lose it like that since her mom died."

Oh fuck is right. The punch to his heart slammed into him. Lachlan closed his eyes and let the memory of that horrible night wash through him. How could he have been so spectacularly wrong? All the tiny indications he'd ignored, that he'd misinterpreted everything, slid into place and formed a solid picture of what a complete jackass he'd been. That intimate, special connection he'd felt with her for those few moments in her apartment, all because of how amazing and strong she was to put her feelings out there. The picture of her sitting on her counter, huge smile glowing as he made promises to her, empty promises he'd shatter the very next day, and again and again.

Coward had never been more apt a name for him. And he'd stupidly thought his heart ached before. Of all the shitty things to do. Across the room, she twirled, full of joy. She'd put herself out there for him and he'd shattered her trust. *Can she forgive me?* He certainly didn't expect her to. He had to pull his act together and apologize. She deserved so much more, but he'd start there.

"I owe you an apology, Noah."

"You don't owe me anything. Ruby's the one who deserves your groveling."

"Yeah." Lachlan traced her with his eyes, wishing he could whisper all the apologies and confessions he needed to in a glance from across the room.

"Thank you—" Lachlan began. He could barely get the words out through the sandpaper in his mouth. "For telling me."

"Do me a favor… After—*if* she forgives you, which she will because her heart's enormous, make up your mind to make the effort or let her go kindly. If you decide to give her what you promised, man up and be all in. She deserves it, and more. And maybe you're the one to give it to her."

This time the smack on Lachlan's shoulder was gentler before Noah walked away. It was the words that stung. *Am I the man for her?* He yearned to be. He *had* fucked up big-time. Now the question pounding with the blood through his heart wasn't only could he fix it, but should he try? *Was* he the man for someone with such depth of beauty as Ruby possessed? He didn't deserve her, but he wanted to. Now he had to figure out how.

Chapter Ten

"Twirl me, Ruby!" Cece pleaded. She grasped Ruby's hands and tried to spin again.

"I'm dizzy, my lovely. No more spinning for a minute."

"But my dress was *made* for twirling."

Ruby giggled at the vehemence of her tiny friend. Seven years old and already the renowned diva of the neighborhood. Ruby aspired to be more like her.

"You look so pretty, Cece. I love that dress." Jill joined their mosh-up.

"Yours is twirly too, Jill! Look at the three of us." Cece danced the trio in a slow circle. "I love fancy dresses. Isn't Ruby's too dynamite?" It was a shame Jill was as nice as she was pretty, because Ruby really wanted to hate her. It seemed as though, in the past, every time Ruby was single, she'd blink and Lachlan would be dating Jill. This time the pinch to her heart was a zillion times worse.

"To die for?" Ruby asked.

Jill grinned. One never knew what was going to come out of young Cece's mouth. "It is gorgeous," Jill started. "Vintage style with a modern twist. Where did you get it?"

"She made it!" Cece let both their hands go and began spinning on her own.

"I only altered it, made it a bit shorter, added flare."

"I love how flirty and sexy it is. I think there is someone else who appreciates it too, or at least can't keep his eyes off you in it." Jill nodded in Lachlan's direction.

Momentarily Ruby was pinned in place by the open vulnerability on Lachlan's face, consuming her with his eyes. They no longer spoke of anger. She couldn't tell what his gaze said. Was it desire, sadness, confusion? All three? He was dressed in a gray suit, with a black shirt underneath, no tie, so handsome. She'd noticed. Now this weird intensity burned off him and it was aimed at her. She nearly fanned herself and took a small step away when reality of standing next to his girlfriend hit her.

"What? Jill, no, I'm sorry…you two are together. There's nothing between us. There never was." How true those three words were.

"Please." Jill rolled her eyes. "The man is pulled to you. And anyone with a pulse can feel the fireworks between you two, and that's with you *not* together."

Ruby shook her head and tried to step off the dance floor. There was no way in hell she was going to break up a couple simply because her heart still ached for what it couldn't have. But Jill took her hand gently and gave it a squeeze. "Lachlan and I are just friends, honey. He's too kind for his own good, and I had a crush on him for about five seconds two years ago, but I'm looking for someone to desire me with the power of all those fireworks lighting up the night sky. He once assisted me with a crappy situation, and honestly, we've only ever been friends."

The music had changed into a slow jazz song and Ruby felt the air shift in the room. Jill's smile and eyes grew huge and she gently nudged Ruby.

"May I?" Lachlan stood right beside her with his hand out.

Ruby stared at his hand, her heart beating wildly to get out of the cage of her chest.

"One dance, Ruby. Please. I know I don't deserve it."

Stuck to the dance floor, her legs wouldn't work. "I...what?" Apparently, her words were out of commission as well. Jill gave her a firm but friendly shove right into the warm, solid body of the man she'd been dreaming about for too long...until he'd burned her.

Jill linked arms with Noah. "Ah, our work here is done."

"For love's sake, let's hope so," Noah replied before he gave Ruby a wink and walked away with Jill.

What madness are they up to?

Lachlan gripped her hand and wrapped his other one around her waist to bring them flush against each other. There was absolutely no hesitation on his part. The contact was almost enough to erase the last few months. Dizzy, confused, she tried to keep up. With four-inch heels she was closer to his height. It felt so natural to rest her hands on his shoulders, to hold on to him, to be pressed up against him. And it wasn't until she did that she realized she was shaking.

"Hey," Lachlan said, gazing down into her eyes.

"What's going on?" she whispered, not because she was worried about anyone hearing them, but because this space suddenly felt sacred, and—because she knew what he was capable of—a tiny bit scary. His hard body moved against hers, achingly slowly as the music led them. God, he was a handsome sight to behold, even more so when he wasn't hiding his emotions away from her in his granite façade. His expression was completely vulnerable, with a hint of…worry?

"You look beautiful." His harsh voice raked over her, stealing its way into her guarded heart.

"What is this? What are we doing? You're talking to me now?" Hope battled with her need to self-protect.

"Your friend Noah illustrated how I stuck my foot up my big ass."

Ruby closed her eyes. She didn't know whether to laugh or cry. She sure as hell didn't know what to say.

For the first time since she'd met him, Lachlan MacGregory did not close off into his quiet stoic nature. "I'm sorry I was such an idiot, Ruby. I'm sorry I made stupid assumptions and didn't ask about your friends that night, that I tried to ignore you afterward. But mostly I'm so sorry I broke my promise to you, that I hurt you. You're this stunning light of joy and beauty that I've hoped to have in my life…" He squeezed her tighter. "For a long damn time. And I screwed up big-time."

"Wow," she said. Her breath came out like she'd been holding on to it, guarding it. *A long damn time?* Her heart peeked out from its hiding place. "You give good apology." She brushed her thumb across his neck. He closed his eyes, sighed and leaned his head into hers.

"Do that again." His voice was both soft and rough as it came out close to her forehead. She didn't recognize this side of him. Her hope blossomed. Ruby held on before she disintegrated into a pile of lust, and, eyes wide open, she stroked Lachlan's neck, marveling at the warm softness of his skin right there. She smoothed along his hard jawline to his cheek.

He braced, tightening his arms around her. The song swept around them. Moody sounds and sparkly lights and Lachlan MacGregory holding her and gazing at her like she was the most beautiful thing the in the world, like she was his salvation. She couldn't help it—her fingers made one soft brush across his lips.

"Jesus, Ruby." He lifted her slightly, for a moment until he slid her body against his, their hard and soft places on fire for each other. "I don't deserve this sweet forgiveness, but I'm not letting it go."

Ruby buried her face in his neck and whispered, "I've wanted you for a long damn time, too, Lachlan. I'm not going to blow my chance after an apology that amazing. We all deserve another chance."

He held her and moved them in a slow circle on the dance floor.

"I don't come from the same place you do, Ruby. I don't know if I can be the man you deserve."

"The same place as me?"

"A solid home life with a strong foundation. You're bold and brave and confident in everything you do, Ruby."

What in the world is this man talking about?

"But I want to try. I'd like a do-over."

That drew a smile from her. "A do-over?"

"Yes, wherein I make a promise to you. Then we say goodnight, to keep up the anticipation. Only, this time, instead of me shattering that for both of us, I get to see you tomorrow for our first official date."

"Wherein?" she whispered. Her heart felt like laughing in relief, in absolute delight. It thundered into hope for this man standing right in front of her. She'd be a fool to say no, to not give this second chance everything she had.

"Need me to define it for you?" He gave her his full, open smile and it transformed all the serious worry on his face into…*talk about beauty. A night sky with the Northern Lights, awe-inducing.*

She shook her head, let go of his hand and wrapped it around the back of his neck to meet her other one, which had the delicious advantage of allowing both his strong hands to grip her waist and tug her even closer. Any closer and they'd be one. And that thought had her dizzy too, dizzy with desire and happiness. She'd had all kinds of lovely dreams about them being one. Now those images could spring into life again.

It was a while before they stopped dancing, holding each other, talking close. She was certain there were a few fast songs in the mix, but she and Lachlan stayed in their own tight bond, their own seductive little world. It didn't feel small. Ruby felt the entire world expanding for her, for them.

Jill had gotten a ride home with the Treversinis and Ruby couldn't decide if she wanted the night to end so she could get that goodnight kiss, that delicious promise, and fast forward their way to tomorrow, or stay dancing under the twinkly lights, secured like a special package in Lachlan's arms forever.

Chapter Eleven

Lachlan's phone was buzzing in his pocket. The last thing he needed to interrupt his first, and especially hours-long, dance with Ruby was a phone call after midnight. There was no such thing as good news at that time of night. And dancing with Ruby in his arms was about the best place he'd ever been. Nothing should end this moment.

"Your pocket is vibrating." Ruby's head rested against his chest, but her hands were snug on his hips. He loved each placement of her body against his.

"Yeah," he chuckled. "It's not exactly the kind of vibrating I had in mind when I pictured you and I together."

Ruby's smile was huge and sexy when she met his gaze with her sea-deep eyes.

"You're cute when you blush. Never saw a blush look so fucking sexy on a woman before." He ran his knuckles over her cheek. Ruby pressed her glorious frame into his, making him harder, if that was possible.

When she hummed, he knew it was. Those sounds she made shot straight through him.

"Mmm, I'm definitely down for having a different conversation about things that vibrate. In fact, I have several items that vibrate we could play with, indeed."

"Fuck, Ruby." He was losing control. It didn't take much with her. This night had been serious and meaningful, and fun. She'd slid them right into the joy of it all.

She giggled into his chest. That was what finally made him stop dancing. "I'm such an idiot. I knew you were classy and smart. Had no idea how fucking sexy you were. Or how cute you are when you tease. Could only dream about it. I'm so sorry it took me so long to apologize."

"Lachlan," she whispered.

"Glad I finally did. Even if it took our friends intervening to make that happen. Now." He traced his finger along her neck, smoothed his thumb over her jaw and sent one soft brush against her lips, like she'd done to him. "I need to get your precious heart home so I can say goodnight and we can see what promises the morning brings."

She nearly stumbled at his words, but his arms caught her. "You make it sound even better than the first time, Lachlan."

He set his lips on hers teasing them both and whispered, "I promise to make it so, Ruby." His phone hummed again. "I should check that. It might be the pub." Last call was at midnight on Saturdays and his bartenders and employees were awesome, but with alcohol involved, he made sure they knew he was always available if something came up.

"You check your phone. I'll grab my coat," Ruby said and sashayed away. He was momentarily stunned in place at the magnitude of this night, what priceless grace she'd given him—the prettiest woman he'd ever seen walking toward or away from him. And this time he could watch with a warm smile, knowing they were finally headed in the right direction. Together.

* * * *

Lachlan pulled up behind his pub and was out of the car door, sliding carefully across the pavement and opening Ruby's for her before she could make a move. The crystal-clear evening had whisked any warmth away and left ice forming on the streets and sidewalks. The tree branches were lit with icicles and sparkled with the glow of the streetlights. Now, clouds were swooping in to cocoon the night. It was quiet, peaceful and deceptive. No way was he letting her slip on those heels. Besides, a goodnight promise was in order before he went in search of his father. *Again.*

Lachlan helped her down but didn't move them away from the door or the remaining warmth of the truck. Wrapped in each other's arms, surrounded by the icy air and stars, their breath whispering between them, Ruby had never looked more gorgeous. It sure felt good having her in his arms. The special touch of hers snuck into him. He'd spent most of his life on the outside, either by force or necessity. And his first taste of being an insider was when his pub began to thrive. He'd worked damn hard to earn the neighborhood's respect. And he had.

But a few months ago in Ruby's arms, right before he'd been a colossal dick, that kind of belonging had topped everything, shoved all other desires out the window. For those few seconds, Lachlan had felt something elusive to him, exactly where he was meant to be. Now he was back there, and the thought of leaving her unsettled him. Her warmth fed his dark soul.

"As much as I am thrilled at the idea of a do-over for a beautiful next morning, I also wish you'd come up right now. Your apology, dancing with you, talking and sharing with you…I don't want the night to end," she whispered, echoing his thoughts. "I think our beginning should happen now."

"Ruby." Lachlan shoved his head into her neck and reveled in the feel of her arms tightening around him. "I hate the thought of letting you out of my sight now that I have you. Even though I'm really fucking looking forward to a promise I made that I intend to keep this time, I can't blow off this phone call. Wish I could."

"Will you tell me what it's about? It's almost two in the morning, Lachlan." Worry crossed her face and he definitely didn't like leaving her with that emotion.

Lachlan brushed his thumb over her cheek, rosy in the cold air, feeling her shiver. "Short version, it's my dad."

"Oh," Ruby said. "Everything all right?"

He didn't want to mar this night in any way, but he also didn't relish lying to Ruby Naylor, the girl he'd been in love with since he was a boy. In the quiet, cold air he silently vowed to always be honest with her. "Nope."

Concern washed over her face and she stroked her chilly hand up and down his neck, searching for more answers in his eyes. "Longer version is for when we have more time and you're not freezing outside in my arms." Lachlan closed the door and, keeping a careful grip on her waist, carefully navigated her to the back door of the pub.

"Mmm, I really enjoy being in your arms, Lachlan."

An icy pavement had its pluses. "Yeah." He was pretty sure he had a goofy grin, and he didn't give a fuck. "Ended up being a great night, didn't it?"

"The best." Ruby ran her hands over his chest, following her hands with her eyes. When she glanced up at him, those deep ocean swirls were clear and happy. "Thank you for apologizing. It means a lot to me, Lachlan."

"Grateful you let me. I…this…it isn't casual for me. The way I feel about you, have felt about you…"

She stopped him with a finger to his lips. "It's not casual for me either. It never was."

"Good. Can I make you another promise?"

"Yeah."

"I promise not to ghost you again if I misunderstand a situation. I may be quiet and spend way too much time in my own head, but I don't deliberately try to be an asshole. Now get inside before we freeze to death. I'm looking forward to that first kiss."

Ruby gave him wide eyes, stood high on her heels and stole a wisp of a kiss, brushing her soft lips ever so slowly against his. Then she waltzed up two steps. Glancing down she said, "That one doesn't count."

Stunned, turned on, watching her walk away with the feeling of her sweet lips on his, Lachlan took one step up to make them eye level, gripped her close with his arms and whispered his words against her mouth. "Oh yes it does." Then he brought his mouth a fraction of an inch closer and devoured her, like he'd wanted to from the beginning.

Sweet, so damn sweet. *Every* kiss from her counted. He savored and explored. She held his head and returned the passion, tasting him, opening to him. When she whimpered and opened her mouth, he was thrilled to take what she offered, diving his tongue in to duel with hers. Was it a battle or submission? *Both.* The two of them taking and giving. The way she gripped his head, kneading her fingernails in, and the soft and hungry feel of her lips while she was pressed up against him almost had his knees buckling.

She shivered and betrayed the heat burning between them, and as much as it hurt physically to pull away, Lachlan slowed down and rested his forehead in her neck. Her neck was becoming one of his favorite places.

"Lachlan?"

"It counts," he said.

"Hmm?" Ruby asked, sounding as lost in a dream as he felt.

"Everything with you counts. Every touch, smile, especially every soft whisper of your lips on mine counts, gorgeous."

"Oh." Her soft voice drifted over his ear. "Yes. I agree."

Lachlan almost tossed aside all his responsibilities and guilt and nagging uncomfortable feeling about his father and chased her up the stairs to her apartment where they could get lost in each other completely. He took a deep breath. The image would have to last him a while longer. So instead, feeling her shivers once more, he gathered his wits, spun her away from him and gently urged her up the stairs.

"Go. Get warm. I'll call you in the morning, and..." He smiled. "And thanks for the dance. It was the best dance of my life."

He was rewarded with her bright smile and breathy "Yeah" before he headed into the frigid night alone.

Chapter Twelve

Almost two in the morning, and Ruby was still twirling, inside and out when she floated into her apartment. *Ahhh, heat, I love you.* The warmth enclosed her freezing but happy body. Absolutely too wired to go to bed, she was overflowing with sparkles and she planned to enjoy them for as long as they lasted. She switched on one low lamp and lit her two favorite candles on her coffee table. The scent of bergamot and rose filtered through the air. A fairy hint of flickering candlelight set the perfect, pretty, hushed mood after a spectacular night.

An exhausting week at work followed by a weekend of busy wedding festivities with two of her greatest friends, on her feet all day yesterday, dancing in heels for hours into the night with Lachlan—Ruby should be exhausted. Instead, her heart swelled, and she danced in her small living room and kitchen, elated, on a love high. She did kick off her heels though. Stupendous though they were, blister-inducing they might also be.

She'd have to assess the damage in the morning. Right now, while she warmed fingertips and toes, she was going to remember a night surrounded by love, a night of beauty, a night of music and bliss in Lachlan's arms.

Noah and Ford had fabulous taste in music and the DJ had been on fire tonight, even before Ruby had been held close in Lachlan's arms. She'd been aware of Lachlan as always, even though he'd mostly stayed in the shadows, but she'd shoved away her feelings toward him and decided to enjoy the wedding. Katie, Leo and their girls, Katie's brother Connor, Noah and Ford, other friends had helped her kick up her heels and have a blast.

Lachlan had put himself out there, literally in the middle of all that chaos, and, with his heart to hers, lifted the shroud of pain and uncomfortableness of the last few months. Memories of Johnny Lang's voice seducing them together in their romantic bubble while they whispered and shared, Lachlan's warm hands never leaving her, had her swaying and capturing the moment into the chamber of her heart she'd locked away from him months ago. Dancing with each other felt better than she'd dreamed.

They'd talked and laughed and teased like people who'd been connected for years. The man had a hidden sense of humor she couldn't wait to explore in depth, and his sexy vibes were intense.

That kiss, wow! She held her hand to her cheek to feel the flush he'd left on her skin. Her bones might have been freezing in the cold night air, but everywhere he'd touched her had burned. And while she wished again that he would have followed her up the stairs tonight and stayed, she couldn't wait to see what his promises brought in the morning. Anticipation might just keep her up all night. It would be so, so worth it.

She opened one of her mini bottles of bubbly and poured it into a special champagne flute to celebrate the moment, the day full of joy. Lachlan had given her his beautiful, vulnerable, apology under the glowing chandeliers, surrounded by their friends, and held her like she was beloved. Ruby had led a pretty fabulous life, but never had she felt so special as the way she had in his arms, with his soul beating against hers. *Tingly* was the best word to describe it.

From her spot in her kitchen, she could see out through the window to the street, and in the glow of the streetlights huge flakes of snow began drifting to the ground. *How perfectly lovely.* She sank onto the cushions in her kitchen window seat and covered her feet and legs with her chunky throw blanket. In the shadowed apartment, glowing with the light of only a few candles, Ruby sipped her celebratory glass of champagne and watched the world turn white and shimmery beneath her.

It truly was one perfect, peaceful moment. There was nothing more magical than watching snow fall. Maybe there'd be enough in the morning for a walk with Lachlan, hand in hand, strolling close to each other. *Or a snowball fight.* She could take him sledding in the park. Ruby smiled and giggled to herself. *Oh my, how we could warm each other up afterward.*

Ruby stood, set the glass on the counter and poured the rest of the champagne. She was reaching for the recycling bin when a crash sounded below her. She jumped and flung out her hand, sending both her glass and the bottle smashing onto her kitchen floor, echoing more sounds of things breaking below her. But downstairs, it wasn't one champagne flute and a bottle—it was loud and frightening, the amount of glass she could hear shattering. *Lachlan's pub?*

"Shit! Shit!" Ruby whispered and crouched, hiding behind her kitchen cabinets. Her blood raced, making her feel lightheaded. The sounds of glass shattering, thuds, grunts and a high-pitched piercing alarm rose from downstairs. *The pub. Oh my God! What the hell is happening?* Frozen for a moment, Ruby huddled and listened to the sounds of things being destroyed one floor beneath her. There was a voice…or two…yelling, followed by more crashing. She closed her eyes tight to the horrible visions of Lachlan's heart and soul being destroyed. Then fear chilled her veins.

Get your phone now! Ruby scrambled across the floor as quietly as she could, Adrenaline and dread racing through her. She bit her lip to keep from crying out as pain shot through her knees. Her purse was on the couch where she'd tossed it. Hands shaking, she fumbled through her password and dialed nine-one-one.

"Someone's breaking into Lachlan's pub at forty-two-hundred Corvallis." She spoke clearly but in a hushed voice over the police operator. "My name is Ruby Naylor, Detective Naylor's daughter, and I live above the pub. Lachlan's, the corner of Corvallis Street and Cedar. You have to hurry." Images of Lachlan's pride being destroyed fueled her emotions. "I'm upstairs."

"Ruby, can you make sure your doors are locked and get somewhere safe in your apartment? Officers are on their way. Mr. MacGregory's security company alerted us right before you called. I'll stay on the phone with you until they arrive and you're safe. You don't have to talk. Get safe and stay with me. They're two minutes out."

"Okay, okay," she whispered as she ran-tiptoed into her bedroom closet, quietly shut the door and sank to the floor by her safe where she kept the gun her dad had given her and trained her how to use—a gun she hoped to never need. She hated guns. She hated them even more in this moment when she might have to use it. Ruby tried to calm down enough to open the safe, just in case. "I'm in my bedroom closet. Please hurry. Someone's destroying his pub. It's his…he built it himself. It's so wonderful and cozy and…" Oh, God she was babbling.

"Police are almost there, Ruby. I know Lachlan's. It's our favorite place to go on Friday nights for the music. And his mushroom pies are the best, aren't they?"

"Yeah," Ruby said, beginning to shake, only not from the cold this time.

"You're going to be okay, honey. We're going to get to you. Stay put if you can."

Taking deep breaths, Ruby rested her forehead on her knees and hugged them close to her chest. Agony sliced through her right knee.

"Dammit!" Sharp pinpricks began to throb in both knees.

"Ruby? Are you okay?"

"I don't know…I…my knees are bleeding." There was something wet on her leg, but she couldn't tell what it was in the dark. Her hands began to throb too. What had she done? Sirens sounded in the distance then, not a few seconds later, landed outside. "I think they're here," she whispered. "The police."

"Yes, Ruby. They're outside now. Please stay where you are. I'm sending a paramedic too. Stay safe, honey." She could hear them now, the police voices in the night and the dispatcher on the phone. And while the shakes took over her body, she prayed whatever had happened downstairs wasn't as bad as it sounded.

"Okay, Ruby, the police are in the pub. They've cleared it of anyone who might have been there, but they're telling me there's a small fire. They've extinguished it and the fire department should be there almost immediately since they're right down the street. Can you hold on a few more moments?"

"Yes," she whispered, having lost the ability to talk through her terror and worry. A few minutes ticked by. Ruby could hear each thud of her heart. It was forever stretched out into infinity.

"Okay, Ruby, two firefighters are coming up to you now. Fire Captain James and Lieutenant Morgan are at your door. You know both of them. Can you let them in?"

Ruby crumpled over her knees and tried to calm the surge that churned her stomach. "Yes…I…I'm going now. Can you stay with me, until…?"

"I promise, Ruby."

She slammed her safe shut, dragged herself up and shifted along the walls till she got to her living room and ran to the door. "Ruby, it's Clara, honey. I'm with Captain James. We're here to help you. It's safe. Can you open the door?"

"Yes, yes." Ruby unlocked her door. She threw herself into her friend Clara's arms and held on tight. The dizziness whooshed in, a banshee crashing into her stomach. "I'm going to be sick." Ruby barely made it to the bathroom in time.

Clara was there beside her in an instant, rubbing her shoulder. "Hey, you're safe."

"Yeah." Ruby sat on the bathroom floor until the nausea had passed. "Thank you."

Her friend's eyes grew more serious as she investigated Ruby's knees. "You're bleeding."

"Oh." It was the only word she could muster.

"I can check you out up here, or we could go down to the ambulance?"

When Ruby closed her eyes all she could hear was the memories of shattering glass and an alarm blaring through the night. "I don't want to be here."

"Okay, outside it is. I'm going to bundle you in this coat and Captain James is going to carry you. Don't worry, we'll take care of you."

Chapter Thirteen

He shouldn't have been surprised that his dad was MIA. The last place Denny had been staying was the small, old Meyer Motel down at the east side of the river. Mr. and Mrs. Meyer had owned if for as long as Lachlan could remember. It was next to the gas station and candy shop Lachlan had used to ride his bike to when he was a child. They took good care of their humble motel, took good care of the neighborhood, which hadn't always been easy over the years. Several times during the last few months, Lachlan had made sure his dad's motel bill had been paid. No sense leaving the Meyers in the lurch because of an irresponsible drunk.

Lachlan hated giving his father money. And he hated himself for feeling like that. Old resentment, long buried, still simmered. But whenever he called, Lachlan still answered. Maybe it made *him* the idiot, not his father. Help the man who was still hell-bent on driving his own life into the ground? Or ignore? Guilt ate at Lachlan no matter what he chose.

"Haven't seen him in over a week, son," Mr. Meyer said when Lachlan buzzed into the motel office.

"I got a message from him about an hour ago, said he'd be here, that he was sick. He sounded awful. But there's no answer at his room. His curtains are open. No one's there."

"Nope. We had to change rooms for him. To be honest, Lachlan, I'm not sure how much longer we can let him stay here. It's not about the money, and you've been good to us, but the state of his room last week when we went to clean it...well, we had to replace the mattress and the carpet will have to be ripped out."

"I'm so sorry, Joe."

"Not your fault. He's sick. Sickest I've seen him. Agitated too. Can't help an addict who doesn't want to be helped. You know that."

Yeah. He couldn't get the word out through the burn in his throat. He knew, yet he kept trying. Some days he wondered how his dad had survived this long. "You have my card on file. Whatever you need. Charge me for all the damages." Lachlan opened the door. "And, Joe, can you call me if you see him?"

"I will, son. You take care now. Anna and I will be there on Saturday for those savory pies you make. Save me and my girl our special table, will you?" Joe winked at him.

"Always," Lachlan said. And even through all the despair in his gut from his father, he left with a ghost of a smile, thinking of Joe and Anna Meyer and how long their love story had endured. The smile probably had to do with the fact that Lachlan might now get the chance for his own beautiful love story with Ruby.

His phone rang again as he opened the door to his truck. A fury of messages beeped in at the same time. *Jesus Christ, why am I so popular in the middle of the night?* He'd been running around like an idiot in the freezing darkness and all he desired was to still be dancing in Ruby's arms or taking that kiss up the stairs with her, into her apartment and all the way into tomorrow.

The ringing and buzzing sounded again almost simultaneously. Grabbing his phone, he saw his security company's name flashing, which meant his alarm had been tripped at the—

"Fuck!" he swore as the security personnel alerted him to a breach at forty-two-hundred Corvallis, the pub. His heart sank to his gut as one image flashed through his mind. *Ruby.*

With his heart pounding, he jerked his truck into gear and put all his focus, his adrenaline on getting to her. The empty road and cocoon of a winter night left space for every single worry and horrible scenario to invade his mind.

Lachlan had never been so scared in his life, not even when he'd been a kid hiding from his dad's angry temper, or when he and his mom had lived in their car for a few months before she'd found a friend to stay with. His heart only started beating again once he saw Ruby outside, sitting in an ambulance, covered in an enormous down coat and holding a mug. He'd barely parked when he threw open his door and ran to her, almost skidding on the slick parking lot surface. Thankfully all the cops and people milling about had melted some of the ice. He ignored everyone else, his focus solely on his woman. Jesus, he wanted her to be his. If they could have a normal date, a normal day…

Christ, he'd take one hour of them being together without the world caving in.

He reached out his hands, uncertain whether to touch her or not.

"I'm okay," Ruby said before he could get any words out. She set her mug down and reached for him.

She looked so lonely and scared and exhausted. Instinct and need had him surging in and wrapping her up in his arms. She exhaled a deep breath and melted into him. Shaking her head in his chest she said, "I'm so sorry, Lachlan, your bar…your beautiful bar…they…someone…"

"Why are you sitting barefoot in an ambulance with the doors open?" His words caught on gravel. Each one a razor on his throat.

"I wanted to make sure to see you, when…" She peeked up at him, her face drawn and void of its usual glow. "When you got here. Someone broke into your pub and the destruction…I could hear it." Ruby shook her head and swallowed. Tears leaked out from her eyes that still held a measure of unease, but also anger. "The sound was horrible. There was more than one person. I heard shattering glass and voices yelling at each other."

In that moment Lachlan couldn't give a fuck about his bar. He held Ruby away from him and took her in. Her face streaked with tears, her warm hands, one enclosed in bandages. "Are you okay? That's what I care about." The reality slammed into him that she could have been seriously harmed by whoever the hell had broken into his business.

"I'm okay. I hid upstairs in the closet until the firefighters came and got me."

Holding her bandaged hand out gently, he brushed light strokes over her fingers, noticed more bandages on her knees and gauze covering one of her bare feet. There was blood streaked on the hem of her dress, marring the sequins and shimmery fabric. *Dried blood on her knees and hand.* Anger surged in his chest. He dropped her hand so he wouldn't squeeze the life out of it or cause her any more pain. *Fuck!*

"Why is there blood on you?" His voice sounded as bitter as the wind howling through the parking lot. "Did they…were you…they hurt you?"

"Lachlan," Detective Naylor shouted and jogged over to meet them at the ambulance. "Have you been inside, son?"

Inside? Inside what? All he could see was the blood on Ruby's dress and knees and bandages while she sat injured in the freezing cold, in the middle of the night waiting for him, fear drawn in the lines of her face. "Why is there blood on her?" he demanded. "Who hurt her?" Jesus, he could barely speak, bellows stoking the rage inside him at the thought of someone harming Ruby.

"You need to calm down, before you head inside, Mac," Isaac ordered.

He was yelling at Ruby's dad who had to be pissed off himself. He breathed in deeply and tried to control his temper.

"I broke a glass and cut myself when I crawled across the floor, Lachlan," Ruby interrupted. She grabbed his hand. "I'm okay. No one did this to me. I was freaked out and got clumsy."

Lachlan had to walk away a few paces and suck in deep lungfulls of cold air because the last thing he was right now was calm. "*I was freaked out.*" His Ruby had been upstairs, terrified while someone vandalized his bar. He'd never wanted to punch someone more in his life.

Isaac followed him and gripped his shoulder. "Mac, she's okay. Trust me. She's the first thing we took care of when we got here after putting out the fire. Now listen to me. It's bad in there, but nothing that can't be fixed."

Lachlan faced the man who'd been a positive influence in his world when he was a child and his life was shitty and scary, and now again, when his life was promising, aside from someone vandalizing his pub and Ruby getting injured. The man had only seen the good in Lachlan. He pointed at Ruby. "She crawled across broken glass and hid in a closet because of me. Her skin, her dress…has blood on it," he bit out. "I'm going to need a moment."

Isaac held his gaze and studied him before a ghost of a smile appeared for an instant. "Yeah. I get you. Scared the fuck out of me when I heard the call. Nearly puked when I saw my baby sitting in the ambulance. But she's okay. And her injuries are not because of you. It's because of the person or people who committed a crime. Get that through your head. Be pissed, then find a way to rein it in, at least for now, because Ruby's okay. Facing what you're going to see inside is not going to be easy. Can you handle it?"

Lachlan let the detective's strong voice edge through the tornado in his mind. Deep breaths steadied him and he banked his rage. The fear was more difficult. *Jesus Christ, what would I do if something happened to her?* Isaac's grip on his shoulders and directness helped. "Give me a minute," Lachlan said.

"Yeah, I'll wait for you at the door, go in with you."

"Appreciate it," Lachlan said.

Isaac nodded and said, "Anytime. We're all here for you. Anything you need, son."

One words, *son*, carried through the frigid night and hit Lachlan deeper than one simple word should. Tonight, in fact most of his life, it had come from two men who weren't related to him, who didn't owe him anything. Not once, in his crappy childhood or successful adult life, had it come from his dad.

"Anytime… Anything you need, son."

Sacred words, meaningful words. He had to find a way to smother the resentment over how lacking his real father was. When he faced Ruby, she was watching him. Fuck, this stunning creature was worried about him and *she* was the one who was injured.

"Do you want me to come with you? Inside? To see it?" she asked, reaching for his hand again. He enclosed her uninjured hand with both of his. "I think it's pretty bad." Her voice was a whisper.

He shook his head, unable to speak again. She amazed him over and over. Here she was injured and stressed after suffering a trauma and she still tried to support him. So much time wasted—him being a chicken, watching her beauty from the sidelines, and months of him being a jerk—passed through his mind. Months that maybe he could have had all that goodness connected to him in a way he wanted more than anything right now. What he didn't want was for her to see what had happened inside. She'd been through enough for one night.

"No, Ruby. You need to get in your apartment and get warm. I can carry you upstairs. Hate the thought of you sitting out here in the cold, injured, exhausted."

"I'm warm enough. I'll wait out here for you and my dad... I'm..." A shudder moved through her. "I'm going to stay at his house tonight...uhm...until they get the pub doors fixed and..." She glanced at her wounds. "I guess until I can wear shoes again."

Jesus, she was scared of her own home. "Ruby." Lachlan reached out and put his hand on her cheek. She leaned immediately into his touch. "I need to hug you again—is that okay with you?"

She nodded and he moved in. They didn't speak, simply held each other for a minute, letting their bodies speak for them, her heart beating against his, finding a rhythm with each other's. This was where he found his calm. He could happily drown in that feeling. "Seems I keep snagging you in the freezing air and making you shiver."

"I'm hoping that means there's cozy around the corner for us soon." Then she whispered, "Go. I'm okay. They have the heat cranked up for me, Lachlan. I'm safe out here. I'm not going anywhere until you and my dad come out, okay?"

"Okay, beautiful." Lachlan brushed his lips against her cheek, gave her one last squeeze and headed in to see what the hell had happened to his pub.

Chapter Fourteen

"Your people are here, Ruby." Her father handed her a water bottle and went to let her friends in. "I'm heading to work. You need anything, you call me immediately. Got a car on the house."

"Dad, I don't need police watching the house. What happened at Lachlan's had nothing to do with me."

"Just being safe with my gem." He winked at her and the moment of peace was tipped upside down when her friends blew in.

"Tell us everything!" Natalie demanded. "How are you? How's Lachlan? What the hell happened?" She had a full wine bag in one hand and a pizza box in the other.

Last night, or in the middle of the early morning, Katie's fiancé, Leo, had found her in the ambulance shortly after Lachlan and her dad had gone into the bar. He'd heard the sirens and seen the lights from their home up the block and he'd come down immediately. He'd informed all their friends. She'd briefly talked with Ford, Katie and Natalie on the phone to assure them she was okay. And now, after a few hours of fitful sleep and too long wondering how Lachlan was, her girlfriends had come to check on her, while the guys finished helping Lachlan clean up the mess at his pub, all except for Noah and Ford who were on a plane to Hawaii for their honeymoon. They'd offered to stay, and she was so glad they hadn't.

Demanding and hardworking like a general, Natalie would probably have been more help down at the pub, but Ruby was grateful she'd come here instead. Ruby needed her friends.

"Are you okay?" Ellie's eyes were huge and worried when she sat next to Ruby. She leaned in for a side hug, her enormous pregnant belly getting in the way. "Your feet!"

"Yeah," Ruby whispered. Her legs were propped on an ottoman, feet bare, one bandaged. "A little cut up from racing across broken glass. My own fault. But I'm going be fine, my lovely friend."

"Thank goodness it wasn't worse," Ellie said. "We all needed to come and make sure."

"I don't think you ladies brought enough food," Ruby joked as Katie waltzed in next and started unpacking food containers from her cafe. Ruby could smell wonderful Italian sauces and her mouth started to water.

"Oh." Katie gave her the mom eye with the raised eyebrow. "We have a lot to catch up on now, don't we? And when have you complained about too much food?"

Ruby giggled. "Never. Especially *your* food."

"I made caramel chocolate cheesecake," Sasha said. She set the platter down carefully and removed the leash from her enormous Boxer.

"You made cheesecake?" Ruby whispered in awe and got to see Sasha's almost-smile. Her eyes were smiling too, which was so nice to see.

"I...I mean..." Sasha eyed the cake then gave a quick glance toward Ruby. "It's my first attempt at anything other than plain cheesecake," she said uncertainly. "New flavors have been floating through my mind.

"I love cheesecake," Ruby and Ellie said at the exact same time. This time Ellie burst into giggles first, but Ruby gave her wide silly eyes and followed.

"I could eat an entire cheesecake," Ellie sighed and closed her eyes, rubbing her baby belly.

Katie gave Sasha's arm a squeeze. "Sasha, this is the easiest crowd when it comes to food. Besides all the other things you've been making at the bakery have been out of this world."

There was a moment of quiet and Sasha gave them all a genuine smile. "Thank you. I love working there. In fact, I... It's... Well, that's all. It's wonderful."

"Good," Ruby replied. "I'm so glad you have that. A job you love, a place to work you feel comfortable and you know you have all of us too. Right?"

Sasha took a step in and sat on the couch, Braveheart at her feet, not quite fully relaxed, but there was progress. Or maybe he was similar to other trauma survivors, a few steps forward, some back.

"Places are easier. People are more difficult still," Sasha said quietly. "I like the busyness of you all." She twirled her hand in the air. "The talking, the noise, but I don't always know how to be a part of it." Sasha had endured a horrible, abusive marriage that had nearly ended her life. Now, even though her evil husband was dead, she was still finding her own new path.

"For a long time, I...well, he cut me off from everyone, and now that I'm alone, I feel...well, like I'm studying, taking notes on it all, on people."

Too stunned to say anything, Ruby felt the quiet settle in the room. This was the first time Sasha had willingly shared any details with them.

"Well," Natalie began, breaking the tension. "If there was ever a group to take notes on, this hilarious one is it." They all laughed, and even Sasha relaxed a bit and gave a small laugh. *Leave it to Natalie to bring humor into any situation.*

Ruby hoped they were what Sasha needed after her horrible past. After all, it was Ruby's favorite group.

"Speaking of people," Katie said. "We have a lot to talk about. And while I think we should get the bad part out of the way first. I'm all kinds of interested in the two *people* who spent hours glued together on the dance floor last night. And how long those two people have been googly eyeing each other and dancing around each other, *instead* of plastered together. And why it took so damn long for the plastering."

"Are you together?" Ellie asked, her pretty glow lighting up her face. "I've been hoping."

They weren't going to let her avoid it. Which was perfectly fine, because she wanted to share now. She couldn't wait to talk about all of it. But Katie was right. *Might as well get the bad out of the way.* Natalie handed out wine and tea then snuggled in right next to Ellie.

Ruby took a sip of her wine and told them everything about last night, which wasn't much more than they'd already learned. "Lachlan texted me this morning about ten to see how I was. He'd been there all night. But I haven't heard much else. Dad brought me here about three a.m."

"Leo said last night that it looked like a tornado had blown through. Liquor bottles and glasses broken all over the pub. The mirror behind the bar was shattered and tables and chairs were flipped over, some broken. The front door was destroyed. They obviously didn't care if there was an alarm, but were hell-bent on even a few moments of destruction. They were gone when the police arrived," Katie said. "All of that damage in the blink of an eye."

Ruby's heart sank, thinking about Lachlan's pub and how special it was. She'd heard the destruction. It was horrible acknowledging that it had really happened. "Who would do that to his pub? It's the foundation of our neighborhood. I don't understand."

"It wasn't quite as bad in the daylight, honey," Ellie chimed in with her sweet, positive tone. "When I dropped Jackson off, all the glass was cleaned up, the liquor too. And the broken chairs had been removed. Connor was already fixing two of the tables and had ordered a new mirror for above the bar. Jackson and Gage were going to install a new temporary door. Sasha, Katie and the Heelys delivered enough food and coffee for an army, Carl offered anything they needed from the hardware store and Mr. and Mrs. Meyer were hovering over Lachlan as if he was their long-lost son who'd recently returned from war. Lachlan has a lot of people in this town who love him. Some of the local bands even showed up to work. Word traveled fast about what had happened. The place was as busy as a Friday night. Gage had them laughing with his tall tales."

"Were you scared? Last night, when it was happening?" Sasha asked. If anyone would understand about terror, it would be Sasha.

"Yes," Ruby admitted. "But it all happened so fast. I heard the break-in, broke my own glass, crawled to my phone, hid in the closet and called the police. I didn't even realize I had cut myself until the adrenaline faded away. But I'm ticked right the hell off for Lachlan. They had to have known about the alarm. Even if they didn't, once they broke in, they heard it."

"You're brave," Sasha said, "staying calm, calling the police."

"You're the brave one, my dear," Ruby said. "We're going to keep telling you that until you believe us."

"Cheers to that!" Natalie raised her glass and they all clinked. God, Ruby loved her friends. "Sasha, you're stuck with us and all our goofy shenanigans."

"Well," Sasha said, a full blush rising up her cheeks. "Maybe it's time to get to the good stuff then."

"*That* deserves a cheers, too," Ellie said. "Now spill. Start at the beginning from last year and don't leave out one single drop of goodness or tension or ogling."

"Last year?" Ruby couldn't hide her incredulous look.

"Uh, hello! We've been watching you two sashay around each other for forever. Last night's real dance was a shock, if you will, but not a surprise to any of us," Natalie said.

"Mmm hmm," Sasha agreed with a smile. "Even I noticed the laser beams you two have been shooting across rooms at each other."

Ruby smiled. Her friends had intelligent spy-like instincts, every single one of them. And she loved them all for it.

"Honestly," she began, "I felt something special the first time I met him, when I rented the apartment from him. But I didn't think he felt the same. He came off so stoic and silent. I thought he was dating Jill on and off. I dated loosely. But once in a while I would feel him looking at me when he thought I wasn't paying attention. I tried flirting. You know I did. I even tried—"

"Flirting with other guys so Lachlan would see," Katie said.

"Yes, which I'm not proud of, but the man is a rock. I figured nothing would happen unless I made a move and threw myself at him. So I did."

"What?"

"When?"

"You didn't! You did?"

She laughed as all her friends chimed in. "It was a few months ago. One night after we all had drinks at the pub. He walked me upstairs and I went for it. Asked him if he was ever going to kiss me."

"Go, Ruby!" Katie said.

"How was it?" Natalie sat on the edge of her seat like she was watching a soap opera, a great keep-you-on-the-edge-of-your seat soap opera.

"The kiss didn't happen."

"No!!!" Natalie fell onto her seat. "Don't tell me he botched it."

"Actually, he was incredible. He blew my world apart! Said he wanted to kiss me, had hoped to for a long time but wanted me to be sober so I would remember it. He said a lot of things." Ruby fanned her face. "I think he was trying to be a gentleman because I'd been drinking. Made me a beautiful promise about the next day. Then left me alone in my apartment."

"It sounds lovely," Ellie said and bumped her shoulder. "Aside from the leaving part."

"It was. I had no idea the man had so many glorious words inside him. Unfortunately, then he ignored me." Ruby didn't enjoy rehashing the ugly, but she felt it prudent to give her friends the whole picture. Not that they would have let her get away with anything less. When she told them what Lachlan had misinterpreted and about their angry conversation in his office in October, they all stared at her with open mouths and wide eyes.

Natalie was the first to break. Shaking her head, she said, "Oh, Lachlan, you foolish man."

Ellie covered her mouth to hide her laughter. Sasha didn't hide her hers which Ruby took as one more baby step of progress and Katie said, "Poor guy, he's been mooning over you for so long I can't even imagine what he must have thought when he came to knock on your door."

"*Poor guy?* He didn't even ask her what was going on, just ghosted her," Natalie said.

"True," Katie began, "but it appears he got all his facts straight, finally."

"So now can we hear about the epic first kiss?" Ellie blinked at Ruby, waiting for an answer.

"Well, first I planted a soft quick one on his lips when he said goodbye last night." She pursed her lips. "Mmm-hmm."

"Good for you!" Ellie gave her a high five. "That's the Ruby I love and aspire to be like some day. Bold, amazing, fearless. Asking for what she desires and getting it."

Ruby was almost speechless. "Me?"

"Duh," Ellie said. "You're my idol."

"But you're the one with your life together. Successful clinic. You found true love, have a baby on the way."

"Ruby," Ellie sighed. "*You've* always had your life together. Men and women fall in love with you at first sight. You're a badass who sets goals and achieves them, with your dream business. And you helped me not ruin my relationship with Jackson. You always see the good in me, in each of us, even when we can't see it ourselves. You encouraged me to be bold—you still encourage me. Plus, you're always glowing and sparkly and beautifully put together. Reminds me, we need another shopping day so you can use your fashion sense to pick out some cute new outfits for me. Maybe after the baby comes."

Ruby's smile was wide when she leaned in and hugged her friend. "You are good for my ego."

"Ha! You don't need any ego boosts."

"I am successful and I love my life, but just because I show dynamite on the outside doesn't mean I'm always confident on the inside, especially about men and romantic relationships. I mean look at me—I've been flirting my way through other men and ridiculous dates trying to get Lachlan to notice me, *hoping* he'd see me, even at times trying to poke his temper so he'd have to *notice* me."

"Oh, he noticed you all right," Natalie said.

"Yes," Ruby sighed. She closed her eyes and remembered being pressed up against his delicious, warm, hard planes last night on the dance floor. He certainly had noticed her.

"So was the kiss as delectable as you hoped?" Katie asked.

"It was." She smiled. "But it was way too short. We were on the stairs last night and he was proving how damn good he was at kissing when I shivered. And he had to go and be a gentleman again and urge me inside so I wouldn't freeze."

"Why the hell didn't he come inside with you?" Natalie asked. "I mean seriously. I'd be all over those lips of yours. And his, his are all thick and broody and gorgeous." Natalie was not wrong.

"Yes, what made the epic make-out session too short last night? Why wasn't he with you when the break-in happened?" Katie asked.

"He actually got a call from his father when we were at the reception. That's why we had to leave and why he couldn't come upstairs. He had to go find him. Something seemed wrong or worrying, but he didn't say much about it."

"Noooo!" Even frowning, Ellie was too cute for words.

Her friends really were full of ridiculousness.

"Gage and I haven't ever met his father," Natalie said. "He talks about his mom quite often but now that I think about it, that's it."

"What do you know about his dad?" Katie asked.

"Nothing," Ruby admitted. "But when he mentioned it was his father he had to go see about, there was a darkness in his eyes, for a moment. If I hadn't been drinking in his gaze, I might have missed it. He told me it was a story for when we had more time. There's so much about Lachlan MacGregory I don't know, but I can't wait to find out. I felt so bad leaving him there in the middle of the night in all that wreckage. He doesn't deserve this kind of thing. I'm so upset for him."

"We all are," Natalie said. "Whoever did this, messed with all of us. The neighborhood belongs to all of us and Lachlan has been so instrumental in making it shine."

"Don't worry," Katie said. "We're all here for him."

"I adore you people for it. But I'm still upset."

"Too upset for cheesecake?" Ellie asked.

"Oh, hell no," Ruby said.

Chapter Fifteen

The day could have been better. A hell of a lot better. He could have spent it with Ruby, flirting, kissing, touching. He could be pulling drafts and making drinks right now while the band of the night charged their music through his pub and people ate and drank and enjoyed a great Sunday night. He should have had Ruby snuggled up next to him at the bar, while he fed her crème brûlée. Then he'd end their night by walking her upstairs and make good on the promise he'd vowed to her.

But it could have been worse. He could have been here all day cleaning up by himself. He could be in a position where a blow this devastating was one his business wouldn't recover from. He could be sweeping up the ashes of his bar from the stupid fire the criminals had set, which had been snuffed out quickly. He could have felt alone, as he often did as a child, with the pull of fear dragging him.

Someone could have been seriously hurt.

His temper did flash then, every time he thought of Ruby scared and alone upstairs, crawling across broken glass to get to safety. But standing here now, in the daylight, most of the mess cleaned up, the place crowded with people helped temper that anger.

It seemed while Lachlan had been busy building up a business and working his ass off to strengthen the community, the people had been paying attention. Today, they had surrounded him. And he knew from Leo that part of that community had also shown up to keep Ruby company, all of which smoothed the dangerous edges of his worry.

With so many working hands, once the police had given them the go-ahead, they'd had the place cleaned up in a few hours. And Lachlan was thankful because seeing what some assholes had done to his bar, well, the images were burned into his mind. But now he could begin to move forward. Or rather, as the voices murmuring around him all morning had said, *they* could begin to move forward. It was a humbling feeling to witness so many upset on his behalf, on behalf of his pub.

Truly, even from the beginning it had been a team effort. Lachlan's would never have been as successful if it weren't for the Corvallis neighborhood. He might have been sickened last night when he walked in to witness the destruction, but this morning and all day his hope had been restored. *More than restored.* These people were his friends, and they had arrived at a moment's notice to help him.

"It's already so much better." His mom, Ava, stood by his side as they surveyed the pub. He paused in documenting all the liquor bottles that had been destroyed. She'd shown up before anyone with strong coffee, a hug and mops. After the glass had been swept, she'd mopped the liquor up from every surface it had been splattered on, cursing the vandalizers. "I still can't believe anyone would do this. Breaking into a place to steal money, maybe, but this type of damage? I'm so sorry, honey. We'll bring it back to its glory."

"Yeah." She was right. But even though his spirits had been bolstered, and no one had been seriously harmed, he couldn't completely wipe out the niggling feeling in his mind that someone had been hell-bent on harming *his* pub, on harming *him* through his pub. And for the life of him, Lachlan couldn't picture anyone he knew wanting to do that.

She gave him a kiss. "I'm going to head home, but you call me if you need anything else. And I'd love to see you for dinner one night this week. You can make me your Guinness stew." She smiled like she was dreaming of his stew right then and there. His mom loved his cooking.

Even though his pub had won awards for its draft beers and ciders, Lachlan was most proud of his food menu. He'd learned to cook from his mother and grandmother, and both women had celebrated his dining awards more than anything else in his life. Shared, good meals were the foundation of a close family, his grandmother had always said. Without realizing the importance of her belief, as a child, he'd taken that opinion of hers and held it close to his heart, made it his own.

"Damn, it looks so much better today." Isaac stood in the front entrance.

"Yeah, the neighborhood crew's been busy. Feels good to have the daylight and busyness." Lachlan strode around the bar to meet him.

"You've got good people in your life, Mac. Just checking in. You doing okay?"

"Trying not to obsess over the why and who. It sure seems, by the way they went at it last night, someone has an issue with me and this place."

"Personal," Isaac said, agreeing. "Sure felt that way when I walked in and saw what they'd done."

"Can't think of anyone who hates me this much, though. Something feels off."

"Add that tidbit to the fact it looks personal, and we have ourselves a puzzle. Somebody intended to leave their mark on this place, scare you in a way that might have a lesser man closing down the pub completely."

"Exactly." Lachlan hadn't once, through the entire ordeal, contemplated closing his pub in fear. One thing his life had taught him was to fight, to stand up for himself. No one, personal vendetta or random criminal, was going to frighten him away from his dreams.

"I wonder if I dragged you into this, by asking you to assist with the neighborhood crime? If this were retaliation?"

Lachlan shook his head. "No way is this your fault. I've been proud to help clean up this neighborhood and keep it safe."

"Mmm," Isaac said, studying the pub. "We'll figure it out. They were stupid, coming in despite the alarm, and either they didn't care, or they didn't know about the new cameras along the block."

Lachlan chose to believe the man. He was good at his job, excellent in fact. And the cold look of steel cinched in Isaac's eyes told Lachlan this case was a priority.

"Anything else you need from me before I head to the station?"

"You really don't take time off."

"Got important cases to solve. Working a double." Isaac himself had admitted to making his career as a detective his life after Ruby's mom had died. In a way, Lachlan had made his pub his life. He'd put everything into it. But not without thought of the future, hopes, dreams of more, of a life with someone he loved. He'd kept those dreams hidden, but they were there, always.

Even as he stood in the mess the criminals had made of his pub, his dreams of finding love didn't hover in the background anymore. Especially not after kissing Ruby last night. And especially not after seeing her in the ambulance and having his heart stop working over her safety rather than his business. His dream was perfectly clear, and it was more than just owning the neighborhood pub. He wanted her. Even with the hint of doubt inside that said he wasn't good enough for someone like her, after holding her in his arms, dancing with her, feeling her words against his neck and her laugh rumble through her to him, he vowed to *make* himself worthy. Or give everything he had trying. Because she looked at him like he was the sun and the moon to her and it was up to him to honor that.

On that last thought he went for it. "I'd like to stop by and check on Ruby, if that's all right."

Isaac didn't even hesitate with his smile. It was like he'd been waiting for the words, and nearly losing his patience. "Couldn't imagine anyone better with my daughter. You were a brilliant kid, Mac, and you've grown into an adult I'm proud of, a man this entire neighborhood is proud of."

Lachlan swallowed. Words hit him in the chest, a punch, a solid force of emotion that nearly crumpled him. The child in him preened. The adult, who'd lived through a lot of grime to get where he was, desperately wanted to believe the man, but also worried about letting him down.

"Haven't always lived an easy life…to get here…where I am now." *Growing up homeless at times. Getting paid to fight when I was a restless and angry young man.* Dropping out of college, wandering the country working in random kitchens here and there until he'd woven his way back to Corvallis.

"You gonna hurt my daughter?"

"No, sir. Not if I can help it." The words were automatic and brought a grin to Isaac's expression. "Although she has had to clue me in on my stupidity once or twice." At that, the detective burst out laughing.

"She suffers no fools, that's for sure." Isaac gripped Lachlan's shoulder. "I'll tell you a secret. I was married to the love of my life for twenty-one years and I was grateful every time she clued me in. Ruby's so similar to her mother, full of love to share and patience for those of us with heads up our asses."

Lachlan appreciated the profound moment, and the humor. "I never met Skye, but I saw you three, when you were leaving the YMCA together, after basketball one night, when you were my Big Brother. That connection you all had? It gave me hope as a lonely kid. Ruby's as beautiful as her mom."

"That she is." And, with one more shoulder-squeeze, the man left Lachlan to his pub and as always with a little more hope in his chest.

Chapter Sixteen

Ruby dragged her eyes open to the ringing of her phone. Daylight had faded into an inky-blue sky to silhouette the trees outside the front window since her friends had left a few hours ago. And as much as she'd tried getting lost in the new Nana Malone romance novel, her mind kept wandering to her own romantic interest. Lost in her thoughts, from wonder to worry, her exhausted body had given in to sleep.

She pulled herself up. Lachlan's name was on her screen. "Hi, there," she answered.

"Ruby." God, his voice was delectable in person, but she'd never had it directed at her over the phone like that. Rugged, intense, like he was relieved, interested and excited to hear her voice all at the same time. His deep timbre did things to her insides. "Mmm, your voice is a balm to my battered mind," he said, echoing her thoughts.

"Where are you? How are you? I've been worried about you."

"I'm here at your dad's. Can I come in?"

"Yes, yes." With a blanket draped like a shawl on her shoulders, Ruby gingerly limped toward the front door, trying to keep her weight off her left foot. Where they'd removed glass and stitched her up was now only a low throb of pain, but she didn't relish putting all her weight on it. It still seemed crazy to her that she hadn't felt the glass cutting her when it had happened last night. Adrenaline was a powerful rush.

They were both still holding their phones when she pulled open the door. "Hey," she said, giving him a smile. God, she bloomed like a flower in his presence.

"Ruby." His lips tipped up at the sides. "Mmm, a sight for sore eyes too, such a pretty one." Whew, even after the night and day he'd had, Lachlan MacGregory's hotness had her falling into a puddle of swoon. Scruff lined his jaw and his hair was damp. He wore his boyishly cute, puffy down jacket—which almost took away from his broody aura—over a worn T-shirt and jeans that showed off all his muscles. *Every single one.* Ruby breathed in and tried to temper her ogling when the scent of his soap mixed with the crisp snowy air hit her.

Without thought, she was leaning into him when she registered *his* smile wasn't soft or swoony. His eyes raked over her and changed from hot and interested to dark. She recognized that expression of his—anger. She'd only seen it once or twice in the entire time she'd known him, and never directed her way. He was a man who kept his emotions in check. *Tightly locked up.* Heck, she'd been trying to provoke emotion out of him for over a year. *Why is he angry?* He slid his phone into his pocket and in an instant, she was in his arms, being carried inside.

"You shouldn't be messing with the stitches on your foot." *Oh, the man has broody-cute and chivalrous in him too.* Ruby took the opportunity to cinch her arms around his neck and snuggle in for the ride. *He can carry me forever, as far as I'm concerned.* Even coming in from the cold, he radiated heat and she was here for all of it. She'd known he would burn from the inside out and she'd been right.

Last night when they were dancing and opening up to each other, during that kiss, and when she'd been sitting in the ambulance and he'd bound her up in an enormous hug, a thread had been woven between them, growing stronger with each encounter. A connection exposed, vulnerable, but also with an undercurrent of strength. Lachlan MacGregory was an affectionate man. *Who knew?* And apparently he enjoyed showering that tenderness on her, which was perfect because affection was essential to her life. Whatever had flipped the switch inside him, she was not about to argue with it.

"Don't worry, I hopped to the door." *Worry all you want, you fine man.* She ran her fingers over the back of his neck and held on, feeling his heat radiating from there, soothing her fingers.

"All this goodness inside you, Ruby, when you unleash it on me, it slays me, gorgeous."

Ditto for when you open up to me, hottie.

Lachlan sat with her on his lap. *Mmm this is even better.* He didn't seem inclined to release her. More goodness for both of them.

She placed a gentle kiss on his cheek. *Might as well make it as obvious as he needs to feel comfortable.* After all, she planned on giving it to him in spades. She nuzzled into his neck and he locked his arms more tightly around her. "You smell good."

"Grabbed a quick shower. Had to wash that part of the day away before I came to you." Lachlan leaned into the couch and surveyed her. One arm held her protectively, his hand resting on her hip, while he roamed his other one lightly over her side and lifted her leg.

"How are you?"

It might have been icicle cold outside and wind whipping through the trees, but inside her dad's house with the fire roaring, it was toasty. She'd grabbed her soft, pink velour pjs last night along with a few essentials from her apartment before her dad had brought her to the hospital to get stitches, then here. The top was a matching cozy cami and sweatshirt, the bottoms shorts, perfect for bandaged knees.

Lachlan seemed unsure of where to put his hands. *All over me, please,* she silently begged. She snuggled in closer. All her aches and pains seemed to melt away surrounded by his warmth, his hard body under hers. Streaks of desire and anticipation shot through her. He gently kneaded her hip with strong hands, his expert thumb drawing circles in the crease of her leg. *If only he'd move it a teeny bit lower.* He had her humming and turned on with that sweet caress, with the promise of all that had been building and was now open between them. No more wondering, no more flirting with other people or angry ignoring. Here they were wrapped up in each other with nothing between them.

"Dammit!" he said. "Ruby…your skin." He flinched as he took in her knees. The bandages didn't cover everything and some of the skin on her knees was raw and red. It resembled serious rug burns. *Racing over glass shards can do that to a person.*

"I'm going to be fine. It's all going to heal." She took his face in her hands and brought his head up so their eyes met. "None of it is serious. I have five little stitches in my foot. That's the worst. I'll have to go without my precious heels for a few days, maybe a week, but it's all going to be okay." She tried to will her thoughts into him. All the shit that had gone down last night, all the wasteful destruction at his pub—her scabbed knees were nothing in comparison.

"You think?" His deep searching eyes told her he wanted to believe her.

"Yes."

"I'm going to hold you to that, but I still want you to tell me how you're feeling? Been worried about you all day."

Mmm, being in Lachlan MacGregory arms while he cared for her, telling her he'd been thinking about her, was almost better than anything she could have imagined. She wiggled in even closer. "It all stings a bit. Mostly I've been wondering how you're doing. I didn't sleep much, because I was worried about you too. But the girls kept me company and fed me, and I napped a little before you got here. And while I napped, I dreamed of you."

"Yeah?"

Poor man, as hot as he was—and as much as she'd love to take advantage of her delicious position sitting right on his lap—a shower hadn't wiped away the emotions on his face. Worry was prominent in the set of his jaw, the night had painted dark swathes of exhaustion under his beautiful, deep-set eyes and his normal badass, confident gaze was shadowed by a vulnerability she hadn't seen on him. Her heart expanded even more.

"How are *you*?" she asked, giving his head a gentle massage.

His eyes closed and he groaned. "God, do that again," he said, and let his head drop forward. And while she caressed his scalp, the breath went out of him. He hugged her closer and let her soothe his aches. It was a moment Ruby wanted to last forever, this enormous, strong, competent man allowing her to care for him. "I'm beat, but better now."

"Hungry?" Ruby let her hands drift down his neck and pushed his jacket off so she could knead his shoulders, which were hard knots of muscle. When she could stand and both hands were healed, she was going to give this man the best massage of his life.

"Mmm." His nod was expected. She was lost in touching his skin and making him feel relief. When he raised his head and took her mouth in a hot, hungry kiss, the surprise only lasted a second or two.

"Oh." Ruby gasped, took one taste with her tongue and all the warm fuzzy tingles he'd elicited in her since he'd arrived tonight—hell, since she'd met him—burst into fireworks.

Catching the back of her head with his hand, Lachlan held her in place, like she was dear, like she was essential. And he savored her. His lips met hers again and again as he roamed and nipped, soft caresses and hard, insistent demands.

"Ruby," he whispered, his voice a desperate plea. When he dipped his tongue in to sample, she met him with her own starving lust. Their tongues battled and danced and he took the breath from her. And *my Lord*, she let him. She let him win. His other hand gripped her waist beneath her sweatshirt, and she craved his touch all over her. The heat, the hunger, the way he explored her mouth, teasing and demanding. She felt pliant in his hands, boneless, while her skin burned with desire.

"God. You taste amazing. Can't get enough." Suddenly he took his lips away and kissed at her neck while his expert hand slid under her cami and up her back pressing her closer to him. Their warmth mingling. "I knew you would be this sweet."

"Lachlan, please…" She could barely talk. She wanted his words as much as his touch, because the way he spoke to her was its own caress. She felt him everywhere against her. His head nuzzled into her like he had to get closer. *I understand.* She angled her body against his to ease the sweet ache, making the thin fabric of her shirt rub against her breasts. He brought his mouth back to hers and each time his lips touched hers, she melted further into bliss. "Lachlan…your lips are magical and…"

"Can't get enough of yours either. Do you know how many times I watched you across the pub, drowned in your smile and *ached*? Could you feel me aching for you?"

Yes. Oh yes.

"You taste sweet and hot. God, Ruby, you're stunning, all flushed and needy for me."

"Uh huh." She was. She'd lost all ability to control her body, unless it meant moving against him. She blossomed at his touch. "I need you…need you to touch me."

Ruby straddled Lachlan but he evened out the frenzy of their make-out session, slowing things down. He gently ran his hands up and down the sides of her hips with the softest caress. "Your knees." One last gentle kiss, then he took a moment and brushed his fingers over her wounds.

God, sexy, thoughtful man. She leaned in to kiss him again. "My knees will be okay." His arms clenched once and he pulled away. *No, no.* "Lachlan?"

He shrugged off his jacket, flipped them gently down on the couch and stretched them out side by side facing each other. Then he slid one arm under her and caressed her cheek with the other. *Oh, wow, okay. I really like this position. I'm here for all of this right here.* "I'm still pissed that you got injured. Trying not to lose my cool."

Oh. Ruby closed her eyes at the emotion in his voice and cuddled in with her entire body. So this was him being pissed. Ruby smiled at all the things she was learning about Lachlan MacGregory. Pissed and snuggling was a position she'd never had the pleasure of experiencing.

"Mmm, Jesus, woman." There was that delicious hum of his again that sang through Ruby. "This, you…" He gripped her neck and brought her closer. "Soothes all my sharp edges. How do you do that, Ruby?"

Her heart, an organ that she'd always thought of as strong and powerful, flopped over, belly up, panting like a puppy for more, more of his touch, more of his kisses, more of these words of his that wove the thread between them deeper and stronger. She wasn't often at a loss for words, but the fluttering of her emotions left her tongue-tied. All she could do was stare at him, wide-eyed, open, full of longing.

This time he held her head and changed the direction of their kiss again, super slow and gentle, determined, as if he were memorizing her. Ruby closed her eyes and did the same with him, feeling the whisper soft caress of his lips against hers. He tasted of cold and snow and the scent of his skin invaded her senses, drugging her. He sampled her mouth at a pace that said *we have all the time in the world* and *I damn well am going to remember every last second of this.*

Ruby's body purred with need to crawl in, to be connected with him. But his warmth and languid, drugging kisses melted her and she savored as he did, slowly, until she ached for more. What a delicious ache.

"Lachlan," she whispered into his neck and brushed up against him. *Oh. Mmm. Yes.* She moved again and let the hard press of his jeans rub against her desperate aching core. He was rock-hard and straining. She roamed her hands lower over his back, his sides, toward his belt buckle when he stopped her, brought her hands between them and trapped them there against his chest. "I want to touch you." *I crave so, so much with you. Everything.* The words stayed on the tip of her tongue. Was it too soon to expose how deep she was already?

"Ruby, you can tell how hard I am."

"Yes. Oh yes." She smiled. "I want to feel you."

"Beautiful, I want that." His voice was rough with need and it gave her a shiver to know she did that to him. "But not on Detective Naylor's couch."

Stunned for only a second at the last words she expected to come out of his mouth, Ruby burst out laughing. She couldn't help it. Lachlan rocked them together.

"Love that sound."

"Oh my goodness, are we sixteen just waiting to get caught?"

"You think this is funny?"

"Uhm, hilarious. I've been waiting a lifetime for you to kiss me and do all the other amazing things. And we're adults, but we're getting blocked by my dad who isn't even here." The laughter poured out of her. Her energy needed an outlet and apparently it wasn't going to happen how she imagined it right this minute.

"A lifetime, huh?" Lachlan's deep, soft voice was a stroke against her skin.

"Yeah," she whispered.

"I've been waiting too." He brushed his fingers through her hair, following their path with his eyes. Pensive eyes. Tired eyes. Ruby noticed the little details. "I can keep waiting."

"Me too," she said, resigned but still in a happy place, lost in him.

"Waiting sucks," he said. And his pout was so darn cute.

"Yeah." Ruby chuckled again. "But this sure is nice."

"Mmm. Maybe you could do that thing to my head again with your hands. Felt damn good."

Her smile was automatic. It felt amazing taking care of this man. She still ached for him, but the warmth spreading through her had nothing to do with temperature or lust. Ruby ran her hands through his hair and kneaded his scalp with her fingers, stroking once in a while with her nails. Soothing, deepening, then soothing again. It was only a few minutes before his breathing changed and his weight settled. Her hottie was asleep. *Oh, you precious man.* She wanted this too, cuddling, making out, watching him sleep. So she snuggled in, smoothed her hands over his back and rested them on his waist.

"Best kiss ever," she whispered as he slept beside her.

Chapter Seventeen

A soft warmth cradled Lachlan. It felt damn good, but a savory aroma of garlic and tomatoes teased at his senses. Lachlan opened his eyes and adjusted his vision to take in the fireplace before him with low, toasty flames. He was on his side on a couch with a soft, fuzzy blanket tucked around him, except for his feet, which stretched out beyond the length of it. He breathed in, smelled Ruby, that seductive perfume that floated in her presence. It lured a man in, made him lose focus on anything else, made him desperate to paw and nuzzle at her heat and skin. To find the source of her scent, to beg for her touch so he'd never be without.

Lachlan yawned and stretched his arms over his head. He'd slept like a dead man. The fatigue had dragged him down into a dark pit of an almost dreamless sleep. Visions of Ruby's bold eyes, on fire for him, her lips parted, skin all flushed after their kisses seduced him while he rested. *Heaven.* But where was she now? He'd rather be snuggled into her softness and heat for real than dreaming of her.

Then he heard her singing, quietly with a sexy, raspy voice. He followed the sound. Sitting on the kitchen counter, she was wearing that sexy-as-hell silky-soft short pajama set. Whatever the hell it was called, it was destined to tempt a man. Lachlan was hard in an instant as his dreams and the vision before him twirled together and seduced him. The long-sleeved top draped, leaving her shoulder bare, and the shorts exposed her gorgeous thighs, her pretty skin and muscles on display for him. Fuzzy pink socks covered her feet. And, eyes closed, spoon in hand, she swayed to her music. Ruby was a woman who knew how to wield fashion like class and power and sex. But casual and soft and completely unguarded, she was stunning.

Pausing, she opened her eyes and blinked at him. "Hey." Her face melted into a soft smile. A smile of secrets especially for him. There was nothing else to do but go to her, the lure was powerful, wiping out every other thought or action. Her eyes widened at his approach and she braced her hands on the counter.

"Hey," he said as he walked right into her, situating himself between her legs so he could do what it now felt like he was born to do—surround himself with her. "You okay?"

"Perfect," she said. Ruby set the spoon down and rubbed her hands over his chest. "You?"

Christ, when she touched him, it both soothed and enticed, striking nerves awake or alive that had been numb for so long. Even his bones moaned their approval. "Better now. Much. Sorry I fell asleep on you."

Ruby shook her head. "No, no. I bet you stayed at the pub all night, didn't you? Do you want to talk about it? Do you know anything about who did it?"

"Nothing concrete yet. But it sure appeared as if someone was hell-bent on destruction, not necessarily robbery, even though they broke the cash register too. There's been more crime in the neighborhood, lately, but this is amped up."

"But haven't the police and the neighborhood watch had been getting that under control?"

"Yeah." He nodded. "It's a helluva lot better than it was a few years ago when I bought the dilapidated building for my pub."

"I remember. I considered a vacancy across town for my salon before the improvements started taking shape here. But I couldn't get the idea out of my head that Corvallis was the place for me. I imagined its rebirth even before things started looking better. I'm sure glad I waited. I love the spot I chose." Ruby wiggled against him. God, when she moved into him that way, rational thoughts flew out the window. "But I remember how things were. Your pub was the beginning of the whole neighborhood's rebirth."

Lachlan didn't know how informed she was about the anti-gang task force and how involved he'd been over the past half a year. He wasn't thrilled to talk about it right now either. They had a connection, and as much as he wanted to confide everything to her, they were both still exhausted and traumatized from last night. But she'd brought it up. Ruby was strong. She could take it. "We don't know who yet, but they might have targeted the pub, targeted *me* on purpose. I'm still angry you were upstairs when it happened, but glad you didn't see the mess. It… it looked like…" Lachlan hesitated. He knew exactly what it looked like. "Rage."

Ruby stilled, then wrapped her arms around him. "Someone targeted your pub, to hurt you." She understood.

He nodded. "Either that or they were assholes on some serious drugs. Or both. Although it seemed too quick and vicious for it to be someone high enough not to grasp what they were doing."

"Dammit to hell!"

She was sexy when she swore on his behalf. She brought her hands up to his neck and head. She did that thing again with her strong fingers against his scalp, alternating with her nails, and he nearly collapsed at the way she made him feel…boneless, tranquil. She could mold him into anything and he'd let her. "Fuck, that feels good," he hissed.

Lachlan let her hands work their magic as he leaned into her and felt the trauma and unknown of last night slip away for a bit. He wanted to kiss her again, get her naked, move their bodies together in the best kind of dance. He'd bet her moves in the bedroom rivaled her moves on the dance floor. He was mostly lost in her soothing, out-of-this-world touch, but he wasn't too far gone to notice her quiet.

"You sure you're okay? I apologize for upsetting you." It was odd for Ruby to be quiet. Even when she'd been giving him the cold shoulder, which he'd deserved, she hadn't gone about it quietly. After all, ice storms weren't muted.

"No, no." She shook her head again. "I feel bad that I didn't notice immediately when you walked in how tired you were. With how much you have going on, everything that happened last night…it's all so much more stressful with this knowledge that it was hate driven, and I...well all I could focus on was you kissing me. I was being selfish."

With his head buried in her neck, Lachlan smiled and enjoyed the feel of her in his arms. He couldn't seem to get enough of her, but he sure was enjoying the challenge. "Not selfish at all. I can't wait to have you be selfish all over me." He let himself dream for a minute and he touched his lips to the soft, sexy skin under her jaw. That skin that was all Ruby. He breathed in her scent, surrounded himself with it. "I keep reneging on my promises," he said. "And you're still here catching me when I fall."

"None of that." Ruby wiggled her hips closer, holding him with her entire body, the way she'd done on the couch, giving him all of her, seducing him into sleep. Fuck, he must have been exhausted to have fallen asleep with all that sexy goodness right there in his hands. But after the night he'd had—hell, after the night both of them had had—sleep was nirvana. No fool would have refused that nap.

"You promised when you kissed me, you wanted to make it special, the way I deserved, and, Lachlan?"

"Yes." He grazed his lips over her neck. "A man could stay right here forever, lost in heaven." He hadn't meant to speak the words aloud, but she should hear them. She should have them, know how much she affected him and how into her he was. *Into her* was a pale phrase for how he felt about Ruby Naylor.

"Mmm, that kiss on the stairs was spectacular," she whispered in his ear. A whisper of breath, erotic. It had him thrusting his hips into her heat and locking his arms behind her. No man could resist her temptation. "The one on the couch, even better." There was only one thing to do—kiss her again. He nearly raced for her lips, but he couldn't resist her jaw, teasing along that strong bone that was covered in smooth skin.

He pulled his head up and, holding hers, ran his thumbs over her eyebrows before he placed reverent kisses on each beautiful eye. He nuzzled into her forehead and traced her cheek with his nose, nearly losing himself in her warm neck again. But the lure of her lips was too much, too powerful to resist. So he didn't. He took her mouth and tasted, dipping his tongue between them to get at her heat. She met his every intention, seducing him with her full, lush welcome, darting her tongue out to taste and tease.

Lachlan used all his restraint to not rip her clothes off and ravish her right there on her father's kitchen countertop. The image alone had him rock-hard and so needy he was shaking, but he wasn't a complete Neanderthal. Lachlan eased them into a lazy, sweet kiss before he stopped and a hazy smile drifted over her face.

"I'd say we've got the kissing down," he said and watched her chuckle with her dreamy eyes closed. She gripped his shirt and plastered her forehead on his chest. Damn, it was fun watching *and* feeling her laugh. Fun wasn't a normal part of his life. He was going to enjoy getting used to it. "Although, I'm a man who believes in practice, lots and lots." He kissed her again. It got better every time.

"I really want to practice all the other fun aspects of a relationship with you and this body of yours, Lachlan." She peeked up at him. "Of course, your mind too, but all I can think about right now is you and me naked." *Sexy and bold.*

"Trust me, if we weren't at your dad's, I'd be all over that, all over you." He smoothed his hands over her back and her arms and rested them on her hips, torturing them both a little.

"Seriously?" Her voice was hopeful and soft.

"Absolutely, Ruby. You're fucking gorgeous. Most men would fall at your feet to give you pleasure. But it's this entire package. When a man gets that, he uncovers strength, kindness, brains and a whole host of other aspects I can't wait to discover. Plus, like I said, I've been dreaming of you for a very long time. You are on my mind. Constantly."

Ruby took his hands and sighed. "I don't want most men, Lachlan. Only you."

"Good. Feels fucking amazing to be that one, Ruby, but as hot as I am for you, and as much as I can't wait to please you, I need to respect your dad and not take you naked in his kitchen, or on his couch, or anywhere in his house."

She smacked him playfully on the chest. "Quit saying these things. They are not helping right now."

He chuckled and gave her a hug. "Smells like heaven in here. Did you cook?"

Ruby pulled away. "Ah, no. Katie brought cannelloni. And that's a good thing, because you might not fall at my feet if you tasted my cooking. I cannot cook. And I'm perfectly okay with that."

Damn she was cute, all bossy and confident even when she was talking about something she wasn't good at.

"Good thing one of us can."

"Yeah," she whispered in that breathy tone he was becoming addicted to.

Chapter Eighteen

"We've got it covered, honey," her salon manager, Sherry, said into the phone. "People will miss your presence, but we'll be fine. Besides you haven't taken a day off in...ever. It's about time you got some rest, although I am so mad at the reason for it."

"Me too, Sher, me too."

For some businesses, January and February were super slow. Not Spa La La. Maybe it came with the need to shed more than holiday blues or pretend not to be buried under the gray weather, or the desire to connect with friends over mimosas and hot tea while someone pampered them. Ruby simply loved that people enjoyed visiting her salon. And Ruby loved her job, but taking some time off and getting to go on a date with Lachlan later...well she was as excited as if it were New Year's Eve and, dressed in a couture gown, she was waiting under starlight for the ball to drop.

"Although, on the other hand, now you get some quality time with the neighborhood hottie. That man may be fine, and he may be a successful businessman, but, honey, he is the definition of turtle, as in S.L.O.W."

Ruby laughed. Sherry was more than an employee. She'd become an honorary aunt figure in Ruby's life. And she'd been nudging Ruby toward Lachlan for almost as long as Ruby had been trying to get his attention.

"Mmm-hmm, you know what they say, though," Sherry continued. "Slow and steady wins the race."

Ruby's laugh echoed Sherry's. She sure hoped Lachlan won the race. Soon.

"Now go primp and get yourself ready and take notes so you can tell me all about it."

Sherry hung up before Ruby could say thank you, but Sherry knew how Ruby felt about her. Ruby believed in showering her love on the people important to her, often. It was a lesson her mom had taught Ruby when she was alive, and when she was dying. *Don't waste a minute waffling. Be honest. Be direct. Share your love and affection.*

Lachlan had spent the night with her at her dad's but not in the way that she'd expected their first night in bed together to go. He'd slept fully clothed and held her tight until the sun came up. Both of them, it seemed, needed to be close to one another. She understood why he'd behaved like a perfect gentleman, and she respected him for it. But she ached. Her entire body buzzed with desire. She'd was high on anticipation.

Maybe because he'd acted so courteously, his exit had been all dirty? *"I'll call you later,"* he'd whispered in her ear after teasing her neck with his lips and breath, in that special way he did. *"Pick you up at four. We'll save the fancy date for when your wounds are healed."* Then he'd kissed the daylights out of her, and before he'd walked out, he'd run his fine fingers down her side and said in a voice full of sin, *"I can bring you back here when the date's over, or, if you feel comfortable, pack a bag. We'll spend the night at my place."*

Lachlan MacGregory excelled at parting shots. And that one had her in her current state all day. *Edgy, uncomfortable, wanting.* It was delicious torture.

Sexy brown eyes danced with heat and humor on her dad's porch. *Goddammit he's cute.* Ruby lost all thoughts but that one when she opened the door to him. His mouth tilted up in that flirty half smile. He wore a wool beanie on his head and his winter coat with his jeans and boots. *All mountain-man hottie.* But it was that secret grin that did her in. It was rare to see a smile on Lachlan MacGregory, let alone one that transformed his entire face and was aimed at her.

She fanned herself and whispered, "Wow." Which turned his grin into one hot smirk, and with those dark eyes of his, his intentions for her were written all over his face.

"Is your dad home?"

"What?" Ruby shook her head. "No, he's—"

A man on a mission, in one smooth motion, Lachlan stepped in, had his arm around her waist and kicked the door shut, whooshing out the cold *and* her breath as he slammed his mouth down on hers for a quick needy kiss. She was grabbing his shoulders to hold on when he pulled his mouth away.

"You always look good enough to eat," he growled. "I feel all my practice at restraint being demolished. Especially after waking up next to you, kissing you goodbye, thinking about you all day. It was a long damn day, Ruby."

It was a good thing he held her up because she swayed into him. *That growl, holy smokes!* It seemed he'd been dealing with the same issue she had all day. *Pure lust and need.* She took advantage of her position and pulled him down for another kiss, never one to waste an excellent opportunity. And the kiss was lightning between them. Lachlan nudged her up against the wall, pressing into her while he ravaged her mouth, stroking his tongue in, all hungry and demanding need. A roaring fire lit through her, coiling in her belly, and she held on to him for the ride, kissing him, sampling his lips. He tasted like mint this time, plus that same cold, snowy goodness as last night. She was surrounded by him.

She ran her needy hands up his neck to his head and under his hat, keeping her mouth locked with his, nipping and sucking. They explored each other on the hot and heavy journey. She pressed her body up against his, expressing this all-consuming need with her movement since his command of her mouth left her without words. Each touch of his tongue on hers, each time he tugged on her lips with his teeth set her core throbbing.

She snuck her hands under his shirt to pull him closer. *Ahh, skin.* His muscles radiated heat. When he moaned into her, she came alive and explored more, skimming her fingers over his back, to his sides, losing herself in touch, feeling his hot aura seep into her, while his mouth and the hard contact of him burning against her sex nearly had her climbing him.

"Whoa." Lachlan chuckled and darted sideways away from her hands. He grabbed them and raised them above her head. "Ticklish." Dark and hooded, his eyes throbbed with desire and pleasure and all kinds of plans. His hair was mussed, hat askew, and he was breathing hard. *Can the man get any cuter?*

Panting, trying to catch her breath, she smiled. "You, Mr. Arms Crossed, Never Smiles, Stoic Statue, are ticklish?"

"Guess so." He pulled her arms down and wrapped them around his neck while he settled his on her hips. The way he smiled at her was so boyish and carefree. She cupped his cheek and tried to see even further into his soul. All these glimpses of Lachlan MacGregory he was sharing with her—each one was a brilliant treasure she was going to cement in her heart.

"You didn't know you were ticklish?"

He studied her, focused on her lips again and ran his thumb over the bottom one. She swooned toward him. It felt right, the acquiescence. A place where giving up control gave her so much. When he met her gaze again, he said, "Guess I didn't. Been a while since someone touched me that way." He gently untucked her blouse and drifted featherlight caresses across her waist and she shivered. Ticklish, turned on…it was all tangled up together.

"Oh, wow," she whispered as his touch matched his words, and was rewarded with his full-on sexy smile. All this talk of tickling and she was panting again, but also struck by his admission. He warmed her with his words, his vulnerability, but she was also curious and perhaps a bit sad. How long had he gone without the kind of soft, intimate touch which allowed him to feel ticklish?

Sex was one thing, its own level of trust and touch, but it could be *just* sex, the act, the function of it. Intimacy, on the other hand, letting go, being vulnerable, dove deeper. And all of those *during* sex took everything to an entirely different level of feelings and risk. So much was at stake, and yet, the way Ruby had always viewed things, there was so much to be gained, to be given, to share. His sensual touch also made it difficult to concentrate and examine all her deep thoughts at the moment. She just knew that even the light-hearted subject of tickling and the few words he'd shared went deeper than what had appeared in this tiny spell in the hallway.

"I better get you out of your dad's house before we discover any other places either of us might be ticklish." *I want that. Oh, yes, please.* He raised one eyebrow like the rogue he was and nipped her lips one last time before he pushed away from her.

At least the moment of intimacy hadn't scared him from her. Especially if he seemed all the more interested in exploring how ticklish they both were.

"And where are you taking me for our first date, Lachlan?"

"Well, we're not going dancing." He scowled at her feet. "But I'm hoping it'll be even more fun." He tugged her winter coat off the rack and helped her into it. "Better dress warm though, at least for the first part. And those cute slippers of yours should come in handy to keep your feet cozy and safe."

Ruby's brain was a bit scrambled by his sexy forcefield, but she wasn't too far down the lust spiral to catch his last words. "I can't wear my bunny slippers out in public."

He laughed and she blushed at her snobby tone. "You won't have to worry about too many people seeing us, but if it makes you feel better, I have faith that you, with your fashion expertise and glamourous style, could start a whole new trend of casual but classy footwear for when all you fashion icons can't wear your sexy heels."

Now she smiled huge. "You think my heels are sexy?"

"Ruby." He gripped the sides of her jacket and tugged her close. He was growling again. She was desperate to get him naked. Naked and growly. "Every fucking thing about you is sexy. But those heels, hmm." His smile was devilish. "You, those high, sparkly things you wear, the black ones with the straps, all of them, what they do to your legs, watching you walk toward me, or *away.*" His focus darkened. "Not sure which view turns me on more. They've starred in more than one fantasy I've had about you."

He leaned in so his warm lips brushed against her ear. "And at night, in the shower, when I'm so hard thinking about you, I have to take matters into my own hands."

"Oh." Ruby was certain her face was flushed and the ache she had for him shimmered in every part of her. She couldn't decide whether to jump him or fall into a puddle at his feet and let him have his way with her. At least he'd roped in his control enough to make decisions for both of them.

After fixing his hat, he grabbed her bag and slung it over his shoulder, handed her her purse, and her slippers, scooped her up in his arms and carried her off to his truck. Then he carefully situated her and her stuff in the passenger seat and started the heat. "Keys," he said.

Still lost in all the sexy, dirty, smooth moves of Lachlan MacGregory, and picturing him in the shower, all sinewy naked form, sleek muscles, eyes closed, while he thought of her and worked himself into an orgasm, she handed him her keys. She watched him jog through the snow to her dad's house to lock up. "Wow."

When he headed back in her direction, his smile aimed at her, she could understand what he meant about having trouble deciding which view was more fun to watch, his sexy, backside or his front. *Mmm, mmm, mmm.* Maybe they wouldn't go anywhere for their date, except to bed with no one else in the world to disturb them. They both deserved that.

Chapter Nineteen

Lachlan had taken a chance on both the weather and Ruby's delight in the weather when he'd planned their date for this afternoon. He'd never heard her complain about the snow, in all the time he'd been on the periphery of her life. And he was banking on her pure enchantment with what the world had to offer helping her enjoy what he had in mind.

It had snowed the night before and on into the morning, but when they arrived at the ice rink down at the river, the sky was clear above them. Candy-colored lights were strung over the rink and began flickering to life. He parked his truck up the hill from the winter wonderland.

Below them, the residents of Corvallis were taking advantage of all the snow they'd been getting. People skated and laughed. Carl and his daughter, Molly, had their hot dog and popcorn stand open. Sasha manned The French Connection Bakery booth with warm cinnamon donuts and hot chocolate. Two of Lachlan's employees sold mulled wine and cider by the ice skate rental, and to their right, people used sleds to slide down the snowy hill into the park. In the new pavilion, a drum circle played while a few kids danced and threw themselves to the upbeat music. The mood was festive-chilly.

He'd hoped the cold wouldn't be a deterrent to Ruby enjoying the evening. Besides, warming each other up later hinted at being a hell of a lot of fun. Not that he was cold. Not one bit. She'd stoked his fire all day. Then when she'd opened the door to him, he'd done nothing but burn for her.

"What have you done, Lachlan MacGregory?" Ruby in his arms was pretty much the best way to experience life. No way in hell did he want her to be injured, but carrying her was not a chore. He soaked up her enormous smile and rosy cheeks.

"I'm sensing I did okay for the beginning of our first date?" He settled her down into the open sleeping bag and pile of blankets he'd put in the back of his pickup. Then he gently placed her cute fluffy pink rabbit slippers on her feet and tucked another blanket around her. "Sweet or salty for snacks, and mulled wine or hot chocolate for drinks?"

Her eyes lit up as she took in the scene below them. She and Lachlan were close enough to enjoy the sounds of laughter and music, close enough to smell the hot dogs roasting and feel a part of it all, but far enough away to be on their own date. Ruby might be the most sophisticated woman he'd ever met, in her designer clothes, those sexy heels of hers she wore like a second skin, head held high, always with a sleek haircut—but he'd seen more than her fancy side.

Not a bit shy, Ruby wasn't afraid to show who she was inside and out. She was fiercely loyal and funny, kind and resourceful. And she loved the Corvallis neighborhood as much as he did. Her salon wasn't only a successful business, with her special parties, mother and daughter days, and the fundraising event she did for breast cancer each summer. It was another gathering place the neighborhood felt proud of.

"Do I have to choose?" So different from the suave expression she always wore, her tiny pout-smile was so cute with delight on her face that he chuckled. *Jesus, when have I ever chuckled or been ticklish in my life?* Her joy for life snuck in under his skin and awoke his own. He'd wanted Ruby Naylor for so long, but he maybe hadn't taken stock of all that would mean. Her beauty and personality shone through for everyone to revel in. These hints of what lay beneath were what fed his hungry soul, made him crave everything she had to offer, not just those ripe lips of hers and that lush body, in her sexy heels *and* out of them, but the entire package.

"How about if I get a combination of good stuff and we share?"

"Oh, that sounds delicious and perfect." She ran her cute mittened hands together. "But first, come here."

Christ, she made *delicious* sound fucking erotic as hell. Maybe he'd toss her over his shoulder and head straight to his apartment. Whether or not they made it to his bed remained to be seen. He had a comfy couch. Hell, his living room rug would do about now. He was still hard as a rock from that kiss, that inferno in her dad's hallway that had swirled them together.

When he leaned in, she gave him the softest touch of her lips. And when she pulled away, eyes still closed, she whispered, "Mmm, best date of my life so far."

He wouldn't be an idiot and ask her how she could tell since the date had barely started, because he felt the same damn way. He grabbed the old milk crate he'd stored in the truck with the empty thermoses, jumped off the bed and waved to her as jogged down the short trail toward the food booths.

Ten minutes later he got to see that smile of hers on the return, watching him. Was she cataloging each part of him the same way he was her? Gently tossing the crate up, he jumped onto the truck bed and got cozy next to her. They'd have maybe an hour before the chill got to be too much, but side by side under blankets with Ruby seemed an excellent way to spend that hour, even if they were both bundled up in warm winter gear.

"Sweet goodness! Sasha makes the best hot chocolate in the world." Ruby moaned with her eyes closed, pure bliss on her face. "Here, you have to try this." She passed the thermos cup to Lachlan and he sipped the thick, rich concoction.

"Damn, she's not messing with powdered crap, is she?"

"Nope. This is pure sin. You might have to wrestle me for some." She ogled the mug of chocolate, caught in its dreamy spell.

When she looked up, he took her lips in a needy kiss, gripping the back of her neck and maneuvering her face. "Yep," he said, his voice deep and edgy. "Pure sin." He dove in and even the cold disappeared as they wrapped themselves up in each other. "And don't make promises you don't intend to keep," he demanded and kissed her ear, down her neck till he rested his forehead on her chest.

"Huh?" She swayed into him. Good, she was as rattled as he was. Lachlan tried to catch his breath. One more slip of his restraint and he'd have her naked beneath him right here for the neighborhood to see. Not a good look for a first date with the woman of his dreams. But damn, she drove him wild.

"Wrestling. You and me, for sinful hot chocolate. You make it sound like a negative." He skimmed his eyes up and down her body, raked his hand over her hip. "When to me, it's all positive."

"Mmm." Ruby smiled, and he realized he'd miscalculated. She wasn't under a spell. She *was* the spell, sinful, like the silky drink. She dipped her finger in the drink, twirling slowly, then she sucked the chocolate off her finger between her kiss-swollen lips. Before she could finish, he took her hand and teased his tongue around her finger, heard her moan and watched her eyes get lazy.

A squeal from a group of kids jolted them both out of their haze. Down below, the horn sounded to announce the start of the neighborhood kids' hockey game.

Ruby adjusted herself in the truck and filled her mouth with a handful of popcorn, waving her finger at him when she was finished. "You are dangerous, Lachlan MacGregory. When you kiss me, I forget everything, where I am, who else is here. How do you do that?"

He took a bite of hot dog then handed it to her. She had the right idea, eating. If his mouth was full of food, he couldn't maul her. After another sip of chocolate, he said, "It's the same for me, Ruby. Now that I have you, now that I intend to make you mine, you're all I see. You zap my entire brain."

Fuck, I said too much too soon. He did intend to make her his, but ah…maybe he could have finessed that a little better or waited say a month or so.

"You intend to make me yours?" There was such hope lacing her words that he wondered if maybe it wasn't too soon. What to do? He'd never felt a connection with anyone the way he did with Ruby. Being without her, hurting her, had been agony. He might as well have been a robot, dead inside. When she let her beauty shine on him, he felt whole and powerful and alive. *No sense wasting a second of our time.* Ruby wasn't the kind of person a man should be wishy-washy about. And that was good, because Lachlan didn't consider himself a flakey person, especially when it came to Ruby Naylor.

He nodded and laced their fingers together. "Give me a chance to prove to you that I can be worthy of you, and hell yes, if that's what you want."

She nodded and her entire face was like a sunbeam. "I want that too, Lachlan."

She made it difficult for him to swallow when she regarded him like that—his heart was thumping all the way in his throat, trying to break free. "Good." He forced the word out and gave her hand a squeeze. "Now, I'll try to keep my lips off you while we watch a bit of the kids' game and get a bit chilly. Part one of our date."

"Get a bit chilly? And what's part two of this delicious date you've planned for us?"

He trailed his finger over her flushed skin. "Warm each other up."

* * * *

Lachlan couldn't recall one play that had happened during the hockey game, or who won. His focus was on getting them home safe and sound in the snow that had started drifting down again, while Ruby held his hand and played with his fingers. Inside he was his own storm ready to boom. How the hell could a light finger caress turn him on so much? *Maybe because everything about her turns me on.*

Home, finally. He parked and gathered her in his arms to carry her in. He barely got the front door to his condo closed before she was kissing him. It took only a second before his brain and libido kicked into gear and they were back at each other, hungry attacking kisses, hands all over. From somewhere in his mind came the reminder to be careful with her foot—still encased in those ridiculous slippers—and her knees, but it was damn hard when she snaked her hands under his shirt and his skin burned with her caress.

"Jesus, Ruby. Your touch." He gripped her head to angle their bodies closer. She kissed like a goddess, powerful, full of desire. He focused on that gorgeous flush he put on her skin and shrugged off his coat.

"I want to touch you everywhere," she said, her voice husky with need.

Ruby fumbled with the buttons on his shirt while he dragged his lips down her neck. Lachlan backed her in against the wall, conscious of the heat between them and the sexy moans Ruby made, which shot straight to his dick. He angled his body against hers so she could feel what she did to him. He wanted to rip her clothes off, have nothing between them. A black shadow darted between his feet and he tripped, taking Ruby with him. He fell into the side of the couch and down to the floor, managing to land mostly on his back with Ruby half on him, half tucked into his arm. Hopefully the cushion of her puffy coat lessened the impact.

"Dammit, Baby," he called to the disappearing fluff. When he looked at Ruby, sprawled next to him, a funny smile warmed her face, her pretty cheeks flushed with heat and desire for him. Her chest beat a rhythm matching his, fast and furious and still not satisfied. "Shit, sorry about that. Are you okay?"

"Yeah. We tumbled?" Even her voice was affected, dazed. Damn she was cute. He felt the same.

His breathing was heavy, and he throbbed with need. Her blouse had come undone and one side fell open to her pink bra. Distracted he traced a finger over her skin to the lace rounding her perfect breasts. "Uh huh." When he lowered his head and followed his finger with his lips, Ruby let out a whimper, arched and held his head to her chest. "This okay?" he paused and asked.

"Yes, please. Have your way with me."

He kissed her soft skin and nuzzled the lace of her bra down. "Not exactly where I planned for us to tumble."

Ruby giggled, a sound he hadn't heard before their dance the other night. Her husky laugh, yes, but a giggle while making out on the floor of his condo? It felt intimate and casual. Damn he could get used to this kissing and talking his way along her skin while she rubbed against him. Lachlan pushed up, gently tugged her hand, and before she was even on her feet, he lifted her into his arms. Lachlan had one destination—his bedroom. He kicked off his boots, dragged off her jacket and this time, when he tumbled her with him, they landed on his bed. "Much better."

"The floor wasn't so bad."

He undid the rest of the buttons on her blouse, flicked open her bra and pushed the fabric away. "We'll try the floor another time, when you're not injured." He raked his hands down her sides and dragged her jeans and panties off, baring her sumptuous body to him.

She did that sexy thing with her hands on his sides, this time snaking over his skin without the burden of clothes. "You lost your shirt," she whispered. Her gaze roamed over his chest and her hands followed, exploring and he wasn't fucking ticklish anymore. He burned for her. When she gripped his belt with her uninjured hand, even the heat of her touch through his jeans was enough to have his cock surging, harder, demanding her fingers on him. "Time to lose your pants."

He took her hands in his, kissed each palm and let them drift down. Then he hurried off with the rest of his clothes and, bracing his arms on the side of her, he hovered over her, taking in every single inch with his eyes.

"Lachlan?" she whispered.

"Worth the wait. Every second, every day, every year of waiting for this moment was worth it, Ruby."

"Come here." Ruby tried to pull him closer.

"Not yet. Let me take advantage of this." He started near the wounds on her knees and kissed and caressed up her thighs, a mixture of gentle on the abrasions and rough on her unmarred skin, which had her writhing and begging. "Please, I need more."

"Shh, beautiful. I'm going to give it to you." Lachlan held her thighs down then nudged them open, his thumbs barely touching while he raked his eyes over her. "Do you know how stunning you are? I want to kiss you here." He placed his lips on her pelvis. "Right here."

He kissed one inner thigh, then the other while he continued to tease and taunt, getting closer to her heat, to her pussy. "Here." He blew soft kisses at first. She tried to bring herself closer to his mouth, and he didn't make her wait. He kissed her sex as he'd kissed her mouth, with a hunger that had her crying out. She lifted off the bed as she chased his mouth, so he grabbed her magnificent ass and held her to him, giving her what she begged for—*more*.

Lachlan devoured her, stroking his tongue along her folds, diving in. Ruby writhed and bucked into him. Her wild abandon was sexy as hell. When he found her clit and stroked her sensitive skin, she came apart, screaming his name.

"Good God, Lachlan," she moaned.

He kissed up her body. "Need to be inside you."

"Yes, please."

He ripped the foil packet open and had a condom on while she whispered her desire. This moment felt damn good. It felt right, Ruby, spread out before him, all hot and soft, desiring him. She was breathing heavily, her pretty chest all rosy. Lachlan raised her hands above her head and lined his cock up to her wet warmth.

"Mmm." His pretty lady wiggled closer. Needy, needy for him, as he was for her.

"Tell me if I hurt you."

"You won't." She shook her head, lost in her bliss.

Lachlan nudged slowly inside, moving against her soft skin. "Anywhere, here." He settled in farther. Sexy as hell, Ruby parted her lips and let out a huff of breath.

"Or your wounds." He thrust in all the way and leaned into her ear. "Don't ever want to hurt you, Ruby."

She shook her head. "Lachlan."

"But..." He pulled out and teased her, waiting, hovering. "There's a storm in me waiting to be unleashed. Now that I have you, I don't want to hold back."

"Don't you dare." Ruby arched up, taking him deep into her, sheathed tight. "Give me everything. Lose control, devour me."

Chapter Twenty

Lachlan was splayed out on his stomach asleep next to her, his arm resting over her waist, the weight of it heavy and hot on her. A lazy smile melted over his face. *Must be having nice dreams. Mmm.* She certainly had been before she'd woken—dreams or memories of his hard body making love to her. She stretched and let the ache in all her well-used muscles remind her of what they'd done. How he'd filled her and stretched her, toyed with her and worshiped her. Made her soar.

He certainly looked how she felt, satisfied, exhausted. She could stare at him all night. But she needed the bathroom and some water. After using his tiny bathroom, she slipped her arms through his cozy zippered sweatshirt and carefully tiptoed into his kitchen, letting the small light over the stove guide her. She hadn't even glanced at his kitchen when they arrived, but it wasn't large, and the bright full moon shone through the window.

She turned on the faucet, and a long black figure jumped from above her, streaked through the water and let out a large meow before it flew off the counter and slid down the hall. "Shit!" Ruby screamed.

"Ruby?" Lachlan yelled. He rushed into the kitchen and flipped on the light. "You okay?" Lachlan stood in the doorway, sweatpants on and nothing else, holding a skinny black cat. He moved closer, roaming his eyes over her. "Scared me."

"I'm okay, just startled." Arms braced on the counter, it took her a moment to catch her breath. He towered over her, a cat tail swishing over his broad, naked chest. "You have a cat?"

"Baby." Lachlan scratched behind the cat's ears. The creature arched under his touch and stared at Ruby. Skinny but healthy, the black cat had two white front paws and bright green eyes.

"You named your cat Baby? That's what tripped us earlier, when we…when we…" *Holy cow.* Her cheeks flushed, thinking of how they'd gone at each other earlier, barely inside his house.

Lachlan's face relaxed into a slow, tempting smile, as if he knew exactly what she was picturing. "Sugar Baby, actually." He sounded a tiny bit annoyed at the animal but the expression on his face when he stroked his cat and the way the cat rubbed against his hand was pure love. *Oh my God.*

"Some days she has more salty than sweet in her, so she gets called Baby." Lachlan smirked at the skinny cat. "She sneaks all over the place, demands food and plays in the water that comes out of the faucet. Goofball. I was too distracted earlier or you wouldn't have tripped me," he cooed to his pet. Insulted, or victorious—Ruby couldn't tell—the cat streaked out of his arms, darted across the floor and disappeared.

She looked up and their eyes met. That zing, that connection buzzed.

Lachlan switched off the light. The click was a shot through the quiet air, tense between them. "So pretty in the moonlight, standing here, in my space." He prowled to her, nestled into her and braced his hands over hers on the counter. Warmth and tingles flooded her. "You stole my sweatshirt."

Oh my. Energy radiated off his body into hers, stirring her desire again. *Guess we didn't completely wear each other out.* "I..."

He pressed into her and Ruby's breath caught. "Hmm?" He stroked his lips up her neck, shooting fire through Ruby's blood.

"I needed...didn't...it's bit chilly to walk around naked."

He used his head to nuzzle the sweatshirt open, while he kissed down her belly. Instinct had her trying to move her hands to keep him right there, but he held her arms captive, sending shivers of lust through her. How could she be so needy again so soon, after the night they'd had?

"I like you naked." When he finally let her go, he used those magnificent fingers to play with the lace of her panties.

"Please," she begged. So soft, the way he touched her, the way he stared at her, like he was lost in a dream. Until his own need took over. He lifted her into his arms and her legs automatically circled his waist.

"Want you right here in my kitchen, but..." He tasted her lips.

"But?" She was shameless, whining at him, a begging woman. He chuckled.

"Condoms are in the bedroom."

* * * *

Damn, the man even made good coffee. She should have guessed. He was a marvel with his hands. Ruby couldn't help the smile that flushed her face while she remembered those extremely capable—one might say magical—hands brushing and stroking her skin, claiming her.

Too, too bad she and Lachlan had to get back to reality.. Ruby loved her work, loved her life, but spending the last two days tangled up in Lachlan had felt like paradise. They'd both taken Monday and Tuesday off. Apparently her salon was fine without her. Well, she had hired a fabulous staff. And Lachlan didn't plan to open until at least Wednesday. Cozied up in his arms, only the two of them, no disturbance, no outside world at all, and she didn't want to leave yet. Lachlan stood at the sink washing their breakfast dishes. That was another thing—the man hadn't let her help with anything. "*Next time,*" he kept saying, "*when you're not injured.*"

With each touch, each kiss, each action, he'd pampered the damn hell out of her. She sighed, wondering if her glow was visible to others. *A woman could get used to this.* Baby danced on the counter next to him, swatting her paw through the faucet every few seconds, then hopping away, acting surprised each time when the water hit her. Lachlan shooed her away and she ran right for Ruby's lap.

The two females had come to an agreement over the weekend. Ruby promised the kitten she wasn't here to steal Lachlan away, and with enough chin and ear rubs, the kitten believed her. *Easy.* Either that or the kitten was still so starved for attention she didn't care. Maybe the soft, skinny fluff actually liked Ruby. She'd never in her life been a cat person, but she'd fallen in love with this one instantly, well almost. It was the way the kitten had purred against Lachlan's naked chest that had Ruby falling.

"What universe have I stumbled into where my badass stoic hottie has a kitten he named Sugar Baby?"

"Your badass stoic hottie?" The grin he aimed her way was scorching enough to set her toes on fire.

Ruby grinned back and raised her eyebrow. Baby was nuzzling into her chest, purring while Ruby stroked her. Lachlan leaned against the counter, arms crossed, watching her. "Mom gave her to me. Said I needed something to take care of." He came around the counter, pushed her knees apart and settled in between her legs. The way he gripped her hips, like she was everything his hands craved. He used his expert thumbs to toy with her hip bones and send all those delicious shivers through her. Ruby's body arched into him as if it had a mind of its own. *More, more,* it urged.

"She said I was lonely."

The man said it not as if it was something to be embarrassed about, but almost as if it were a question.

Lachlan lifted Baby off her lap and set her on the floor. He tugged Ruby off the stool and twirled her. *Mmm, closer.* She liked closer.

"I laughed, but indulged her," he said. "Cat was tiny when she arrived, starving." He pulled Ruby tight so her back rested against his chest, "But now…" With his soft lips brushing her ear, that deep voice of his, her breath caught. Lachlan moved their bodies as one so they could both watch Sugar Baby prance across the arm of the couch. "I'm wondering if she was right. Not sure if I knew what lonely felt like or could define it. Maybe I just tried *not* to acknowledge it. But having you here, in my arms, in my bed, on my counter…"

He nipped her ear and she laughed at his teasing. They'd eventually initiated the counter and it had been stupendous. "Digging under my skin. Something clicked inside me. Now I feel the opposite of lonely."

God, she felt it too. It scared her, the enormousness of her feelings for him. These feelings were unrecognizable. Intense lust and deep love all tangled together. "Is it soon?" she whispered. "*Too* soon? Do you wonder? Question it?"

"You feel it too, don't you." It wasn't a question. He seemed certain she understood. That instinct he had, how he could read her and feel her emotions, smoothed over her fear and insecurities, and allowed her to be fully in the moment, to embrace the feelings simmering between them. It was the way she lived her life, never shying away from true feelings. He *had* been watching her, learning her. What a sneaky magician.

Ruby turned so she could wrap him in her arms and see his face when she answered. "I feel it too."

His heart thudded against hers, and he sighed. "Good." His voice caught on that one single word. Ruby burrowed in tighter, communicating how special this moment was for her too. She held on tight to the best thing that had ever happened to her.

Lachlan cleared his throat and lifted her head with his hands. God, the man could slay her with a look, with those intense dark eyes taking in every inch of her face before he locked his hands behind her head and devoured her lips with his in a slow tango. When he pulled away, her eyes were still closed, holding on to all that was passing between them.

"Love my pub, but I sure do wish we were on an island vacation together with absolutely no responsibilities, except giving you pleasure." Damn, he was hot when he was mad on her behalf.

"Uh huh," she sighed into him.

"Got to get to the pub so they can install the new mirror. Should I take you to your dad's or your apartment? I'll be there all day. In case you're still feeling uncomfortable."

"My apartment. I don't think I'll be scared anymore, especially if you're downstairs. But maybe…can I stay with you again, tonight, if you…if that's what you want."

He tightened his hold and the smile he gave her was fierce. "I do. I want you with me every night. Your place or mine. Doesn't matter. I'm still angry this happened while you were there in your safe place. Don't like the thought of you worrying about staying at your own home."

"Well…" Ruby danced her fingers over his chest, hesitant to tell him her news. "It's actually not going to be my place much longer."

"What?" She felt him brace, watched the smile change. Curious intent took over his expression.

"I bought a house." The excitement hadn't lessened from it yet. Two months had passed since she'd put in the offer, which had been accepted. Then she'd gone back and forth with the seller over the price after the inspection showed the extensive chimney damage. But now she was days away from closing, from twelve fifty-two Ash Street being hers. "I'm moving. Not far," she rushed to assure him. "Actually, a few blocks from Katie and Leo. Up Ash Street, behind your pub. I can still walk to work. It needs some love and care, mostly the Ruby Naylor touch, but it's old and charming and grand. It has a yard." She squealed and closed her eyes, picturing the lush green beauty she was going to transform that yard into. "I'm going to plant a garden full of roses, lots of peonies, anything that blooms and smells wonderful."

Lachlan gave her a gentle shake and she opened her eyes to see his shining at her. "Ruby, that's great. I figured you weren't going to stay above the pub much longer. It's not a forever home for someone like you. Bet you picked something spectacular to fit you."

"I close next week. It's so beautiful, I can't wait to show it to you," she whispered.

"Can't wait to see it." His ease had returned. The way he gazed at her as if she were his star guiding him. And he had no problems letting her.

"What about you?" Ruby inspected his condo in the daylight. Efficient, small one-bedroom with white walls, doors that might as well be made from cardboard and a kitchen with appliances older than she was. The popcorn ceiling dated back to the late seventies. Although it was clean and clutter-free, nothing about the place said Lachlan MacGregory and all his sleek, strong, creative, hardworking self who'd rehabbed the pub from disgusting to urban cool. "When I see you and your impressive bar, I don't picture you here."

Lachlan rotated her again, so she faced out. He rested his chin on her head. "It was a cheap place to sleep when I returned to Corvallis. Bought the pub and put all my time and energy and money into it. A home was always going to be next if I could make the business successful."

"I'd say you've accomplished that goal."

"Hmm." His chest vibrated and she loved that she was snuggled up against him to feel it. "Seems the only goal I can focus on is making your body sing." His gave her neck a quick nip, sighed and grabbed her jacket. Still reeling from his erotic words, she let him put it on her and pull her in for a hug.

Whew! The man had mad skills, and she was a puddle again. It was time to show him she could play at this too. "I love how you seem to enjoy cuddling with me as much as fucking me."

Lachlan's arms gripped her tightly. He buried his head in her neck and burst out laughing, then kissed the hell out of her.

Chapter Twenty-One

Most mornings there was a buzzing energy when Lachlan walked into his bar. Even empty, void of people, music and laughter, there was still a murmur of anticipation for the day to come, whether it beat from him into the space or the space into him, he wasn't sure…but it met him there, welcomed him. A sense of friendly ghosts, slumbering, waiting to stir to life when the day began, like a stage crew that merely hibernated overnight and with the flip of a switch, came alive in the morning. Walking in each day, it surged over him.

He'd hit the lights, make a pot of coffee, put some music on and get to work. A few of his employees would begin to arrive. Someone would take the chairs down and set out the salt and peppers. Another person would unload the dishwasher, the clink of glasses heralding the fresh new day, the beginning of something great.

Today it was quiet. Dark and quiet.

With the low gray clouds outside, not much light filtered through the windows. He was waiting for the replacement front door, so absolutely no light came through the plywood makeshift. The mess had been cleaned up, much of the damage had been repaired, but something had snuffed the life out of the place.

Above him came the muffled sounds of Ruby moving, getting ready for work. The faint lilt of music traveled down from her apartment. It sounded like she was singing. That brought a smile to his face. The woman had moves and a voice and now he got to enjoy all of her without being some creepy stranger who was caught staring and drooling.

He shrugged off the damp and dormant feeling of his injured pub and got to work. Unlocking the door, he propped it open, then he began taking the second door to the bar off its hinges so the men delivering the long mirror for behind the bar could get it through. The air was calm but bracing and he welcomed the fresh chill, something needed to wipe out the gloom hovering over him and his bar. He wondered if this was how Ruby felt upstairs now. It was good she wouldn't be living there long. She could make a fresh start without the lingering unease and trauma. Being the recipient of a random act of crime sucked. It wasn't good for anyone. But the knowledge that people had targeted him and his pub directly, for such nasty destruction was a twisted, churning ball of unease inside him.

Huh. Lachlan paused with his screwdriver and took a deep breath of cold winter air. That unease had stilled during his date with Ruby. It wasn't until he'd left her at her apartment and walked into the front of the bar that the churning had started again. Maybe she had magical powers. He shrugged and wrote the whole thing off to them being completely fucking lost in each other. Not just the sex, although it had been phenomenal, but him simply being with her the last few days had enclosed them in a safe bubble of pleasure and ease. When he studied his thoughts, it wasn't only the mess of his pub—she'd lifted weights from his entire life.

Even the night he'd showed, exhausted and cranky, at her dad's, she'd soothed away all his rough edges with her warm embrace, her sexy voice. Damn, the way she'd massaged his head. He'd napped. Lachlan chuckled to himself. He couldn't remember the last time he'd been relaxed enough to nap. Sleep at night didn't always come easily or smoothly for him, let alone the middle of the afternoon.

"Hey!"

Lachlan followed the voice. Connor Duggan was jogging toward him, his oversized blond lab at his side. "Kitten, sit," Connor commanded. The dog, gazing and drooling at Connor, plopped her butt down, but Lachlan could see the quivering mess of energy she still was. Although she'd come a long, *long* way in her training. "Good girl." Connor scrubbed her head and the dog beamed, like she'd entered the gates of heaven.

That's exactly how I feel when Ruby rubs my head, girl. Maybe that was what it was. Maybe it had nothing to do with magic—maybe Lachlan was simply a beast craving her attention.

"Kitten seems calmer."

"She behaves for me, mostly these days. Don'tcha, girl? What else does a man need but a good dog?"

Hmm, Lachlan might have agreed a few years ago, hell, even a few weeks ago, but finally connecting with Ruby had him rethinking a whole bunch of things.

"Mirror guys should be here any minute. Came to help you get it installed," Connor said.

"Don't you have a million jobs to work on?" Lachlan asked.

"Something close to that, yeah." Connor smiled. The man was an army when it came to renovations, and, thankfully for the neighborhood, Connor Duggan had taken Corvallis under his wing and had been restoring the buildings to beauty over the last several years. He'd consulted on many of Lachlan's projects when he'd bought and restored his pub. It was like Connor created more than twenty-four hours a day to get stuff done. And yet he always appeared happy-go-lucky and was endlessly available to help anyone.

The mirror showed up, and it was a good thing Connor was there. It took four of them maneuvering through the tight entryway and behind the bar to get it hung. It didn't take long, but it was damn heavy. Lachlan was sweating by the time they finished.

"Looks as good as the old one," Connor said, slapping Lachlan on the shoulder. They stood in the open doorway, admiring their work, Kitten sleeping in the circle of sunshine at Connor's feet.

"Better," Lachlan admitted. "The scrollwork you suggested for the corners was spot on. Appreciate it."

They walked out into bright sunshine and a blue sky above them. "Day's warming up," Lachlan said. "Christ, we could use some sun." His phone beeped in his pocket and he read the text from Ruby with a smile.

Ruby: Hey, handsome, could I get that ride to work you offered? Pretty please.

Lachlan: Be right up, gorgeous.

"Are you blushing?" Connor punched in the arm.

Lachlan grinned. No sense hiding how happy he was. "Maybe."

"Heard you and Ruby are together. Happy for you."

"It's new," Lachlan said.

Connor rolled his eyes. "Please, you two have been circling each other for at least a year, with a temperature hot enough to leave scars."

Lachlan laughed. They had been, but he was just surprised so many other people had noticed. He'd been so entrenched in his own narrowminded desire for her without being able to have her. "You writing romance novels now?"

"Ha. I'm not ashamed to say I have enjoyed reading a few, but man, you forget, up until a few months ago, I was surrounded and groomed by a strong pack of females. It doesn't take a romance novel for me to see what's been simmering between you two. That expression on your face tells me things are good. You gotta hold on tight to it."

"Yeah." Lachlan didn't intend to do anything but.

Kitten started jumping and whining, her nose pointing across the street.

"Kitten, stay," Connor commanded. The dog vibrated with the desire to move. On the corner across from Lachlan's pub and down was The French Connection Bakery. Sasha Kincaid and her dog were exiting the front door and heading toward the park.

"Seems like a good time to go say, 'Hi.' What do you think, girl?" Kitten bounded up and down.

"You using your dog to get a woman to notice you now?" Lachlan teased.

Connor didn't smile. Not so much as a grin. The serious nature of his stance was unlike Lachlan's friend. Gone was the goofy, suave, not a care in the world man. "Maybe," he said, uncertainty lacing his voice. But he didn't give Lachlan another glance when he and his dog set off in the direction of Sasha.

Huh. Maybe a man does need more than a good dog. If Connor was interested in Sasha, he had a mountain to climb to earn the woman's trust. Speaking of women, Lachlan had his own to take care of. And didn't that make him grin again.

* * * *

Grin wasn't what happened when he opened the door to her. Shit, his heart stopped. She was so fucking gorgeous, naked and mussed up in his bed, or classy and all put together as she was now. The woman could pull off a combination of glamourous meets sexy for a day at work like no one else. Resting on the arm of her sofa, waiting for him, she exuded royalty.

Her teal dress with small pink flowers had sleeves that came to her wrists and small pads at the shoulders to give her a strict, sexy-professor presence. The flowy fabric tucked in with a thin black belt at her waist and draped to her shins, with an enticing slit up the side, hinted at all that skin and curves underneath. Shimmery gold and teal makeup highlighted her eyes. Lachlan dragged his gaze down and lost his breath at the heels. *Strappy gold heels with her toes peeking through.* The bandage showed as well, but apparently she wasn't going to let a few stitches stop her from wearing her sexy shoes.

Lachlan strolled over and she automatically opened her arms to him. Wrapped up in her felt as natural as breathing. *Better.*

"Your foot okay in those?"

"I wanted to see your face when I had them on, now that I know how you feel about them," she whispered into his ear.

Lachlan dragged her up to standing, taking most of her weight so she wouldn't feel the pain in her wound. He made his appreciation for her heels obvious with the look he stroked down her body.

"Besides"—she held up the pink fuzzy slippers she was carrying in her hand—"I'm taking these to work with me. My winter boots are still too tight for the bandage."

"I'm sorry, Ruby." Christ, he was glad she hadn't been injured more seriously than she had been Saturday night, but he wasn't ready to get over his anger and guilt. He might never be.

"I'm not. I still got to see your reaction and we have all the time in the world for me to wear more heels for you. When I can actually walk in them. For now, your slipper idea has grown on me."

"It's a deal," he said. He held up her jacket and when she was all bundled, he grabbed her bag, slung it over his arm and lifted her.

"Although..." She nuzzled her lips against his neck. "I've become a huge fan of you carrying me."

"I like having you in my arms too." He meant it. The world was a different place when she was touching him. He couldn't get enough of that sensation. Her nearness, the hint of perfume she wore that teased at his senses and almost made him walk her right back upstairs to bed, remove all her clothes, explore and kiss her all over, to discover all the secret places she'd dabbed that scent.

He rounded the corner from the hallway where her back stairs were located in relation to the bar. "Oh, it's wonderful," Ruby exclaimed. Her fingers were rubbing his neck, distracting him. She was gazing at the new mirror, but all he could see and feel was her. She was so warm and sensual. Every small and large caress of hers was significant to him. He was stunned silent with the force of his feelings.

"Connor's friends did such a good job." She cupped his cheek and faced him. "I know it's not the same as the original. I'm so upset all this happened to you."

He closed his eyes and rubbed his face against her hand. Yep, his need was as basic as a dog seeking her caress. "It feels better with you here." Simply having her in the room wiped away the gloomy unnatural quiet he'd felt this morning. "Place felt dead, weird when I walked in this morning. That may seem odd, since it's empty, but it felt lifeless. Usually when I arrive, even before we open, it has this beating anticipation for the day ahead."

"Hmm." Ruby examined the pub. He could see her mind working, gathering her words as he walked her out and across the street to her salon. Two of her employees were already there, attending to clients. They gave small waves and hellos from across the room. Another client waited on the plush blue velvet chairs Ruby had placed in the front windows. A soft pink wallpaper shimmered in the sunlight. With Ruby's knack for style and design, the warm grays and off-white paint worked with the soft pink color scheme and the pop of blue. The addition of several glittery chandeliers, oversized drapes with the old high ceilings and crown molding, and her place whispered softly, but stylishly, "*Pamper me.*"

"You do know the life, the humming in that place across the street is because of you, Lachlan MacGregory?" She poked him in the chest as he set her down on her stool behind the counter. "Don't you?"

He grinned at her vehemence. "You don't think it could be from the Friday night crowds and live music and knit nights full of customers?"

"That adds to it all, of course, but you are the spark. You are the heart beating in that place. You always have been. You built it up from dust to make it as wonderful and successful as it is today. You've created something many people crave, a place to belong. It's the Cheers of the neighborhood. It's the family-owned pizza restaurant that's been there for generations. When people walk into your pub, they don't simply see how broody-gorgeous you made it, or enjoy fabulous food and drinks and world-class bands—they've come home. Don't let some butt sores take that away from you."

He laughed outright. "I love your descriptions. And butt sores?"

"I try not to swear too often in my salon." She twirled her pretty red nails. "Plus, I love it when you laugh. I don't think I ever heard you laugh before this weekend. And it is a sound and sight to behold."

He hugged her and said in a gruff voice, "Well, us stoic hotties can't be seen laughing too often, especially not in our broody-gorgeous bars."

This time he got to watch her laugh, and he had to agree, it was a sight. *A beautiful one.* He gave her a kiss and she play-shoved him away. "Let me get to work. And you, go find the life in your pub again. Don't be afraid," she whispered. "It's right here." Ruby set her hand on his heart.

He was at the door when she called his name again.

"Lachlan, you also know most of those people who come in to your pub aren't simply customers, don't you?"

"Oh, what are they?"

"Family, my love. Family. And they're all rooting for you to open again so they can support you the way you support everyone in this neighborhood. Maybe they'll help you bring the life back."

Fuck, he was choked up listening to her words. Speechless, he gave her a small smile and a nod. Lachlan let the sun beat down on him on this chilly day, but it was Ruby's words that warmed him. How she viewed his customers and his heart, but also that she'd called him, "*My love.*"

He let that feeling carry with him as he surveyed his empty pub. Then he smiled, put on some Alabama Shakes and got his tools out to install the new front door. It was time to get this place open, for his customers. His neighbors. His family.

Working on his pride and joy, Lachlan realized Ruby *was* magical. She had burrowed her way into his soul. She made him feel happy and ten feet tall. She could convince him of anything, and if she said he was the life in his pub and that the people who frequented his pub were family, he was damn well going to believe her.

Chapter Twenty-Two

Ruby despised tennis shoes—could barely bring herself to utter the words—but even two weeks after she'd sliced her foot open on broken glass, her wound still throbbed if she stayed on it too long, especially in her heels. *Why couldn't it have been my elbow that was cut? No one needs an elbow.* But she'd been missing her strolls in the park with Ellie and her dogs. Things would change any day, when Ellie had her baby, and Ruby was determined to soak up every last second with her friend right now, even though she was also excited to add more love to their group.

Secretly she could admit her sparkly new silver skids, as she preferred to call them, were definitely more comfortable to stroll in than her heels, no matter how much she adored her pretty shoes. Bonus, Lachlan seemed to love her sexy heels as much as her goofy slippers *and* skids. She suspected he liked her feet bare best.

"He has a kitten," Ruby sighed. "She's the scrawniest, softest, cutest, weirdest thing I've seen."

Ellie had her arm twined with Ruby's. They were two hobbling fools carrying each other along. But the exercise and fresh air with the sun warming them was too wonderful to miss. With her other hand, Ellie held the leashes of her two dogs, Buffy and Chewie, along with two puppies from her clinic who were learning how to behave. It was fascinating how Ellie got them all under control.

Many of their friends in the Corvallis neighborhood had jobs they loved and were good at. Ruby guessed that was one of the reasons the neighborhood was becoming so vibrant and healthy. But Ellie was on another tier altogether. All she had to do was talk to them and the animals listened and obeyed. She was their rescuer, their angel and they adored her. Truly, they could be wrestling with each other during a live squirrel chase, and all she had to do was open her mouth and poof! It was like she was Glenda the Good Witch waving the wand and her smile and her sweet voice over them saying everything was wonderful. And they'd stop their misbehavior, listen and believe her.

"His mother gave her to him because she said he was lonely. I have to admit, lonely is not something I associated with Lachlan MacGregory. He puts on this larger than life, super strong persona, Ellie, but I think he might be. I mean his pub is impressive. But his home is, well…not a home. Not comfy and full of who Lachlan is. It's clean and plain. Those are the nicest things I can say about it. Almost as if he's holding back from making it special."

Ellie nodded. "Sometimes it's hard to see what people don't want us to, or don't even realize about themselves. He doesn't project lonely, but then again, most of us probably don't."

"Isn't that the truth. And I don't think he realizes how big of a family and friends he has in this neighborhood."

"Are you going to show him how much looovvve he has? Help him get un-lonely?" Ellie teased in her sing-song voice.

"Well, I am perfect for the job," Ruby bragged and got a laugh out of her friend. They giggled together, but Ruby added. "To be honest, I've been lonely too."

Ellie glanced at her.

"I mean I have a wonderful life. I love my life. But being with him the last few weeks feels soul-opening, freeing, wonderful. It's exhilarating and at the same time I feel more comfortable than I ever have. I want to be near him all the time. Do I sound loopy after only dating him for a few weeks?"

"I'm not sure how to answer that. Part of me thinks love *is* loopy, in a good way. It does fill us up. But also, I wouldn't call what you and Lachlan are doing dating."

Ruby laughed. "Well, cocooning ourselves and having lots of amazing sex isn't a phrase you go tossing willy-nilly into normal conversation."

Ellie laughed. "You do if you're Ruby Naylor."

Ruby pinched her side. "Hey."

"I'm teasing you. I just mean you're brazen and you say whatever you feel, although always in a cultured, I-know-everything voice, which I adore about you. What I meant was, dating is too simple for what's going on. I think you two were meant for each other. One of the grand loves you only see in the movies lit by starlight." Ellie sighed. "Lachlan has this tough outer exterior and harsh good looks. A man who hardly smiles or uncrosses his arms. He's all buttoned up. We know almost nothing about his background. Maybe he was a spy? He secretly fights crime, takes care of his neighbors and has been harboring a torch for the neighborhood fashion model, savvy businesswoman, genius hottie who has men dropping like flies at her feet." She fanned her face. "It's all so romantic."

Ruby's smile grew huge with Ellie's image, and she patted her friend's arm. "That was quite a script you wrote there. You are my hopeless romantic, now, aren't you?" Ruby *didn't* know much about his life before. She'd heard him mention his mom, but she hadn't met the woman yet. Although, to be fair, when they were together, they ignored everyone else and climbed into bed to explore each other's bodies. Oh, those images heated her right up.

And his dad was that conversation they still hadn't gotten to, she remembered now. How Lachlan had gone to meet him the night of the attack. Ruby had completely forgotten to ask him about what had happened, if his dad was even okay.

"Oh, no, not hopeless at all. Not anymore." Ellie gestured to the bench. "Must sit down," she said, arching her back and groaning. "I'm so heavy. Even my bones ache. Will it ever end?"

"Soon, my precious friend. Then you are going to be the best mommy in the world."

The glow on Ellie's face completely obliterated the discomfort she seemed to be in. "I'm already so in love with him or her and the munchkin isn't even here yet. I never dreamed I would get to be a mom, until I met Jackson."

Buffy groaned and rolled over onto her side by Ellie's feet. "At least not to a human." She rubbed her dog's belly. "Wasn't sure I would be good at it."

It was only recently in their going-on-seven-years' friendship that Ruby learned about Ellie's past. She could understand why people didn't share their ghosts. She felt grateful she didn't have too many buried in a closet somewhere. The absolute worst thing that had happened to her was losing her mom to breast cancer. That ache still resurfaced, even though it had been years. But she'd never shied away from telling people about it. It was their own problem if they couldn't deal.

Ellie had been ashamed of her past, even though it was Ellie's mother's burden to bear. Now Ruby wondered what ghosts Lachlan had and whether or not he might be ashamed of them. She didn't care how bad they might be, she wanted to learn everything about him and be a place he felt safe sharing. Maybe that was a part of real love too, being open and prepared to share your partner's ghosts. Being that protected place for them to land.

"Are you falling in love?" Ellie's question startled her out of her reverie.

Ruby leaned into her friend's side. "I think I've been half in love with the man since we first met. Now that he's opened up to allow me in, it's the only path I see. And it shimmers."

"Yeah!" Ellie squealed.

Although Ruby had a lot of ground to cover in getting to know everything about Lachlan. But that too was a gift, not a burden. What about his dreams for the future? Did he share hers? Did he want marriage and kids? She'd love to get married someday, but kids weren't necessarily part of her dream. At least not yet. Learning, growing together, that was the journey she dreamed of with him.

"It feels fabulous!"

"Are you going to come up for air and hang out with the rest of us ever again, or does he keep you locked up in a tower somewhere, so he doesn't have to share you?"

"Mmm, now that's another image I'm enjoying." It felt good to laugh over her new love with her best friend. "But, no, you're right. I miss you all. We're coming to Natalie's party this weekend for you and Jackson before the baby comes."

"Any news yet on who broke into his pub?" Ellie asked.

"Honestly, we've both been so busy with work and when we're not, well, there's no fairy tale tower, but we have been…focused on learning about each other."

"Is that what we're calling it these days?" Ellie laughed.

"The police have been keeping him in the loop. And I'm sure he'd tell me. Did you know he volunteers at the Opal City Clinic for drug and alcohol rehab?" Ruby had learned that nugget last night when their date couldn't begin until after midnight. He'd used the key he had to her apartment, climbed under the covers naked with her and woken her with his mouth and strong hands exploring her body. Midnight dates, it appeared, were up there for number one or two for her favorites.

"It doesn't surprise me," Elle said. "I'm telling you, tough exterior with a superhero heart inside. Trust me, I'm an expert now." Ruby grinned. Another plus of Ellie's relationship with Jackson was how much her friend's confidence about her own inner beauty had grown, or maybe come out from under its hiding place. Ellie did the same for Jackson. *Talk about a true love match.*

"But now that you mention it, we haven't talked much about the break-in. I need to ask him. I have so many things to ask him, to discover about him. He knows my dad, but I can't wait for him to hang out with him as simply my dad, and for serious Detective Naylor to see how important Lachlan is to me. These important people in our lives—I'm meeting his mom this weekend. She's making dinner for us. I'm so nervous."

"You?" Ellie gave her a suspicious glare that made her look cross-eyed.

"Oh, my darling, you are so funny when you try to give me that silly, sneaky side-eye."

Ellie fell into giggles and a puppy jumped up, trying to get in on whatever adventure was happening. "Settle down." Her soft voice had all four animals sitting immediately. "Good dogs." She pulled out small treats from her pocket and fed one to each dog. "I mean it though, I've never once seen you nervous about anything. Except maybe whether or not the gel polish you chose would match your heels."

"Oh, please," Ruby scoffed and playfully smacked Ellie's arm. "It's whether the color matches my dress. Seriously, though, of course I'm nervous. It's clear from the way he talks about her that she's very special. He adores her. What if she hates me?"

"I highly doubt that's going to happen, especially when she sees how happy you make him."

"I hope you're right," Ruby said, and her voice had lost all casualness. "Having a good mom in your life is special."

Ellie leaned her head on Ruby's shoulder. "Yeah," she sighed. Ellie's mom was a monster and out of Ellie's life for good, and Jackson's had died years ago in prison. They understood that there were no guarantees in life when it came to having a mom who loved them, or who wasn't dead because of a tragedy. "Does Lachlan know you're nervous?"

"Well, I haven't said those exact words, but he's pretty intelligent so the fifty or so times I've asked him if she'll like me probably clued him in."

"Probably." Ellie chuckled. "Well, this mama has to go to the bathroom so we'd better head to my clinic. You're going to have to help me up."

"Anything for you." Once standing, Ellie looped her arm through Ruby's again and they wobbled their way out of the park talking about love and motherhood.

Chapter Twenty-Three

"What is this?" Lachlan choked down his laughter. Ruby was waiting for him when he entered her apartment, coat and new plush winter boots on. She'd graduated from her furry pink slippers to furry winter boots. *Cute, sexy.* In her arms were two bouquets of flowers, two bottles of wine and a box from The French Connection Bakery. One thing he hadn't seen before and never would have guessed he'd see—Ruby Naylor worried about someone liking her. He knew his mom was going to fall right in love with her. Did this incredible woman not understand that everyone who came into her orbit fell hard and fast?

"I want her to like me, *them* to like me," she rushed out. Lachlan took pity on her. His heart gave one giant thud against his chest. There was no *slow fall* into love with this woman—he'd exploded into it with her, and with each new day, he tumbled all over again.

Lachlan set down the litter box and cat carrier and unlocked a crying Sugar Baby who immediately pranced out and began investigating Ruby's apartment. One by one he took the gifts out of Ruby's hands and set them on her coffee table. Then he got in close, snuggled his hands in between her coat and her top, some dark pink wrap design that hugged her body and put her curves on display.

"You're a gift," he said, fingering the tie at her waist. "All wrapped up for me, hiding away all these delectable secrets." Damn, it was easy to get lost in her. They'd been discovering each other for the past few weeks and tonight was the first time they were breaking out of their bubble to include someone else in their space.

Ruby relaxed an inch as she leaned into him. She rested her hands on his neck and stroked the skin along his jaw. He closed his eyes at the healing, sensual touch, let out a sigh and leaned his forehead down to meet hers. "I promise you, Mom and Nana are going to love you, Ruby. Mom's been not so subtly asking me for years why she never gets to meet any of my girlfriends."

"Oh?" Ruby's head popped up and he opened his eyes to see her face tight with worry, another emotion she rarely displayed.

"Do you want to know why?"

"Maaaaybe…no, I don't. Don't tell me. Oh my God, this is worse than I thought." Ruby tried to pull away, but he tugged her into his arms, locking her to him. He loved the way she fit, how she settled him, at the same time as she heated his blood with desire for her. He'd never felt both simultaneously before and it was exhilarating.

"She hasn't met any of my girlfriends because I haven't had that many. I haven't had *any* since I've been back in Opal. But I've always wanted her to meet you."

Ruby sucked in a breath and her eyes got wet.

"Hey." He gently shook her. "You're gonna ruin your makeup if you start crying." He couldn't have given a fuck whether her makeup was perfect or not, but it mattered to her.

She shook her head and waved her hand in front of her eyes. "Waterproof mascara. It's only for serious occasions because it's ridiculously unhealthy for the eyes, but I planned ahead for tonight." Now he didn't know whether to laugh at her again or not. But since he still didn't quite understand everything that was going on in her head, smart man that he was, he kept his laugh to himself.

"So, you planned on crying tonight?" he asked. She was gathering her defenses to head into battle.

"Yes! I mean no. Of course not. I just…it's…" Ruby sealed her lips and her eyes got huge. And he couldn't help the chuckle then. "I prepared in case she and your grandmother didn't like me and you decided you couldn't be with me if your mom didn't give her approval and we broke up and my heart stayed shattered forever." The words rushed out fast and furious.

Jesus, she was seriously worried. "Ruby, babe, come here." Lachlan sat on her couch and pulled her down onto his lap.

"I know it's all completely ridiculous and I'm being foolish, but my stomach's all stirred up, which has never ever, *ever* happened to me in my life. I like you so much it hurts. What we have, it's something unbelievable. It's different from any relationship I've experienced before and after only a few weeks. I feel like we were waiting for each other, like we found the most amazing, special person for each other. How ridiculous is that? I worked myself into a tizzy. But it's because it's your mom and her mom. Moms are precious."

"Deeper and deeper," he said, his voice gravelly. She slayed him over and over again. And it hadn't even occurred to him that the reason she was worried was because she knew how special moms were. She was the kind of person who lived each day to the fullest, who took every relationship she had, friendships, neighbors, family, seriously and took the utmost care with them. He didn't know if she had those qualities because she'd lost her mom, or if she'd always been that way. But he'd been a fucking idiot not to have made the connection earlier, seen what a sensitive topic this was for her.

"What?" she whispered.

"I really, really"—he enunciated each word with a kiss in between—"like you too. I *know* I've been waiting for you, not anyone, *you*. For someone as beautiful inside and out, for someone who looks at me and gives everything she has to making me feel like the most spectacular person on the planet. I'm in love with you, Ruby Naylor."

It was brilliant to say the words while he held her. Her face blossomed into her intimate, vulnerable, smile and he knew he'd made the right decision telling her. "If we had time, I'd do more than give you the words. I'd show you how much I'm falling for you. Deeper and deeper. Every day. Every moment. What I failed to convey to you is that I will take care of all of you, your cut feet and scraped knees, but this too." Lachlan put his hand on her heart.

"And I would not take you to meet my mom and grandmother if I wasn't one hundred percent certain that they are going to adore you. I'm sorry I didn't do everything in my power this week to calm your worries. I didn't think about how you must be feeling with regards to losing your own mom, Ruby. That was careless of me. But if you trust me, if you give me a chance, if you go to dinner with me at my mom's, I promise you'll see. I promise to be careful with you."

She nodded. This time she didn't try to fan away her tears. And when one spilled over he leaned in and kissed it away. "You've been careful with me," she said. "And not only with my feet, but with my heart. I want to impress them. I understand how special they are to you."

The shudder that Ruby let go with her words struck him. Elegant, perfectly put together, confident on the outside, inside his woman had a fragile soul that he was still learning about every day. And he'd never realized how important that would be to him.

"Then let's go eat dinner with them and get that taken care of, okay?"

Ruby took his head in hers and gave him one of her soft, lingering kisses. "Okay," she whispered.

"Something else I didn't tell you." Lachlan stood and grabbed the gifts Ruby had gotten for his mom.

"Oh?" she said and took his hand and he led her into the chilly night.

"She's a better cook than I am."

"Really?" Her pretty green eyes lit up. Another score for him was one of the ways to her heart was food.

"Oh yeah. She and my grandmother taught me."

"I wish I could have seen that," Ruby said.

He smirked and squeezed her hand, warm and soft in his. He played with her fingers and smoothed his thumb over her knuckles. "I was twelve when they started lessons. They got sick of me grumbling about doing the dishes, so they took pity and made a deal. If I made dinner, they'd do the cleanup."

"That's a good deal."

"My grandmother, sweet as a flower, said it was important I learn to feed myself, have a skill besides complaining and being a pain in the ass."

"You?" Ruby laughed and he felt her relaxing bit by bit. Maybe, hopefully he made her feel safe, the way she did for him.

He nodded and maneuvered the truck through the few inches of snow that had fallen that afternoon. "I was a serious grump at that age."

"Why?" Huh, it was easy to try to sooth her worries and have a casual chat. But with that question it would bring the serious back.

"My mom and I had finally left Corvallis. Her mom, Nana, took us in, saved us really. We'd been staying with friends…And…" So much had changed in his life so drastically. Even though he'd been safe from his dad's unpredictable behavior, even though he'd had a roof over his head and food to eat, it had taken him months to adapt to their new life and actually feel okay. Plus, when they'd left Corvallis, he'd lost things too, the routine of a familiar school, basketball and Big Brother nights with Isaac. Things that a twelve-year-old boy found difficult being ripped from his life suddenly. "We're here." He parked the car in his mom's driveway.

Ruby didn't even flinch. Her eyes were still on him, her hand linked with his, holding tight. "I'm so sorry, Lachlan." His name on her lips was the balm he needed. "Want to tell me about it?"

He pressed his lips to her hand. "Yeah, but right now, I'd rather take care of my woman, alleviate all her worries about a special night and feed her. Can you give me that?"

Ruby's smile, aimed at him, especially *for* him was prettier and more spectacular than the starlit sky. She leaned in and kissed him. "Yes, Lachlan, my love." He closed his eyes to take in the sensation of her speaking against his lips, sensual, soothing touch of hers. "But you should know, I want to learn everything about you, okay?"

He opened his eyes and met hers when he answered, "Okay."

All her worries had been ridiculous. Well, not ridiculous—she didn't consider her worry about something special between her and Lachlan wasted, but she may have gone a tad overboard with the whole "almost had a panic attack at her apartment when Lachlan picked her up". Ruby took deep breaths as they walked to the front porch. Before they even made it up the walkway, his mom opened the door with a huge smile aimed at Ruby and said, "I have been looking forward to this all week."

"Mom," Lachlan said. "This is Ruby. Ruby, my mom, Ava MacGregory."

"Nice to meet—" Ruby started to say, but was enveloped in a quick, warm hug from his mom.

"Sorry," Ava said and let her go. Her enormous blue eyes were wet. "I'm a bit emotional. Hey, honey," she said to her son and gave him a peck on the cheek. "Nana's in the living room."

"Mom," Lachlan said. "It's just dinner."

"Right." She nodded. And even Ruby could tell she was totally pacifying her son.

Ruby stared, wide-eyed and with a huge smile. Her nerves steadied immediately. "I thought you might like these." She handed one of the wild bunches of dried flowers Clare's Floral had made for her this afternoon.

Ava fingered the blue thistles that stood tall in the bouquet. "So beautiful," she said.

Lachlan winked at Ruby and held up the wine and sweets. "These are also from Ruby."

"I wasn't sure what would go with what we we're eating. So I bought both red and white. And chocolate truffles. I probably over-bought. My mom taught me never to show up emptyhanded. And well..." Ruby shut her mouth. For glitter's sakes she was rambling again. *Guess my nerves are still there beneath the surface.*

"A woman after my own heart," Ava said.

After Lachlan set the gifts down, he took his and Ruby's jackets and hung them in his mom's hall closet. Then he took Ruby's hand and led her into the living room.

"Mary!" Ruby exclaimed.

"I was so hoping you were *the* Ruby Ava was talking about. How lovely to see you, dear."

"You two know each other?" Lachlan asked. He leaned in and gave his grandmother an enormous hug and kissed her cheek.

"Ruby used to come to my apartment at the nursing home to give me the world's best pedicures. She takes good care of me and she makes my toes sparkle. Now that I'm moved in with Ava here in Corvallis, I can come visit your salon and see how lovely it must be. I have heard stories, oh my! Come sit by me."

Ruby sat next to Mary and gave her hand a gentle squeeze.

"You drove two towns away to make house calls?" Lachlan asked with that husky voice aimed her way.

"Well, it started as a project when I was in beauty school, before I even had my salon. And once I met some of the residents, they became my friends."

Mary patted her arm. "It's so good to see you.

"You look wonderful. When did you move?"

"Last month. Ava's been searching for a house closer to Lachlan for some time now. I'm just lucky she let me join her."

"I wanted you here, Mom," Ava said and hugged Mary's shoulders from behind. Ruby was surrounded by happiness. She caught Lachlan's gaze, shining with love for her. Wow, it was a good thing she'd put on waterproof mascara. Happy tears could ruin the perfect makeup as easily as sad tears. She'd felt his love, but him saying the words at her apartment, it was a gift she'd treasure.

"I'd still make house calls for you any day, Mary, but I'd love to show you my salon too. I think you'd adore it."

"I peeked my head in last week and, Ruby, you have something so special there," Lachlan's mom said. "I didn't want it to appear as though I was lurking or stalking, but now that we've met, I'll make appointments for Mom and me."

"It's a date," Mary said.

"It smells wonderful in here," Ruby said. "I'd offer to help, but I'm not the best cook. I am expert at pouring wine, though."

Ava waved her offer away. "You get to sit and enjoy tonight. And tell me all about yourself. Here, honey, you open these." She handed the bottle opener to Lachlan. "I also have that new cider from Freshwater Orchards you told me about."

"Wine's good, Mom. What are you making? I'm starved."

"A new curry recipe with lots of ginger and shallots. Felt perfect for a freezing night."

"Your home is lovely," Ruby said. It was a charming bungalow that had been completely updated. The sleek kitchen was a mix of traditional and modern with bright marble countertops and open shelves. The soft scalloped tile behind the hood and for the backsplash was spectacular. Off the kitchen, the cozy living room had matching white sofa and loveseats with throw pillows in a teal batik print. They were set in a u shape in front of a restored fireplace. The entire place said classy and cozy. Ruby loved it.

"Isn't it," Ava gushed. "We moved in last month. Connor Duggan did the renovations. It had been sitting on the market and I snatched it up. I can't wait for spring to actually get here so I can play in the garden. Wait till you see it. It's dreamy."

"Connor's amazing, isn't he?"

"Yes." Ava smiled at her. "The neighborhood is so different from when I lived here all those years ago. I was almost afraid to return because of, well…memories." She waved her hand as if brushing the past away. "But it's become so cheerful. And now I get to have my mom and Lachlan closer. It feels right."

It does. Everything feels right.

Chapter Twenty-Four

"I'm going to be full forever." Ruby kicked her boots off and fell onto her couch, coat still on. Lachlan lifted her legs and, sitting down under them, pulled them over his lap. "That dinner was exceptional. I'd do it all over again, eat too much, devour that chocolate pudding cake she made for dessert. Mmm, mmm, mmm." Lachlan dug his fingers into the pads of her feet. *Oh, wow, delicious.*

"It's my favorite," he said.

"What? Why have I never *ever* had chocolate orange pudding cake before? I mean it was glorious. It would be such a hit at the pub."

"Can't make it as good as my mom does. She's got the magic touch with that dessert. It always tastes better under her hands. Keeps it special."

"Can you believe I know your grandmother?"

"Small world, isn't it?"

"Yeah." She smiled at him. She was so in love. He gentled his movement on her feet, giving them a light massage. She closed her eyes as his touch soothed her.

The night had been beyond anything she could have imagined in her dreams. Not over-the-top fantasy dreams, but comfortable, loving, his mom and grandmother approved of her dreams. Ruby was so glad he had these two spectacular women in his life. Lachlan hadn't been shy about holding her hand or touching her when he was near, as if to reassure her at each step. Ruby had laughed, talked, eaten and been completely charmed by his family dynamics.

The only teeny-tiny part niggling at her brain was the role Lachlan's father had played in his life, or hadn't played. More so, that Lachlan hadn't trusted her with the information yet, deflecting every time she brought it up. Ruby didn't want to make him relive nightmares, but she wished to care for him, for whatever demons he had from childhood.

"Cute when you're full," he said. She could hear the smile in his voice. His big, warm hands moved up and down her legs.

"Cute?" she asked indignantly. Or she tried. She didn't even have enough energy to muster a pout.

"Full and happy," Lachlan said. He climbed over and lowered down next to her. She smiled and drifted on the high. He was so big and all-encompassing. She let him all encompass. He ran those strong fingers over her cheeks. "Cheeks are all flushed, eyes on fire, entire face lost in a dream. You're all loose and relaxed, not tied up like this shirt. I love this shirt, but I need to untie you."

When Ruby brought her focus back, his brow furrowed, his gentle touch became more intent. His needy fingers started a fire in her belly as he worked the sash at her side while kissing her neck and whispering dirty things to her.

"I want to untie you, get you naked while you're here at my mercy, taste every inch of you with my tongue. Hold you down and watch this flush take over your breasts while I play with your nipples, make you arch into my hands, make you beg me to let you come, do what you do to me, make me lose my mind with need for you.

Dirty, beautiful things. "God," she moaned and did what he commanded, arched into him. With each phrase he growled, he sank his hard body into hers, mimicking what he intended to do to her, plunder, take, make her his. When his hands finally untied her wrap and met her bare skin, his touch shocked, sent lightning bolts across her skin.

He angled himself up and knelt over her, boxing her hips in. Then he pushed open the side of her top, ran his fingers up her chest and shoved the top down her shoulders, locking her in place, baring her to him. She squirmed to touch him, rip his shirt off, get them both naked. But he held her there, that dark lust glazing his eyes, all for her.

"When I used to watch you, when I wanted you, but couldn't touch, I used to wonder if the rest of your skin got this rosy flush your cheeks do." Lachlan splayed his hand on her chest, spinning circles on her skin with his thumb. So close to her breasts, to her aching hard nipples, teasing her with that whisper of space. Her skin burned and she writhed again trying to communicate without words. *Touch me, touch me everywhere.*

His smile was lethal. He knew what she craved. "Are you needy yet, Ruby? The flush definitely comes here, and here." He stroked down between her breasts, missing her nipples again. Deliberately.

"Lachlan, please," she moaned. He played with her stomach.

"So beautiful." He leaned down and kissed her belly. "This flush right here. And here." He blew on her nipples, caught her eyes and held them while he grazed his fingers down her sides, making her squirm for more, for his fingers to quit teasing and hit their target. She felt his touch, his breath, her nipples straining against her bra. Slowly, he dragged her jeans off, savored her with his dark eyes.

He covered her breasts with his amazing hands, and kneaded, pinching her nipples through the lace of her bra, making them even harder. "Fuck." His own moan echoed hers. Done teasing, his touch wasn't gentle anymore, but powerful and insistent. Still kissing her stomach, he dragged one hand from her breasts, shoved aside her panties and used his extremely capable thumb to rub her clit. "So fucking wet." He used her then, used her wetness to toy with and seduce her, rubbing along her folds. "Always wet for me, Ruby. Do you know what that does to me?"

"No." It was a plea. He was building an explosion inside her. Gentle, hot, needy, caressing, insistent, a bit rough. She loved every single touch he gave her, showered on her. And she needed more. She needed everything.

Arms free now, she shimmied out of her jacket and shirt, grabbed his hand that was feasting on her breast and brought it to her mouth. Ruby sucked his thumb in and thrust her hips into his other hand. He met her need and plundered with his finger, one then two. But it wasn't enough. "More," she pleaded.

She watched his gaze darken, their eyes meeting in this erotic mating ritual. Then he parted her legs farther and stroked her sex with his tongue, answering her plea. He licked and sucked with his hands gripping her bottom, holding her to him, like he couldn't do anything but feast on her.

"God, Lachlan," she moaned.

"Yeah," he whispered against her thigh. "What do you want, Ruby?"

"You. Only you. Always. I need you always. It's not enough, and yet it's everything." She lost his hand when he dragged her panties off, and when he came back to her, he was naked. *Glorious naked body.* "How is that…" She panted. "How is that possible?"

"It's the same for me, beautiful woman." He opened the condom and dragged it over his magnificent cock. He wasn't even touching her, and she moaned at how erotic it was. She didn't have long to linger before he dragged her up and placed her on his lap, so she was straddling him. As soon as she felt him at her entrance she could no longer wait. His demand met hers, and as he gripped her hips, she sank down onto him. Lachlan held her there, both of them breathing heavily. Then he lifted her up and tugged her back down, urging her on until she couldn't take it anymore, her body shaking and desperate. And when she flew apart and screamed his name, he held her still and surged his own release into her.

* * * *

"How can I be hungry?" Ruby licked the ice cream off her spoon and loved how Lachlan's eyes got hooded at her movement. When she dipped the spoon in, he took her hand and fed himself. He stirred her up again. They'd worked off a ton of energy on the couch and on her rug. That was how she could be hungry after that enormous meal at his mom's. Lachlan wore only his jeans, unbuttoned, and an expression that she thought must mirror hers, satisfied, dopey, still pumping desire. She had her satin robe on, but she might as well have been naked the way he devoured her with his eyes.

"Loved sharing you with my family tonight."

She blushed. "They are so lovely and funny, Lachlan. You didn't tell me how funny they were. Where'd you come from?" she teased.

He stole her spoon and the bucket of ice cream this time. "I can be funny." His grumpy pout said otherwise. He fed her and she caught the smile in his eyes. He was teasing too.

"Lachlan." She had to get it out there before he distracted her again. "In case I haven't been communicating well, I am so in love with you too. You made my heart soar with those words earlier tonight and I feel the same." She placed her hand on his heart. "I want to learn about you, not only how your fingers feel on my skin, or your lips on…" She sighed and smiled. "Well, all over me." His gaze heated again. They did this to each other, stoked the fire, sent each other into flames. "Or how cute you are when you tease me, when you laugh."

When he leaned in to kiss her, she had to chant in her head, *Don't lose focus. Don't lose focus.*

"You love me?" His grin was so dang cute.

She nodded.

"Beautiful body," he said and ran his finger down her chest. "Beautiful heart, beautiful mind." He set the empty ice cream tub in the sink with the spoon. "What's going on in that mind of yours? Your thoughts are like a race car. Smooth and sleek, but intent."

"Not a freight train?" she teased. That was how they felt, railroading through her brain, clamoring to get out.

"Nothing about Ruby Naylor is even close to a freight train. Every single inch of you is all class, with the perfect touch of dangerous seduction."

Just because she showed class and calm to the world didn't mean she wasn't a hive of nervous bees sometimes. "I…when we start to talk about your dad, something happens, or it isn't the right time, and I don't want you to think for one second it's because I don't care about your past. All of it, the good, the bad, where you came from. Every bit of it shaped you into this special human being and I want to know it. Be your safe place."

At first, she wondered if she'd made a monumental mistake when Lachlan's face morphed into a crazy look of confusion before settling into an easy smile. Then he tugged her legs around him and leaned into her

"You're right that it hasn't been the best time to talk about my dad. That's because it is never a good time to talk about Denny MacGregory."

"Oh, honey." Ruby ached to wrap him up, but his arms were heavy and locked in on her hips. He enjoyed this position. It was what he needed, so she'd give it to him. She placed a gentle kiss on his mouth.

"I have very few memories of good moments with my father. And the ones I do have are most likely tinged with him being either barely drunk enough to still feel happy, or still being on a high from some grand idea he'd worked that had gone well, usually a con."

"You grew up here, before your mom took you and left, you said in the truck tonight."

"Yeah. I knew these neighborhood streets like the back of my hand. Took my basketball with me everywhere. Short and unsweet, Ruby, my mom did the best she could working and trying to pay the bills, but my dad couldn't quit the gambling, the schemes. We got evicted from our apartment when I was eleven. Dad had deserted us for good that time, or was too drunk to figure out what the hell he was doing.

"Mom had a job, but after Dad cleaned out our account it was difficult to get back on our feet. Finally, we left and went to Nana for help. It was the best thing to happen, but didn't feel that way for any of us at first. Mom and Nana had a lot of work to do to repair their relationship, but they did it."

"For you." Ruby tried to will away her tears, but one slid down her cheek. Lachlan growled and brushed it away lightly with his fingertips. *So gruff and gentle at the same time.*

"Don't want you to cry over this," he said.

Ruby caressed his cheek. "Can't help it, you mean too much to me. I ache for the child you were, for your mom and your grandmother. But I'm also so amazed at the man you have become, and thrilled that I get to be here with you trusting me."

"I do trust you. It's a heady feeling, Ruby Naylor." He rested his forehead against hers.

Ruby ran her hands over his shoulders. His muscles were tight, bunched. "So Denny's still here, in Corvallis?"

"Some days. He wanders, I think. Didn't see him for the first two years I was back. Until the pub got successful and he was interested in me again." He laughed but there was no humor in the sound. "And still," he whispered. "No matter how many times the man hurt me, physically or emotionally, or disappointed me, I can't seem to cut him out of my life.

Which might make me the dumbest person on the planet."

"No, honey." Ruby gently moved her forehead over his. "It makes you human. It makes you a son wishing for a good father, wanting to feel worthy of love and respect and caretaking. All kids should have that."

Growing up, Ruby had believed everyone had a dad similar to hers, loving, funny, warm, larger than life. She'd seen enough over the years as an adult to know that was the farthest thing from the truth. And it broke a tiny bit of her heart that Lachlan had grown up without his own Isaac Naylor.

Lachlan brushed his lips over her head. "You make me feel worthy. You beat back all the horrible from my past all my grief. Is that silly? Grief for a father I never had."

She shook her head. "You can tell me anything, Lachlan. And I'll take it for you. I'll beat anything back for you." Her hands had made their way to his scalp to massage, the way he loved. "You do the same for me. Now it's your turn."

"Pardon?"

"Come with me." Ruby hopped down and led him into her bedroom. "Lie down on your stomach, naked."

Lachlan leaned in and stole a quick kiss. "I like the sound of this."

Ruby slid the pillow away, lit her candles and grabbed her massage oil. She put on a mellow Blues CD and dimmed the lights, then she shed her robe and climbed onto Lachlan's back. *Perfect.*

"Ahh, perfect," he said. *Wonderful man reading my thoughts.*

Ruby rubbed the oil between her hands to warm it up, gave thanks for this magnificent man before her, his body, his heart. She started with his shoulders and his deltoids and he moaned under her touch. "Sexy, hardworking, tight muscles," she cooed. He was so responsive to her fingertips as she alternated between deep massage and light caress, the oil slicking over his skin. Knots loosened and his limbs gave in.

"Ruby." The way he said her name in his deep, strangled voice. "Feels damn good."

"You deserve good, Lachlan. You deserve wonderful." She soothed with her voice, softly, grounding his emotions even while she worked his muscles into a euphoric state with her hands. *A lovely balance.*

"You have superpowers."

"Shh," she whispered near his ear as she gently stroked his scalp and down his neck. After she paid reverence to his strong arms, she climbed off and worked his legs from his toes up his calves and thighs to his glutes. And when she arrived, she kissed his magnificent butt. The man had the best butt, two tiny dimples, one on each cheek.

"Ruby." His growl returned. Ruby felt her cheek, finding it flushed. She'd never gotten turned on from giving a massage before.

"I don't do massage very often anymore." She straddled him again and stretched, using all her limbs to snuggle him. "It's hard on my body." She kissed his neck, his ear, got lost in his scent. So lost, she was unprepared for him to spring.

A man on a mission, Lachlan twisted out, grabbed her and had her under him in two seconds flat.

"Oh," she said on a sigh as her breath left her. She was pinned beneath him, facedown in the same position he'd been in. Lachlan MacGregory was straddling her. And he was hard, so hard and hot. He vibrated over her, sending arrows of desire licking over her skin.

"This body..." He stroked down her spine, kneaded her butt. "Deserves to be pampered now too. Need to take good care of this body." He warmed some oil, the way she'd done, then took his time stroking every inch of her into pleasure. The flames on her skin licked and leapt. Ruby couldn't help her soft moans.

"Oh!" she squealed. Sugar Baby had leapt onto the bed.

"No, Baby." Lachlan reached for his cat, but she danced over Ruby's shoulders, then leapt to the pillow beside Ruby, and started pawing at Ruby's face.

Laughter bubbled out of her.

"Ridiculous cat," Lachlan said, humor in his voice. "Shoo, go away." He tried sliding Baby off the pillow, but she meowed and pranced up and down the bed, investigating what was going on.

"Did you..." Laughing on her stomach, with over two hundred pounds of man on her back was a feat. "Did you just shoo your cat?"

She felt Lachlan's laughter rumble out of him as he sprawled over her. Tears leaked out of her eyes from her own amusement.

"Get out, you feline nuisance." Lachlan grabbed Baby and set her out of the bedroom. "Never thought we'd have to close the door to the cat."

"That was..." Her giggles wouldn't stop. "That was the most ridiculous thing...I..."

"Mmm." His tone had changed to serious again. He climbed back on and caressed her butt, so soft, then deeper, intent. "Ridiculous, huh?" He lifted and stroked his cock through her folds.

"Yeah," she moaned, drawn into her lust fog.

"Made me lose my focus." He lined up at her entrance. His hands on her were rough, thorough in their pursuit of giving her the best massage.

"Oh, no." She pouted when he stroked his fingers through her wetness. "Please don't lose your focus." Her entire being was aware, shaking, craving his touch. She closed her eyes and let her body hear and feel. He was breathing heavily. He rocked into her. She could feel him take his cock in hand and stroke it with her desire, slicking himself with her. Even the sound of the condom package opening was erotic.

He was giving her such a sensual, erotic massage. She felt like flying. If only he'd let her.

"Lachlan," she moaned.

"Yes, Ruby. What do you need?" His hands were working her legs apart. He stroked her inner thighs, getting so close, then teasing away, until it must have been too much for him and he placed the tip of his cock at her entrance, captured her hips and thrust in.

"God," she moaned and held on to the sheet while he used her body and brought them both pleasure. "That feels…so…good, honey."

"Yeah, it does. Hot and slick and tight. The way you pull me in," he said. "It feels like everything."

Ruby had no warning before the storm burst through them and sent them spinning into space together. His weight was heavy and lovely on her as she floated.

Lachlan rolled onto his side and smoothed his hands over her skin. "Wow," he said, taking a deep breath.

Ruby chuckled. "You can say that again. Mmm, I love the way you caress me. Feels so good, dreams coming true." Sleep was sneaking over her.

"Sweet, sweet, Ruby." He trailed kisses down her backbone as she drifted. "You'd battle my demons for me, huh?"

"Mmm-hmmm." She smiled and closed her eyes.

As Ruby was drifting off, she felt his lips on her skin and his soft whisper humming through her, "You're my dream. A dream come true."

Chapter Twenty-Five

It had been a long time since Lachlan had woken up with his father on his mind, although the negative effect was nearly washed away at having Ruby sprawled out on his chest. He stroked her back, loving the little noises of pleasure she made in her sleep. Her love, being in love with her, felt fucking fabulous.

She'd drifted off quickly, but he'd been restless all night. Memories could do that to him, steal his rest, bang on his head until he paid attention to them, pieced them together and remembered, whether he wanted to or not.

It had been weeks since he'd seen, heard from or heard talk of his father. Normally that wouldn't be weird. But it occurred to Lachlan that the last time had been the night that his pub had been vandalized. Not only had he been unable to find his father that night, but he was remembering what Mr. Meyer had said about the state of his room at their hotel.

Sick, or drunk-sick—it was too difficult to tell the difference anymore—his father had needed something, usually money. And Lachlan had learned over the past year of visits and interactions from his father that when his father needed something, he didn't disappear and go radio silent.

So why hadn't he been where he'd said he was going to be that icy night? And why hadn't Lachlan heard from him since? Neither question had any good kind of answers. The whole thing churned in his gut, in his instincts, trying to tell him something, convey some message. Unfortunately the pieces weren't fitting together. He needed a workout. Not a sexy one with his gorgeous girlfriend, but one that involved a punching bag and a gym and Lachlan's absolute concentration.

* * * *

Apparently beating the shit out of a leather bag hadn't been enough, because two hours after he'd slipped out of bed, leaving Ruby a note on the coffee pot, Lachlan was sweating profusely, shooting layup after layup on the basketball court. His legs were beginning to burn now with the punishment, but still Lachlan hadn't been able to work out the problem signaling at the base of his skull that he was missing something.

"You punishing yourself? Hopefully nothing to do with my Ruby." Isaac Naylor jogged onto the court and motioned for the ball. Lachlan shot it to his chest and bent over to catch his breath.

"Ruby's good, I swear. She's giddy over us having dinner together Friday."

"Yeah?" Isaac smiled. "Sounds like that's a good thing, not a negative." The man eased into his layup and sank the shot the same way he'd done it a thousand times over the years. He could probably play blind, he was so good. Not Lachlan, he had to work for every shot. But it was awesome to watch a genius at play.

"I haven't told her about us."

That caught the man off guard and brought a chuckle to Lachlan.

"Us?"

"That I'm assisting with the anti-gang task force, have been—"

Isaac waved his hand and lit a three pointer that sank as if it were reaching for salvation. "She knows about that."

She was aware of the neighborhood watch, as a Corvallis business owner herself. But her dad was right, she probably knew all about the anti-gang task force as well. She'd been so cute and adamant last night that he understand she was there for him in all ways. He felt the same for her. He wanted to be her world, and he was going to do everything he could to hold tight to that feeling and nurture it. They hadn't much come up for air or out of bed since they'd gotten together. *Best damn month of my life.* He'd happily stay under the blankets with her. He'd better school the grin off his face or Ruby's father would know exactly where his fantasies had gone.

Connor and Jackson had actually been most instrumental in the renovation of the neighborhood, because they'd been dealing with absentee landlords and vacant properties. But Lachlan had offered Isaac his support with the seedier bits, the gangs who'd been pissed when their drug turf had begun to get cleaned up.

"I haven't told her about you being my Big Brother." *That my mom and I were living out of our car. That the YMCA was where I got to be a kid, take a shower, breathe.*

"You embarrassed by that?" Isaac shot him a dark glare, calling him out on his bullshit.

"Hell no. You're the one who has the right to be embarrassed." The old wounds spilled out unbidden, rarely, but it happened.

That had the man traveling and losing his grip on the ball. He didn't even bother to follow its path as it rolled across the court. He met Lachlan where he stood. They were equal in size and height, but Lachlan, even now, as a grown man, would always feel smaller than Detective Isaac Naylor. *No way to compare to a hero.* "Seems ridiculous to have to say this to you right now with all you've accomplished, but you are not your father, Mac."

I sure as hell hope not. "I know." The lie came easily. He'd been telling himself the same thing since he was twelve. *Easier to chant the words than actually believe them some days.* "I never want her to see how needy I was as a kid. How much I lacked."

The admission spilled out and fuck, did those words sting. Here he was at thirty-three, a successful business owner, proud of his neighborhood, had a woman he was head over heels for. It was more than most people got in one lifetime. And yet it seemed to heighten all his old insecurities.

"You think she'd care any less about you? Do you think I cared less about you as your Big Brother?" Isaac didn't let him answer. "I was proud of you because you were an amazing kid. Yes, you needed support. We all do at times. Now you're the one giving to the community." He grabbed the basketball. Without pause, he shot it to Lachlan. "If you're as close to my daughter as I'm guessing, you understand not only how strong she is, but how much compassion she has in her heart. Anything you went through as a child, anything difficult you will continue to face in life, as long as your heart is true, she could not do anything but love you more."

Lachlan had to choke back his tears. *There's no crying in basketball.* She did love him, showered her love on him every day since they'd been together.

"And the love of a good woman," Isaac said, "is the most beautiful thing in the world." He took advantage of Lachlan's distraction to steal the ball and run through another perfect layup.

Isaac had lost his love too, too early. But the smile on his face when he talked about Ruby's mom spelled out how rare it was, how it should be cherished. And Lachlan wished for that kind of love with Ruby.

"Now, enough stepping into the past. Let's talk about what specials you're cooking up for me Friday night at the pub. Haven't had a night off in weeks. Looking forward to dinner with you and Ruby, some of your magic in the kitchen and listening to that young band you have scheduled. Heard they're a mix of vintage rhythm and blues meets New Orleans jazz funk. Now that I have got to see."

Isaac was right again, time to step out of the past and head toward his future. And that future included the love of a good woman.

Chapter Twenty-Six

"When are you moving in?" Katie asked and ran her hands over the curved banister.

"Next week, as soon as the floors are done. Everything else can wait, or happen while I live here."

"Holy smokes," Katie said and sighed. She fanned her face. "Hot and cute is coming up the walkway right now." They watched Lachlan approach Ruby's front door. "That's a lethal combination." Katie bumped Ruby's shoulder. "The sexy, dangerous kind." They peeked through the old lace curtains in the front room of her new house like two teenage girls spying on the super-cute older guy next door.

"I know." Ruby's words came out all breathy and she had to clear her throat. But Katie was right. The man was lethal. Even more so now that Ruby knew what all the leashed muscle and energy felt like, tasted like when he loosed it on her. All for her. She'd never been in love with someone who was also in love with her. The constant wire of energy that flowed between them, even when they were separated—well, she could understand what people meant when they spoke of a drugged feeling, a high. The hotness factor wasn't a secret, with his good looks, intensely delicious eyes and ripped body. Cute wasn't a word Ruby would have associated with Lachlan MacGregory, but the more she learned about him, his cuteness showed up all over the place.

"Are you going to ask him to move in with you?"

Ruby startled and faced her friend. "I want to, but I'm a teeny bit afraid. What if he doesn't..."

"Pshaw." Katie rolled her eyes. "He'd be stupid not to. And that handsome specimen does not strike me as stupid, especially not since he made you his."

Mmm, he sure did make me his.

He was smiling. Maybe he could see them drooling and gossiping over him. His hair was still damp from his shower—she nearly pouted, a shower he'd taken without her this morning. He'd left her warm and satisfied in bed to go work out and check in on his grandmother. She'd had her own coffee date with Katie to show off the wallpaper samples for her house. But now he was meeting Ruby here to walk her to work, as he'd done every day this week. No matter if he had appointments or morning commitments, no matter where she was, he walked her to her salon.

His navy hoodie stretched over his shoulder muscles and his dark jeans fit him so, so well. And he carried two large black plastic pots with plants in them. *For my garden.* Ruby's heart lodged in her throat. *Sweet, sweet man.* At breakfast one morning last week she'd gushed over the plants she was going to buy, her eyes full of stars at getting to reshape that space into her dream garden, lush and romantic and sensual. Climbing roses and peonies and jasmine. An entire herb garden and poppies of every kind and color. And here he was already making her dreams come true.

She never knew what to expect with him, his heart so ready to give her the world. Hot and cute and loving, how much of his life he'd opened up to accommodate her. Altogether, the intense combination was breathtaking. Her heart knew it. Her heart welcomed it.

Ruby opened the door and they stepped out onto the porch. "What are you doing?"

"Ladies," Lachlan said. "Morning, Katie." He set the pots on the porch, and leaning down, touched his lips to Ruby's. "My gram gave me these for you. A Royal Sunset, which, according to her, is the best climbing rose with scent that blooms all summer long. And the Ruby, the prettiest rose she's ever seen."

"I have to run. You two lovebirds have a good day." Ruby barely registered Katie's hug before her friend walked off.

"You brought me plants for my garden?"

"Yeah." Lachlan tugged her into him. "You said you pictured climbing roses dancing over the entire garden wall. Perfect time of year to plant bare root roses. We could do it this weekend. If you'd like."

Breathless, held tight against him, she caressed his neck. "You paid attention when I went off on my crazy garden dreams?"

"I pay attention to it all. When you talk about the ideal light fixtures, or how you picture the garden on a hot summer evening, the way you take care with every touch, every word you bestow on your friends, on their kids, on me."

Katie had been right, hot and cute. *But so much more.* He practically laid his heart bare for her daily. And still it surprised her. "Thank you."

A wide smile warmed his face. "I enjoy making you happy. Best feeling in the world."

"Move in with me. Here," Ruby blurted. "Is it too soon? It doesn't feel too soon. I don't care. I want to live with you, start our life together, you and Sugar Baby and me."

She shouldn't have worried, because his smile didn't change, if anything it got softer and sweeter, melting her into a gazillion pieces of mush before she had to go work.

Lachlan snaked an arm around her. "Is that what you want, Ruby?"

She nodded. "Oh, yes. So much."

"Why, Ruby Naylor." He kissed her. "I've never had such a beautiful proposal before."

"Really?"

"Nope." He ran his fingers over her cheek and cupped her jaw. "Couldn't care less where we live, because you're all I need. But I'd be honored to move in with you to your dream house."

"Yay," she whispered and shooed the tears away. "Beautiful dreams coming true."

"Yeah," he said, held on tight and planted a deep wet kiss on her.

Then, gentleman that he was, he took the keys from her and locked her door, while she stood there winded and breathless from what had just transpired. He grabbed her large shoulder bag, took her hand and walked her to work. And it was a damn good thing he held on tight, because again she was putty in his hands. He flipped her world upside down and made her dizzy. When she finally pulled herself together, somewhat, it seemed she was always floating on some level or another. She peeked at him to see a grin on his handsome face, so much more relaxed than when they'd been in their stupid avoidance dance.

"What's that smirk for, handsome man?" He held her hand but had his entire arm snaked through hers holding her close. All these weeks later and he was still worried about her injured foot. Boy, did he pay attention.

"You." He waved to Carl, who was setting up his brisket cart outside the hardware store. Tradition on the first day of March, rain or shine. It was clear and sunny today. And Ruby breathed in the sunshine. "Your dreams." Jackson was lifting Ellie down from his truck in front of her clinic. Her dogs bounded after her. Lachlan and Ruby reached Spa La La and she unlocked the door. He pressed his body up against hers. "Everything about you. This classy outfit of yours." He brushed his hands up against her skirt. "Those shoes that can make a man fall to his knees and beg." He twirled her in his arms.

Lachlan's toyed with her bottom lip. "Pretty ruby-colored lips." His voice had taken on a hushed tone. And she felt naked as he dragged his eyes down and back up to take all of her in. "You stun me every time I look at you, all put together like a fashion stylist, prim and proper."

But it was that sexy way he had of sending her lusty messages simply with his mouth quirked up at the side and those dark, serious eyes burning into her skin that spoke more than his words. "But I also know how enticing you are when you're all undone. Mine. My secret knowledge. Love that you have all these contrasts. But all I can think about is getting you all mussed up again." He tugged her close and she could feel how hard he was for her.

"Lachlan," she said, sounding desperate. He did that to her, stirred her up into a tornado of lust only moments after sending her heart soaring.

"Peeling off this satiny blouse that gets to be intimate with your skin all day while I'm at work thinking about you. Sliding this skirt off to see what you have on underneath for me." He fingered the fabric of her skirt again between his fingers like there might be gold if he could dig deep enough. And he was right. It was for him, all the silky pieces of lingerie she decorated her skin with these days, was for him. He stepped into the salon with her, locked the door behind them and walked her into the shadows. "Can't get enough. Want to mess you up right now. Too bad you have to work."

Bad? Too bad nothing. Ruby grabbed his sweatshirt, pulled him close and sealed their lips together. And with every ounce of coordination she had left, she walked them backward toward her office. They bumped into the door frame.

"Sorry." Lachlan's voice was muffled against her throat.

"Uh huh," she moaned as he bent down, palmed his hands under her skirt and lifted her onto her desk. He shoved her skirt up, locked his body into hers and teased her neck, her chest with his famished lips.

Ruby rubbed against him trying to get closer, trying to align her swollen clit to the hard, rough thrust of his jean-clad body.

"Fuck!" He tore his lips away and held her hips open for his inspection. "Was expecting one of your sexy panties. You're naked under here."

"Surprise," she said and tried to arch closer to him again, to his touch. His thumbs were hot and probing, so close, so close, but always teasing, short of where she craved them. Hot on her thighs, sparks lit her up as he stroked leisurely lines as if they had all day. He knew how to torture her.

"Not torture." She must have begged that all out loud. "Stir you up, entice, savor you." And he did. He did all of that with those sexy thumbs while his fingers gripped her ass and worked into her. He knelt. And God, that pose, him on his knees searing her with those intent, hooded eyes of his. "Look at you all splayed out and bare for me."

"Uh huh." She leaned onto her hands and nodded. And when he quit torturing her and met her pussy with his mouth, when he took one long erotic lick and tasted her folds, her body bowed up into his mouth. She moaned. "Fuck, Lachlan." All she could hear were her cries and his feasting. She rocked and tried to claw into him. His grip on her was just as fierce. Until he rose and, with one hand still holding her, undid his jeans.

"So fucking beautiful, undone and glowing." He tugged her closer, gripped his cock and slid it along her sensitive skin, teasing, caressing.

"Condom. Now. I need you," she pleaded, gripping onto his hands at her hips. On fire for his touch, she pleaded for him to make them one.

"Mmm." That fucking cocky smirk was in his words. "Didn't bring one with me, Ruby," he ground out, teasing her slit with his hard cock. So hard. So thick. She needed it to fill her.

"I'm so empty." She squirmed. His touch had her pliant and burning with desire. "My…bag…I have one…" Ruby tried to gesture.

He leaned down over her, his cock at her entrance, tracing slow circles on her wet pussy. "Dropped your bag at the front door, Ruby. Want me to go get it? Want me to leave you here, skirt shoved up, your gorgeous body displayed here, all flushed and begging?"

"No...yes..." *I don't know.* He started to pull away and she couldn't stand the cold, the emptiness. "No, no, no." Ruby grabbed his arm and brought him back to her. "That..." She made a desperate attempt at a twirling motion with her hand. "What you're doing. Keep doing that."

"What's that, Ruby?" He made one long erotic circle with his cock on her skin. She might explode if he made one more movement, one more caress. "Coating your sweet juices all over me. Making myself all wet with you. Getting us both all fucking mussed up."

"God, yes, please."

"You don't have to beg for it. But damn I love how you show me with your words and your sensual movements, trying to climb me. What can I do for you, Ruby? I'm dripping with you."

It was intense and he wasn't even inside her. "I need you. You're everything."

With his cock fisted, he found her clit and rubbed it with his thumb. So good, so amazing. Her body shaking, she screamed and splintered into a million pieces.

"Fuck, Ruby." Seeing her, so erotic, so powerful, made him lose control and he climaxed in his hand. "Christ, you destroy me." He leaned into her, as undone as she was. *So sexy.* He bent over and gave her chest a kiss. "Be right back."

"Huh," was all she managed to get out. But when he returned, all cleaned up and tucked into his jeans, she almost wept at the loss. Then he placed a warm cloth between her legs and cleaned her up, tenderly, reverently.

When he was done, he pulled her up and stepped in between her legs to enfold her in a huge warm hug, running his large hands down her back in soothing motions, as if knowing she was still coming down from the cliff he'd shot her off. "I love walking you to work," he whispered into her hair. Ruby clutched him tighter and giggled. *Giggled?* God, she was a helium balloon let loose, flying ridiculously and squealing through the air. She slumped into his broad, powerful, safe chest and let herself enjoy the ride.

"I got my test results. All clean," Lachlan whispered in her ear. "We could go without condoms now, if you want?"

Ruby chuckled again. "I want. You could have told me that a few minutes ago, when we were…"

"When you were ravishing me and shattering all my rational thoughts?" he asked. "The last thing on my mind was speaking coherent sentences, especially about something so important."

"Yeah." Ruby nodded.

"Besides, I like what we just did. A whole lot."

"Yeah," she said again, still floating on her sex high. "Me too." She'd told him she was on birth control, and her tests were clean, but he'd been determined to wait for his test results to prove to her that he was serious about their relationship. Her chivalrous man, giving her fantastic orgasms and caring for her at the same time. All her dreams were coming true and it felt fabulous, to see them happening, to share them with Lachlan. Life had never been more spectacular.

Chapter Twenty-Seven

Sugar Baby was dancing across his shoulders when Ruby's car pulled into the drive. He opened the door and watched her walk to him, happiness radiating from every pore.

"My absolute darling goodness, I'm so in love," Ruby said and threw herself into his arms, sending Baby flying into the dark kitchen. It was after midnight. He'd gotten home from the pub a few minutes earlier.

Her light was so brilliant that it slayed him. "Everyone okay?"

"They are perfect! Baby Alexander is seven pounds exactly. He has the biggest cheeks and this tiny, soft, scrunched-up face. Ellie's glowing. Even Jackson is beside himself with joy. I don't think the man has ever smiled so much. He's in awe."

"That's good, honey. Glad you got to be there." Lachlan was in awe too. *Of Ruby's body, her heart.*

"Me too, it was so special. And I get to be an honorary aunt." She threw her purse down and gave him a loud smacking kiss.

He nuzzled into her and guided her toward his bedroom, his need for her in overdrive. He listened to her talk, while he undressed her. Her joy heated his blood and set him on a mission. *Get Ruby naked.*

"Babies make you happy?" He'd give her her heart's desires. He stripped off her sparkly red lingerie till it was her and nothing else, bared to him. He nudged her down to his bed and shrugged his own clothes off. Her eyes were hooded, her skin flushed and waiting for him. "Do you want babies, beautiful Ruby?" He stroked his hands up her legs, over her belly and cupped each breast.

"Mmm," she sighed. "Maybe someday. Maybe not. You?" She curved into his touch, all glorious soft planes and angles rubbing against his hands.

"I want two things, Ruby. You and to make you happy. Whatever that takes. I'll do anything for you." He teased open her legs, blew soft kisses up her inner thighs and reveled in her moans.

"Anything?"

He grinned.

"Then come here and give me that body of yours with nothing between us."

Lachlan climbed in beside her and rolled them so they were on their sides, facing each other. He dragged her leg over his hip and smoothed his hands over her body, letting the heat of her skin sink into him.

"I want to spend my life with you, Lachlan MacGregory. How does that sound?" She kissed his chest and wiggled closer, rubbing her soft folds over his erection while she dragged her nails over his skin. The combination of her softness and her hard nails was as erotic as hell. He was hard and burning for her, to sink into her, feel her clamp onto him in all her beauty.

"It sounds…" He thrust in, claiming her, connecting them. There was no time for foreplay. The last month had been foreplay, teasing each other, devouring each other, lighting each other up. "Like everything." His voice came out harsh and intent. He gripped her butt and centered himself deep inside her. "I'm never letting you go, gorgeous woman." Lachlan found her mouth and drove his tongue inside, mirroring the movements of his body. She braced around every inch of him, and when she came undone, she lured him along with her and claimed him as hers.

* * * *

Lachlan paused for a minute and basked in the glow of the din of the pub on a crowded Friday night. Mid-March and outside it was one of those winters that was determined to charge hard all the way to the bitter end.

Winter was such a sneaky witch. Since one day of sunshine on Monday, there'd been cold freezing rain for days, no sun in sight through the low, dark clouds. More snow was predicted for tomorrow.

Inside, his pub was filled with warmth. The best decision he'd made was creating a secluded entryway so the wind wouldn't blow them all down every time someone entered on a night like tonight. The low lights cast a seductive ambiance across his patrons, the heaters were pumping and one of his new favorite bands, the High Jinx, jammed on stage.

As crowded as the eleven members were up there, they played and sang like it was a jam-packed music festival on a summer day and they were all flying with happiness. People ate and drank, friends, strangers, neighbors. A seamless, perfect night at his bar, exactly what he'd imagined when he was writing his business plan and building his dream.

He took pride in the fact that what he'd created could provide people with a reprieve from the gloomy weather and loneliness of an unrelenting winter. But damn, he couldn't wait for the outdoor patio to open. They all needed a good long thaw, the whole neighborhood.

He wiped a glass and shelved it before taking in the corner table. His Ruby sat on the end of the booth, enjoying happy hour with Natalie, Ford, Noah and Katie before her dad arrived. Isaac was due to meet them later for their first official dinner together. At least that was what Ruby was calling it. She'd been giddy all week about her two favorite men finally getting together. It was important to Ruby that he and Isaac got along. He hoped she'd be pleasantly surprised to discover he and her dad had been friends for a long time, that her dad was already important to him.

The wall sconces lit up her face, which was full of laughter and happiness. Somehow his gaze pulled her attention and she smiled at him. Damn, that sexy, knowing, intimate smile she gave to him, *only* him. It hit Lachlan in the chest again and again.

For too long he'd seen that smile and tried not to drool and pant for it to be aimed at him. What he couldn't have fathomed was how her entire expression would grow even more lovely when she sent it his way. Even across the room, they were lost in each other. This time he didn't hide how it affected him. He smiled too and rubbed his chest. It made her laugh again. He couldn't hear it over the noise of the busy pub, but he knew it was soft and throaty. Everything about her was soft, except the parts that were powerful and strong. She was all tangled up in beauty and complexity and he was enjoying untangling and discovering every bit of her. He cherished each part she shared with him.

No amount of freezing rain and relentless winter, no matter his past or his fears of being unworthy, Lachlan MacGregory took in the setting and allowed a glow of happiness to seep into his bones. His pub was part of that, but Ruby exploded his joy into outer space.

He took a breath and planted the moment in his heart, happiness, peace, love. Damn, he loved her. She'd made it so fucking easy to fall deep. He'd been falling since he was a boy. Never had he known such a feeling comfort him the way her love did. Despite his shitty childhood, Lachlan had been shown love, from his mother, from his friends and brothers by chance. This was different, *more*. To have his own place to fall, to fully be himself, and have someone appreciate and nourish him in the way only Ruby could—it wiped away every last hint of doubt, of searching, of that feeling that he'd hovered in limbo for so long.

Someone called his attention at the bar. He blew her a kiss, and she gave him a small finger wave and returned her attention to her friends while he took drink orders and filled pints.

"Got any of your famous Guinness stew tonight?" his friend Charlie asked as he grabbed a recently emptied seat and helped his enormously pregnant wife in.

Lachlan shook his friend's hand, leaned over and gave Charlie's wife, Davinia, a kiss on the cheek. "Always for you two. And I made a dark chocolate cake with a smoky coffee buttercream frosting." He winked at Davinia.

"Now you're speaking my language. I'll have cake for dinner with a side of fries and a cup of your caramel apple cider. This baby craves all the sugar all the time."

"A pint and the stew for me. It's frigid out there." Charlie shivered and rubbed his hands together. "Toasty in here. I may not leave. Place looks great, man. Glad you were able to get up and running again so soon."

"Couldn't have done it without everyone. Appreciate you working your magic for the liquor discount."

"Anytime."

"How are you? How's Ruby?" Davinia asked.

"Good." Lachlan smiled. He nodded in Ruby's direction. "She's there bundled in with her friends. We're having dinner with her dad tonight."

"Ooooohhh." Davinia swooned. "Meeting the parents already. I sense love in the air." Davinia was a hopeless romantic, but she wasn't wrong.

"I've known Detective Naylor since I was a boy." He felt his gaze pulled Ruby's way again, and put his hands on the bar and indulged his friends. "But yes, it's definitely an important step. Ruby's been gushing about us getting together for weeks now. He's important to her. Hopefully I won't screw anything up."

Davinia's smile softened. "How could you? You're an amazing man and friend, Lachlan. Ruby's lucky to have you." Her words soothed his insecurities, but he knew he was the lucky one.

"We're moving in together," Lachlan told them. "She bought a house up the street and I'm going to help her restore it. The old Poole house."

"Another house with lots of charm," Charlie teased. "Sucker." But he shook Lachlan's hand with a warm smile.

"Yes!" Davinia cheered. "Buh bye, lonely old condo. Hello, true love."

Lachlan indulged them with a smile. It *was* love, and dreams coming true. He was surrounded by it. He had much to be thankful for. He left his friends to place their order and get their drinks.

More people straggled in. The band took a break. Laughter thrilled over the crowd. His kitchen was jamming, and his bartenders and waitresses would make a mint tonight. Good, they deserved it. Everyone felt the buzz.

Something drew Lachlan's attention toward the front. When the pub door opened this time, despite the two-door alcove, a bitter wind snaked in like a banshee, heralding something dark and dangerous.

Even standing all the way at the end of the bar near the busy, loud kitchen, surrounded by the warmth of all that was good in his life, Lachlan felt the chill try to suffocate him. He glanced up and saw two police officers. The one in uniform was unfamiliar, but he recognized Detective Mimi Shillings. She was the only female detective in their precinct and had been assisting Detective Naylor with the anti-gang taskforce. She lasered in on Lachlan, her face pale and drawn. He might have said *haunted*. Or was that a ghost that skittered across his heart? Something ominous was in the air. He could sense it. And it had nothing to do with the freezing rain or bitter wind.

The police approached the bar. "Lachlan," Detective Shillings said.

"What's wrong?" His blood hummed with dread. It was no ghost, whatever bad thing they'd dragged in with them. It was a live, beating beast.

"We're looking for Ruby. She's not answering her front door, and…we need to find her, talk to her. It's urgent. Thought you might be able to check her door through the pub, or that you might know where she is."

"She's here. There." He pointed toward the booth. "We're waiting for Isaac to show, to have dinner." *Fuck!* All color drained from her cheeks.

"There was an incident. It's bad." She turned in Ruby's direction. Lachlan nearly vaulted over the bar to join them.

And fuck if Ruby's smile that lit up the entire world didn't fall from her face as she took in the scene approaching her. She was standing, leaning against the table, relaxed, warm. She tilted her head at the approach of the police. Sounds muffled into a tunneled drone. People were blurred. His sole focus was her, getting to her.

"Mimi?" Ruby questioned.

"Your dad's been shot, Ruby." Detective Shillings didn't beat around the bush. "We need to get you to—"

The wineglass slipped from Ruby's fingers. Slow-motion understanding changed her expression in a heartbeat as she screamed, "No!" shoved off from the booth and ran out through the back of the pub.

Lachlan took off after her. She was on her knees in the parking lot, icy rain blowing sideways as she shoved her hands over her ears. He slid on the ice beside her and pulled her into his lap. She wrestled and tried to get away, screaming "No, no, no!" but the slick, wet ground made it difficult. He enclosed her in his arms, offering shelter.

"Ruby!" he yelled, trying to get her attention, brushing her wet hair off her face. "Ruby!"

"No! Go away! I don't want to hear… I can't… No!" She screamed and beat at his chest.

Rain pelted them and soaked straight through to their bones while he rocked her and called her name, "Ruby, I'm here. Ruby, Ruby." She beat at his chest until she couldn't anymore, then buried her face in his chest and sobbed.

"I've got you," he called into her ear. Lachlan looked up. The police stood there. Her friends too, while the storm raged and shocking awareness bled through his veins. But it was the burn of her tears on his chest that, no matter how many lifetimes he lived, he would never forget.

Chapter Twenty-Eight

In her cloudy mind, Ruby wondered if she was numb. Had she ever been numb before? There was that one time, as a child when she'd played outside for hours in the snow, building igloos and snowmen. Maybe her fingers had been numb then, although she hadn't realized it. They'd felt weighted and heavy and they'd barely tingled through her damp gloves, but it wasn't until she'd come inside and run them under warm water that the sharp daggers had streaked through her nerves and shredded her fingertips.

Her father had come running at her scream. *"You have to start with cool water, baby,"* he'd said. *"Until the feeling comes back into your fingers. Or it'll sting like hell."* He'd cradled her fingers in his large warm hands and had gently caressed them until she was all better.

He'd always been there, her foundation.

There were eerie similarities to this moment right now. A weird, bloated calm-before-the-storm engulfed her. *Camouflage.* She'd stopped shaking, finally, and had settled into a hushed trance-like state. The quiet only added to this out-of-body feeling. She rested her arms on the bed by her father. The only noises she heard were the routine humming of the machines keeping him alive and, once in a while, a voice passing outside the door of his hospital room. Otherwise, nothing, not her dad's laughter or gentle teasing.

She kept her eyes tightly shut, but held her father's hand in hers, knowing if she faced the truth, it would be the explosion, nerves cracking and thawing with the scalding water of reality. This time there would be no soothing comfort from her father.

"Hey, Ruby, honey. It's me, Lachlan. I brought you some soup." He cupped his hand around her neck.

She kept her eyes closed but stretched into his touch. Her body battled between leaning in and hiding from the warmth. "Not hungry," she mumbled. She didn't know what she was, but she didn't want food. She might never be hungry again.

She heard a scuffling sound and felt his hands on her waist. She was lifted then surrounded by more soothing heat as he placed her in his lap, all without separating her hand from her father's. He leaned his chest into her. For a moment, she let herself accept the warmth, but there was a nagging pull in her brain. His embrace almost dragged her under, into sleep. She was so, so tired. *No!* She couldn't let go of the anesthetized feeling. She struggled out of his grip to stand instead. "No. Don't do that. I have to stay right here. Don't make me feel like that."

"Like what?" His gentle hands on her hips grounded her.

Ruby tried not to cry, but tears broke through. "Good. Safe." The words were torn out of her and she lost it. The shell shattered and all her numb pieces splintered into a million lacerations. "Lachlan," she moaned and covered her face with her hands.

"Ruby, babe. Come here. I know you're worried." He gently pulled her down to his lap. "But he's stable. They got the bullets out. He's out of ICU. These are all good signs. And you need rest and food."

"No, I can't leave him."

"I won't make you go anywhere, but you need to eat, and I think you're still cold from being out in the freezing rain and from the shock. You're shivering again, even with this blanket on your shoulders. Soup will help, Ruby. You need to do it for your dad."

Worry lined his face, her stalwart giant, worry for her. Ruby rested her head against his cheek. She was in dry clothes and at the hospital because of him, that much she knew. When she'd run screaming from the pub, he'd been the one to care for her, to move her forward, to tell her Isaac was still alive. To give her hope.

Exhausted, feeling the weight of tears again, she gave in. He handed her a tissue then and she sat in his lap, like a child, with tears running down her cheeks, while he fed her and wiped her tears and all the feeling came thundering back into her, cracking her ribs open to make room for all that was good and horrible in her world. And she cried some more because it hurt like hell, her heart crying out for her dad to be okay. But she let Lachlan take care of her. No matter what she needed, he'd been there for her. So she slowly settled and allowed him to warm her up this time.

* * * *

Ruby woke, startled as her dreamless nap rushed away. She blinked and felt the soft blanket tickling her face. And it all came flooding back, breaking through the last dregs of sleep, a dam bursting. Her father had been shot multiple times, had survived surgery, and was now lying in a hospital bed with a chest tube. She and Lachlan were here with him. Lachlan had fed her, and she must have passed out because she was resting on the small couch, with her head on a pillow and blankets warding off the chill.

More lucid, more rested, images from last night played in the forefront of her mind. The police approaching her table with a ghostly pallor shadowing their expressions. My God she'd known. And she, Ruby Naylor, tough, independent detective's daughter had completely lost her shit. Although, who would want to calmly remain in place and let officers announce the death of a loved one. *Run!* That had been her first instinct, screaming into her head.

Now she reached inside herself for deep grounding breaths, because her dad wasn't dead. He'd been alive when they'd brought her to the hospital last night, and he was still alive this morning. Or whatever time it was. The curtains in the room were closed, but a large slash of light peeked through the small slit, casting rays across the floor. Ruby used the bathroom and brushed her teeth with the toothbrush and toothpaste Katie and Leo had brought last night.

Lachlan slept in the chair by her father's bedside. His arms were crossed over his chest, legs stretched out. He'd told her he wouldn't leave her, and aside from getting her food and coffee, he hadn't, not for one second. He was the reason she was here in the first place, and not passed out or hiding like a chicken, frozen to death behind the pub.

The soup and bread he'd brought her last night had soothed the last bits of her that were frozen, frozen from the cold and from the fear. With his touch and comfort, his assurance that he'd be there, he'd cracked her wall open and let her fall apart completely. Then he'd sheltered her so the healing could begin, or at least bring her to a place where she could shore up her defenses.

Now she remembered him tucking a blanket over her on the small, hard sofa, then blackness. Apparently, no matter how uncomfortable the vinyl-covered furniture was, it held nothing against her physical exhaustion. But she ached today. Aching was good. It was better than the paralyzed state she'd slipped into last night. She couldn't face the present or the future if she remained frozen—another nugget of wisdom from her love last night before he'd kissed her cheek and she'd drifted into oblivion. He'd urged her to keep up her strength, to rest, to lean on him, in order to help her father through his recovery.

Her dad was still asleep—the word was unconscious, but she chose to believe he was sleeping until he had enough strength to wake up. She gave him a gentle kiss on his cheek, careful not to jostle his shoulder where one of the bullets had driven through his body. The other one had shattered two ribs and collapsed his left lung, narrowly missing his heart. His beautiful heart that had stopped beating for a few precious minutes when the bullets had penetrated.

All her life she'd been aware of the risks that her father faced as a detective investigating special crimes and gangs, but he'd always, *always* been heroic, untouchable. She squeezed his fingers. An old ache beat in her heart. *Until Mom died, that is.* Skye Naylor's death had been its own kind of assault on him, one Ruby had thought neither of them would recover from. But this felt so much worse. At least when they grieved her mom, they could talk and yell and cry together. Now she was alone in this nightmare. *No.* She glanced over. *Not alone.* Her heart softened at the hard planes of Lachlan's face, still so handsome even while he was all disheveled.

"Hey," Ruby said. She wrapped her arms around Lachlan from behind and nuzzled her face into his neck. Mmm, she could stay right there breathing him in, taking his comfort. Or return to a few weeks ago, when they'd spent every second together, lost in each other, ignoring the rest of the world.

"Ruby." His deep, sleepy voice undid her every time. The way he said her name, like it was warm sun on his cold skin, ocean water soothing over his bare feet, every brilliant star in the sky. He lifted her arms over him and brought her to sit on his lap. It was where she'd been in the storm, her heart breaking in half with the knowledge that her dad might be dead, where she'd ended her night before she'd fallen asleep, and right now, where she started her morning. It was where she belonged, secure in his arms, his love, his safety. "Any news?"

"I just woke up. Haven't spoken to any nurses or doctors yet. Wanted to hug you first."

He tightened his hold on her.

"Thank you," she whispered. "For looking after me when I couldn't take care of myself." With Lachlan, she often felt so much more vulnerable. She could let go of her independence and power and togetherness, because he would never take advantage of her vulnerability, it made her also feel cherished and protected.

"I will do anything for you. Always, Ruby. Do you understand?"

"Yes." And she did.

They sat together and Ruby took solace from his presence and his love and they waited for her dad to wake up.

Chapter Twenty-Nine

"I wanted…*want* you to know him." Her voice was so quiet, a shell of his confident, bold woman. Although he didn't enjoy her suffering, he loved this part of her as much as the sophisticated goddess she portrayed. Ruby was one hundred percent authentic with him.

"Hey." Lachlan leaned forward. They were lying face to face on her bed, fully clothed. The nurses had kicked them out, ordered them to leave and get a good night's sleep. Her dad still hadn't woken up. They'd only planned to run home, grab quick showers and clean clothes before they made it back to the hospital, but they'd taken their shoes off, fallen into bed and both had napped for a few hours. Hers had been fitful, and he hadn't left her side.

"I mean, obviously you know *who* he is, and you probably see him at the neighborhood watch meetings, but I've been so looking forward to you getting to know him as my dad." She reached out and rested her hand on his heart. "And for him to meet you as…mine. I'm sorry, I can't seem to quit crying." She grabbed the box of tissues from her bedside table. "For him to see how important you are to me, for you to see how amazing he is."

Lachlan had planned on telling her about that awkward year of his life. But he found it difficult to admit that he and his mom had been homeless, that they'd often stayed at shelters or slept in his mom's car. He'd had a crush on Ruby, heck, on her entire family. He'd longed to be a part all their light and joy and warmth and goodness, like a stray dog, begging for a home.

But Ruby treated him like he was made of gold, no matter what side of his life he shared with her. And he was his own Big Brother now to two kids. He never once thought of them as not good enough. Their crummy circumstances were no reflection on them at all. It was odd how it worked, though. He actively believed his Little Brothers were incredible, that they were destined for greatness and could be whatever they dreamed of, that they should expect wonder and beauty in their lives. But telling those same things to himself…well, the last dregs of shame were difficult to scrub away.

But none of that mattered anymore, especially not his feelings. This was about what he could give her. After all, she had a way of washing away all his burdens. It was his chance to ease her worries. Maybe he could take that haunted shadow away from her, bring her joy even while they waited in this in-between space of concern and uncertainty.

He leaned up against the headboard and pulled her in close, so she was tucked into him, her head on his chest. Then he snagged his legs around her and pulled the covers up over their bodies. "Did you know, when I lived here as a kid, I used to belong to the YMCA downtown?" Lachlan spoke into her soft hair.

Ruby pushed up part way and looked at him. "So did I."

"Yeah..." He hesitated. "We couldn't afford the membership, but kids who were a part of the Big Brothers and Big Sisters program got in free." He smoothed his hand over her back, taking his own comfort too from her warmth.

"Mmm." Ruby snuggled into him. It was one of his favorite things about her, how she did that. No matter how close she was, she always tried to burrow deeper "Dad was a Big Brother there."

He put his lips on her head and whispered the words, "Yeah, he was mine." She stopped snuggling and her hands clenched on his sides. "For almost six months the year I was twelve. Every Tuesday evening, he played basketball with me."

This time she sat upright completely and rested her hands on his stomach. "You knew him?" God, she was so damn hopeful and happy. It unleashed all his worry. "All those years ago?"

"Yeah, honey."

"Tell me." Ruby straddled him and brushed her fingers over his neck so their eyes were only inches apart. God he could get lost in those eyes—already had a million times over—how they swirled from blue to green depending on her mood. "Tell. Me." She shut her eyes tight. When she relaxed and opened them again, she added softly, "I mean if you want to, please."

How could he deny her? He never would even if it meant hurting himself, but this wasn't that at all. This was him sharing a part of his childhood and moments of her father's life with her, for her. *Easy.* She did that, made life seem easy.

"I think he saved my life. Not in any sort of physical-harm way, but by being there, being so solid, such a stand-up guy. He was the best ball player I'd ever seen and I..." He chuckled with the memories. "I was a disaster. I was all gangly uncoordinated limbs and felt as if I had five feet instead of two. I was shy, which Mom jokes was code for 'sullen and angry'. As far as basketball was concerned, I loved the game, but I didn't have anyone to play with. God, I was such a cheeseball."

She gazed at him with those beautiful eyes, full of hope.

"He taught me how to play, how to handle the ball, how to be patient, how to shoot a layup like nobody's business. He worked the summer fundraiser that year too, and there were a few nights I think he delivered food to my mom. Although he never said. I only suspected it was him. We were...we lived in our car some weeks. It sucked."

Ruby gave him a gentle hug, rested her head on his chest, worked her love into him.

"But going to the Y, spending time with your dad...he was a huge inspiration to me."

"He loves playing, but he loves teaching more," she whispered. "I sometimes wonder, if he hadn't become a cop, maybe he would have become a teacher. Wait..." Her head shot up. "I remember that year. Little Mac. He talked about you." Her eyes shimmered with unshed tears, but it was her smile that dug into his heart.

Lachlan chuckled at the nickname Isaac had given him. It was the first time anyone had given him a nickname and coming from Detective Naylor, he'd drunk it in.

"You were his favorite. Said how quiet and focused you were, how you listened and tried all the suggestions he gave you."

He laughed again. "I was partly in awe and partly scared to death."

"Scared?"

"That he would decide I wasn't good enough." There was the truth of it all, why he'd become so stoic, as Ruby liked to tease. He had been, *still was* quiet and on alert. Pretending he didn't care what people thought, but secretly always waiting for someone to decide he wasn't worth it.

When their eyes met, he could tell she understood so much more than his spoken words. "Lachlan." She sighed and snuggled into him. She got him—she always had. As soon as they'd gotten together, she hadn't let one moment go by where she didn't show him, not only that she saw him, flaws and all, but that she loved the vision, loved even what he kept hidden until he'd been brave enough to share with her. She hadn't let one moment go by when she didn't try to draw him out of his stoic shell of uncertainty and what he'd never admitted to anyone was his low self-confidence. It all stemmed from his childhood. Fucking wounds were sneaky bastards. Lachlan squeezed her tight and let out a breath.

"It's ridiculous, isn't it? I've been carrying that feeling with me since I was a kid. Taught myself to shut up and listen, to never let anyone get close."

"It hurts me that you would have believed for a minute you weren't worthy, but I am so infinitely happy that I get to be the one you open up to, share with, laugh with, love. That kind of trust is brilliant and now I know how much more special it is. And how hard I have to work to make you believe that every day."

Lachlan belted out a laugh. "You don't have to work hard at all. Just being who you are, the way your smile lights up when you see me, the way you enjoy touching me when I'm near as if I'm the most important being in your orbit, you do show me. One look from across a crowded room and it's like you've injected all your joy into me. Makes a man feel ten feet tall. I'm putty in your hands, woman."

"Oh, really?"

"I always have been." He held her head and rubbed his thumbs over her rosy cheeks. She leaned into his touch and gave a soft moan. "Ever since I was Little Mac."

"What?" That lazy, sweet smile she gave him, how she got lost in his touch the same way he did hers.

"I met you once, at the Y. Well, we didn't actually meet. You were at swim team practice and you were walking out of the locker room. The floor was all wet. We were passing by each other, but like the pre-teen idiot who comes across the prettiest girl in the room, I froze. You were so damn pretty, and you sparkled with happiness. You still do."

"Oh!" She sat up. "You saved me from falling. I remember you. You didn't say anything. But you had these huge eyes, beautiful eyes." When she snuggled in, it was with a smile. "I remember you. I wondered who you were, where you went. I never saw you again. We would have been friends. I can feel it."

His voice was gruff when he replied, "Glad we found each other again, babe." He wrapped her up in his arms where they could shut out the rest of the world for a little while longer.

"Lachlan?" She was tucked in close, surrounded by his arms, his warmth. As soon as sunrise came, they'd make their way back to the hospital. She both wanted to be there and was frightened of what was to come. Right now, this cocoon was the safest place to be.

"Hmm?" He tightened his grip on her and brushed lazy fingers through her hair. He made her feel protected. *He makes me feel alive.* She untucked his shirt and brought her hands to his skin, smoothing her touches over him. She closed her eyes and day-dreamed of his naked body.

"All those weeks ago when we finally connected." Ruby reached his shirt up over his head. Then she started to unbutton her blouse.

"Yeah? Hey..." He stopped her hands. "You sure about this right now?"

"Yes, Lachlan. I want you. Please love me, make me feel alive. Can you do that for me?"

He took over and helped her off with her blouse. When she tried to unhook her bra, he brushed her hands away and did that for her too. They he gently pressed her onto the bed and dragged her jeans and panties off. "Remember when you said, 'I've wanted your beauty and joy in my life for a long damn time?'"

"Yeah." He brushed a kiss over her mouth, stroked his lips down her chest and warmed her with his hands. When he stood and shrugged out of the rest of his clothes, she nearly lost her ability to breathe. He was simply magnificent, on fire for her, caring for her in the way she'd asked him to. Then he was on her, connected to her, skin to skin. She stretched deeper into him, as though he played a note and she responded with one of her own. This perfect melody between them, the music they made. This was exactly what she craved, to feel beloved.

"Did you mean…"

He licked and suckled that spot on her neck that made her delirious, distracting her. That, coupled with his naked form snaking over hers, had shivers of desire streaking across her skin. He rolled them so he was on his back and she was splayed over him. *My favorite.* They were all her favorites, all the ways he handled her, all the positions in which they discovered more of each other. He raked his hands over her body, teasing, soft touches intertwined with insistent urging. Urging her closer to him, to his hard, glorious body. So needy for her.

"Did you—"

He held her head and took her in a long drugging kiss, diving his tongue in to spar with hers, to tango, to seduce. "Hmm?" He dragged her up, set that hungry mouth of his on her nipple and she almost came right then. Oh, her man with his hmms and mmms, seducing her with his confidence and tongue and heat, even as she tried to speak.

She could take it. She loved his version of teasing. She could give as good as she got. Ruby massaged her core up and down his hard cock while he played with her breasts. When he moaned and thrust against her, she knew he wasn't as in control as he pretended.

"Have you, my beautiful love. Oh." Grabbing his shoulders so she didn't fly away from the pleasure, she arched into him again. "Have you had a crush on me since we were kids?" Her words were a whisper of breath, and he caught them and set them flying away.

"No." He surged up and entered her at the same time. Ruby held on while he plundered her. This was it. This was the only thing that mattered in the world that could change in an instant. This connection, this all-consuming, brilliant love.

"Oh!" He was so deep inside her. Then his word penetrated her lusty fog. "No?" She was confused but it didn't stop her from enjoying what was happening to her. Pleasure exploded, fireworks streaking through her blood.

"No." He lost control and thrust into her over and over again as she came. "I did not have a crush on you." She shook her head as if agreeing with him, *of course not*, completely lost in the moment. "I've been *in love…*" He clamped his hands on her hips and held her there while his own body tightened and coiled underneath her hands. "With you, Ruby Naylor." He shuddered and came apart in her, locked with her. Their breathing was heavy as they rocked into each other. Lachlan peppered along her neck and shoulder. "Since that very first time. The very first."

She clung to him, feeling his heart thudding against hers, feeling his voice murmur through her, his words circle her heart. He loved so big and so hard. And to know that she got to be in that mystical space—the old world she'd inhabited shattered, only to be sewn together piece by piece with his love and tenderness woven through all the fragments of her soul.

Chapter Thirty

Ruby shouldn't have been surprised. She had great friends. She *and* Lachlan had great friends. But still, seeing the amount of people and trucks here helping her and Lachlan move into their new house, after the week from hell she'd had, almost made her cry. But she was determined not to ruin her eye makeup this early in the day. She hadn't even had her coffee yet, and she'd shed enough tears this week to last a lifetime. It sure felt like she'd lived a lifetime in that week. Ruby basked under the sunlight and let it ground her.

Happier times ahead. She'd just left the hospital to get here before anyone arrived, but it appeared she was late to her own party. Her dad had been awake and responsive for three days now. His chest tube was out, all his tests had gone well and he would be getting discharged tomorrow.

Today she and Lachlan were moving in together. They'd decided to work on renovations while they lived in the house. He and Connor had refinished the hardwood floors this week and more projects were happening today. The rest they'd be able to do in time. They both felt it unnecessary to waste one more moment on the periphery of life. They were charging ahead with all their plans, together, in love. *Win. Win. Win!*

Jackson and Gage were carrying in her sofa. Connor was on the roof with a few of his employees, installing the last of the new chimney section. She saw Leo's truck, so he must be here somewhere. Talented metal artist that he was, he'd designed a new gate for her garden. Even Ford and Noah were here. Well, Ford, wearing an outfit too nice for moving, was sneaking a pastry off the table Sasha must have set up with all kinds of goodies and coffee. Katie was there with her truck, and another huge table set up with her delicious spicy chicken getting ready to go on the grill.

Ruby didn't even have enough stuff to warrant this much to-do, but they'd all insisted on helping. And the sun was out, so any reason—after the snow and rainy season they'd all endured—to celebrate nice weather, her friends would capitalize on. She suspected they came mostly to surround her and see how she was doing. She adored her friends.

Today she was going to see if she could wrangle a bunch of them to attack the wild, overgrown jungle in the yard. And maybe some of them could work their magic with the side of the porch that was sagging a tiny bit. Ruby was both in an excited rush to get their house beautified, and looking forward to the journey.

The only person who wasn't working was Ellie, who sat in a large outdoor chair with her newborn snuggled on her chest. Her dogs, Sasha's dog and Connor's dog all sat, worshiping at her feet, or basking in the sun.

Most likely both. Ruby gave a few waves, and made her way over to sit with Ellie. "You're glowing, new mama." She touched her lips to Ellie's cheek and softly on Alex's head, then pulled a chair in close.

Ellie blushed and gave her a huge smile. "How's your dad?" Ellie propped Alex on her shoulder and gently patted his back. His bright eyes were open, a pretty blueish-green, they wandered, taking in the world, his tiny mouth opened in an oval.

"So much better," Ruby said and sipped her coffee. Creamy, still hot in her travel mug. *Divine.*

"He comes home tomorrow?" Ellie asked. "Will that be difficult for him? Will he need a nurse?"

"No nurse, although Lachlan and I might spend a few nights at his house with him to make sure. The difficult part will be making sure he doesn't try to go back to work immediately. Stubborn, stubborn man."

"I guess that's a good sign, if he can put up a fight, huh?"

"Yes." Ruby relaxed for the first time in seven long days. She didn't know if it was because her dad was going to be okay or because of Ellie's calming presence in the warm spring day, but Ruby gathered her strength and breathed deep. "He's doing so well. He'll be tired and achy, especially when he quits taking the pain meds. But the doctors say he's going to be fine."

Ellie gripped her hand and squeezed. And Ruby smiled huge in relief and happiness. Alex scrunched his face up and small explosion came from his baby butt.

"Oh my God," Ruby gasped and started laughing. Ellie's mouth formed an open-mouthed shock, but humor danced in her eyes. Before either of them could move, Jackson Kincaid, real life superhero husband, and now father, swooped in, grabbed the diaper bag, carefully snuggled the baby from Ellie and walked away. The ladies watched as the enormous man made googly noises at Alexander while he changed the baby's diaper on the front seat of his truck.

"Wow," Ruby sighed.

"Right," Ellie agreed. "He's such a good dad. Can you believe him, making those cute faces? He says he's teaching Alexander how to smile. He wants him to grow up loved and happy."

"Precious man. I guess life is a constant combination of love and anguish, weird and good, difficult and silly," Ruby said.

"Yep." Ellie sighed. "And hot! I mean whew." She fanned her face. "Pay attention to all that scorching maleness headed your way."

Ruby turned, and there was *her* man, walking through the front door, T-shirt already sweaty, a *short-sleeved* T-shirt showing off his powerful arm muscles. He noticed her and gave her that subtle, boyish quirk of his mouth with the one eyebrow raised that she'd fallen in love with before she'd even heard him talk. Then he came right to her. Sweaty confident grin, hot muscles and all.

"Hi." Ruby breathed out his name and tried to act normal instead of a drooling fool batting her eyelashes.

"Hi, yourself." He took her hand and lifted her to standing. "How's your dad?"

"Huh?" Ruby swayed into him.

He grinned and raised that sexy eyebrow again. "Your dad, at the hospital?"

Right. Focus. She chastised herself. Oh, but now that her world had calmed again, it was so, so hard to pay attention to anything except how much she wanted everyone to leave this minute so she could get Lachlan inside to their bedroom and get him naked. "Good." Lachlan's scent was making her dizzy. Hopefully, if she swooned all over the lawn, he'd catch her.

"Good." He smiled. "Can you come upstairs and check out the wall before we knock it out? The one between the bedroom and where the master bath might go?"

"What?" Oh, hearing him talk construction with her while he stood in the sunlight all strong and sweaty, smelling like sin and wicked dreams…

He chuckled. "Thought we'd bust it out today and clean up the mess before we sleep up there tonight."

"Do we have to wait till tonight? I mean…"

Ellies soft laughter reminded her where she was. *Right, renovating my dream house with this wonderful man. Standing in my front yard surrounded by people.*

She gave Lachlan's hand a squeeze. "Uh huh, yes, I do want to get it knocked down." Ruby nodded. She gave Ellie silly wide eyes and let Lachlan lead her into their house. Inside she tried to calm her hussy libido. Seriously, she might not get any renovations completed if she tried to do them with Lachlan. *And is that really a bad thing?*

* * * *

"I always believed the world was a brilliant place, probably because of all the joy my parents showed me." Ruby rested her head against Lachlan's chest. She had no curtains on the windows yet and the night sky through their bedroom window sparkled with stars. It was so refreshing to see the sky after the long dark winter they'd had. They were tangled together in her sheets after a fun day with friends and a dreamy night of making love in their new home.

"Hmm." Lachlan stroked his fingers across her collarbone. "I watched the three of you once, walking out of the Y. There was definitely joy there, but honestly, Ruby, I think you were born to be spectacular."

She smiled and kissed his chest. "I understand how lucky, how fortunate I am. But over the years, I often met people who told me I shouldn't have such high expectations, that the world was gray as opposed to all the colors in the rainbow."

"Bet they didn't last long in your life." His smile was evident in his voice. Happy, soft, loving.

She chuckled. "Nope. Even when we lost my mom, even that horrible, tragic experience was sacred and tinged with beauty. Not the sickness or that she died, but that I got to be with her when she died."

He flipped them over and gave her forehead soft, gentle kisses. "I'm sorry you had to go through that, Ruby. To lose your mom. Bet you took good care of her, my brave beauty."

She closed her eyes and, in the safety of his arms, let the memories score through her. "I miss her. She taught me so much. She taught me to see the world in a magnificent palette. So many people go through life not seeing the beauty and brilliance in things, and I don't know why. But because of her, I've been confident in the fact I would find a love like no other. And I did." She watched him, then ran her fingers over his face, cementing his expression of love into her heart.

"It's all because of you, Ruby. You painted my world with light. I knew it was out there, especially when you walked across my path all those years ago. But I rarely hoped or believed it could belong to me. Or maybe I kept my head down until you showed back up in my life."

She wiggled into him. "Lachlan. You don't realize how brilliant you are, have *always* been too. Don't you think all children are born into beauty? It's the world that screws us up along the way or doesn't. Your amazingness, it has nothing to do with me. You simply were, *are*."

"After that day I talked to you at the Y..." Lachlan tucked them together, side by side. "I used to watch you swim. When basketball was over, for a few minutes before my mom came to get me, I'd climb up into the bleachers and hope I'd get to see Ruby Naylor before I went home. Some nights...when we didn't always have a place to go. That was such a difficult, weird year for my mom and me."

"Honey." Ruby kept her arms around him.

"But I had this image of a pretty girl—the prettiest girl in the room—to carry with me."

"I remember how bummed my dad was when he found out you'd left town, that he didn't get to be your Big Brother anymore. He was cranky and broody for weeks. I overheard him and my mom talking late one night. He said it wasn't any kind of life for a child to be moving so often to have such an unstable life."

"He was right. But even though I didn't realize it in the moment, when we left Corvallis, we moved far enough away that my dad's drunkenness and gambling couldn't hurt us anymore. And we moved in with my grandmother, who is one of the best women in my life. So I'm luckier than I ever imagined possible. Seems my luck keeps getting better." *Maybe luck has nothing to do with any of it.* But he felt kissed by the golden goddess these days with Ruby in his life.

"I think we were meant to be together. That's what I choose to believe. That *we* deserve each other." Ruby's smile was so soft and sweet. It always was after he made her come…and when she was talking about them and love.

Chapter Thirty-One

"I'm the lucky one. You'll never have my luck." His dad's voice was close, then drifted away again and the sound was muffled. *Words from my childhood, weird.* Lachlan felt as if he were holding his breath under water, listening as the words came to him, distilled through the waves. Words he wanted to ignore. He swam deeper into the darkness, trying to rid his space of the creeping snake.

"Maybe your luck's about to run out."

Jesus! Lachlan surged up in bed, trying to ground himself in the here and now. *Where the fuck am I?*

"What is it?" Ruby squeezed his arm. "You okay, honey?"

I'm with Ruby at her place. He must have yelled out, or maybe his movement had startled her, because nothing woke Ruby when she was deep asleep.

"My dad. Christ!" Lachlan swore as the images surged into him, unwanted, angry, like choking on his own bile. He swung his feet over the side and let the cool hardwood floors seep into him, ground him. Something was cracking a sledgehammer against his skull. *Jesus.* He jumped out of bed. Sugar Baby leapt after him, meowing her dislike. He tugged his sweats on and stormed downstairs into the kitchen. When he leaned over the sink, his hands were shaking so badly that he had trouble filling a cup with water. *Fuck it.* He dropped it into the sink and drank from the tap.

"Lachlan?" Ruby called after him. She followed him and pulled his sweatshirt over her head. "What's wrong?" She came directly to his side. He gripped her shoulders and put his head to hers, finding that settling, that peace, that strength she fed into him. Then he set her away to listen to his thoughts. No matter how dark they were, here, right now as they drilled into his head, he had to pay attention.

He paced and started putting together the fragments of memory and intuition, from the past few weeks, no, *months* of upheaval in their lives. All the damaged or buried clips of an old movie being spliced together. It made his stomach churn as they all slipped neatly into place. *Too fucking neatly to be a coincidence.*

The night his father had been waiting on his front steps. The cigarette butts in his backyard. His dad hadn't dropped by for a friendly visit, as he'd claimed, like the actor he was. He'd shown up to Lachlan's and broken in. What had Denny originally planned, if Lachlan hadn't gotten home earlier than usual?

But really, things had started before that night, maybe last summer when Denny had come into the pub, drunk and unruly and indignant, expecting Lachlan to fall at his feet? *Shit, is this what it's all about?* The uptick in crime in the neighborhood, the graffiti, the drugs, the destruction at his pub—did it all have to do with some vendetta his dad had against him? When little things here and there had started happening, a break-in, a car vandalized, the graffiti, he and Detective Naylor had attributed it all to flushing out the last dregs of the Lucciano gang.

Lachlan massaged his head to still the racing, gut-wrenching clarity. Could all those incidents be traced to his dad, rather than a gang?

The night of the wedding when Denny had texted Lachlan. He hadn't needed his help at all. He'd sent him on a fucking wild-goose chase. He'd taken advantage of Lachlan's relationship with the Meyers, had believed Lachlan would come running. Then Denny'd broken into the pub. He'd fucking put Ruby's life in jeopardy. *Christ!* Lachlan kept walking out to the patio. Damp, the stones were cold against his bare feet, but it braced him too, centered the mess in his head. *Click, click, click.* The fresh night air cleared his vision so he could see. Everything was shockingly clear.

"Do you want to tell me what's going on?"

Ruby stood in the doorway with Sugar Baby on her neck. The cat was pawing at her clothes, unsettled, worried.

He stopped pacing and, hands on hips, faced her. "I think it was my own father who vandalized my pub."

"What?" she whispered. "How can you be certain?" Her face was blanketed in shock.

"I was dreaming, trying to swim away from his voice...memories of things he's said to me over the years... It all came together in my mind. Things that have happened since...well, mostly since last summer, if I'm correct. My father came to the pub, wanted to be a part of it. He was wasted, so I tossed him into a cab and told him not to return. Then, the night I was supposed to keep my promise to you, when I was an asshole instead, I ended up at my condo earlier than normal. My dad was there, begged me for money, whined about how successful the pub was, how selfish I was. When he walked away, he mumbled something to the effect, *'Your luck might be about to run out.'* I realized later he'd broken into my place. Didn't focus much on it then because it was typical Denny and I was upset about..."

"It's okay," she said. "We're past that. Go on."

"There have been random acts of crime, stupid, small. You and I haven't talked about all of it. Right before Christmas, the stupid shit amped up, especially on my side of the street. You might have seen the front door tagged with graffiti. I had to replace it."

Even as he illustrated the picture for her, it grew in precision. "The night of the wedding, when you and I got to dance. I think he lured me away..." The image solidified in his mind. It hummed with electricity. The Meyers' motel was thirty minutes away from his condo, twenty from the pub on a snowy night. And Denny hadn't even been there when Lachlan had arrived. "From the pub. I'm certain of it. I can feel it in my gut, Ruby. He was nowhere to be found that night. I didn't get a chance to tell you. In fact, I put it out of my mind, almost completely."

"That's why he didn't care about the alarm. If it was him, or whoever attacked your pub. They busted in and caused all that destruction as fast as they could. Just to be the absolute slime of the earth. A person shouldn't be allowed to be such an asshole. I am seething," Ruby said.

Without hesitation, she clued in to the entire picture. She believed him. That was a heady feeling. And she looked pissed as hell for him. Shit, it cooled the raging menace inside him at his father. Barefoot in her sparkly, silver baggy sweatpants and his oversized sweatshirt, drowning in comfy clothes, as she liked to say, with his cat snuggling up and purring on her. Here she stood, outside, in the middle of the night, prepared to charge into battle for him.

The anger flew out of him. He couldn't help but smile at the glowing picture she made with the light behind her. He made his way to her and took her hand. "There aren't enough words to describe how magnificent you are. How much I love you."

"Lachlan." She set the cat down and stepped into him.

"Every time I blink, you are there for me. When things are good, when disaster happens, even after I've been a complete jerk to you, you keep standing by my side."

She smoothed those magical healing arms around him. "You weren't a complete jerk to me."

"Ruby." He squeezed her to him. "I—"

"Shh." She put her soft fingers to his mouth. "We're not going there again. And the rest? It's what we do for each other. We take care of each other. You have been doing the same for me. I wouldn't be standing if it weren't for you."

Just when he had his emotions controlled, another wave surged. Here stood the most precious thing in the world to him. *Beauty, love, joy.* And he'd put her in danger.

"You were injured because of him." He tightened his hold.

"Hey."

"And it could have been so much worse. And it guts me to imagine what could have happened. I left you there that night. I fucking left you."

"Honey." Ruby pushed against his chest. "You're going to have to let me breathe." He immediately loosened his arms, but she grabbed them as they fell to his side. "A little loose, not all the way. Now, what your father has been up to is not on you at all. You're not the one committing crimes."

"Still makes me rage inside to think of what went down that night, *how* it all went down, that I could have at least been with you when it happened." Lachlan brushed his fingers through her hair and over her cheek. "I could have been there with you."

"It's over now. As soon as you knew something was wrong, you came for me, and you've been taking care of me ever since."

"With every touch, every smile, every word, you've been doing the same for me. Feels fucking phenomenal, to have all that shining down on me. Never had that before, from a woman. Not in my life."

"You'd better get used to it, my beautiful love, because I'm planning on a lifetime with you."

Damn, her words felt good. Wrapped in her warmth, he could stay in this moment forever.

"Now, I'm freezing, and we have to figure out what the hell to do about Denny MacGregory. I'll make coffee. You call the police. I'm ready to put all of this behind us. We have so many more important things to concentrate on. Like what kind of soaking tub we're going to put in the master bathroom."

She was already moving on, facing the action. And she was right—they did have much more important things to do with their lives than to be caught up by

Denny's shitty behavior. And Lachlan wanted every little and huge experience with her. He took a deep breath and let her lead him into their warm life together.

Chapter Thirty-Two

"I'm so sorry you got caught up in all of Denny's mess, Ruby."

"You have nothing to be sorry for. You didn't gamble away the most important things in your life, your marriage, your son's welfare. You didn't stay drunk and angry for decades and vandalize a pub." They still hadn't been able to find Denny MacGregory. The weather had calmed down. So far spring had decided to roll in gently. But there was an odd peace about the neighborhood because it felt like they were all waiting for something bad to happen.

All had gone quiet after her dad had been shot during a drug bust related to the Luccianos, the old Italian gang trying to hold on to a part of town that no longer belonged to them. It belonged to the people in Corvallis who had been working tirelessly to make it safe and wonderful. The silence was disarming. The entire neighborhood was on edge.

Ava smiled and put her hand on Ruby's. "Believe me, I know I'm not responsible. Took me years of therapy to be able to move forward and tell myself I was doing the best for Lachlan. But a mom never stops worrying or caring."

They were sitting in one of the small curved booths against the wall at the pub. It was one of Ruby's favorite places to sit, so she could take in the entire crowd, especially her sexy man standing at the bar, supporting his bartenders since a group of twenty had rolled in for a birthday party. She, Ava and Lachlan had had a delicious Sunday lunch, but as soon as the party had stumbled in cheering and hungry, Lachlan had kissed her cheek, grabbed their empty plates and gotten up to help his staff. His employees had stepped up when her dad had been shot, covered for him so he could be there for her and Isaac, and she owed them all an enormous debt of gratitude.

"You did such a great job raising him."

"I'm so glad he has you, Ruby. He's so happy and at ease. You did that for him."

Love, kindness, caring, passion. That was what they had between them. Ruby watched Lachlan carry an enormous tray of food out of the kitchen. He caught her eye and winked. "He does the same for me."

A movement outside the front window of the pub caught Ruby's attention and all the fine hairs on her neck stood up. She'd felt the same sensation two additional times the last couple of days. She shot her gaze to Lachlan. He stood behind the bar, caught in some moment of thought perhaps, motionless, frozen. *Coiled,* was the word that came to mind. Did he feel it too? And what the heck was *it*?

He'd been like this since his revelations about his father the other night, replaying information and moments in his head in order to fit them together, to solve a puzzle. *Tense and exhausted, overprotective of me.* She didn't mind the overprotective, but she didn't like the source of it—fear. He was such a foundation of this new, beautified, healthy Corvallis. She wanted that happiness and peace back in town, for his sake and for all their sakes. This edgy zone of distress was for the birds. *Big-time.*

"Shall we go work on that surprise you have planned?" Ava asked.

That brought a smile to Ruby's face. "Absolutely."

* * * *

Ruby was doing the dishes when he came in through the back door. He shook his jacket off and reached down to let Baby nuzzle his hand. "What smells so damn good in here?" When he stood, he gifted Ruby with that sexy smile, stalked to the kitchen and cornered her up against the counter.

"Sorry I'm so late again." It was the third night this week he'd missed dinner with her. One night he'd been at his volunteer work, the last two he'd been at the pub. He'd needed to return to work, give his bartenders a night or two off, but she definitely missed their evenings together. They hadn't found his father yet, and she could tell it was eating at him.

"It's okay, my darling. You do own a pub. This will be our life some nights." Ruby put her hand on his cheek.

"Mmm, love it when you get all cultured on me and call me your darling or love. I get to slide into your embrace, take your words to heart." He kissed her, took any response she might have given and stunned her with his touch. "I fucking love the words *our life* coming from your beautiful mouth." Lachlan traced her lips with his thumb. "I know how much you hate doing the dishes. You could always leave them for me."

Beautiful man. She moved fully into his arms, so he could feel the laugh move through her body. "You do them all the time, honey. Believe me I am fully aware of that, and grateful." Besides, she'd made something special for him. It would mar the treat if he had to clean up after her. "You're exhausted. Look at you, you're so cute when you're pouting and grumpy."

He made a mock offended face. "Pouting?" He leaned in and nipped her bottom lip. "Grumpy?"

"Even when you're grumpy at yourself." She slid her hands up his neck and into his hair.

"Hmph. Better I take my mood out on me than you." He nuzzled into her neck. Talk about love—her neck adored the attention he paid it. He hadn't shaved today and his skin was rough. It sent delicious shivers through her body.

"If this is you being grumpy, I think I can handle you taking it out on me. Please..." Ruby said and rubbed her body against his. "Use me however you desire."

"So true with your words and movements, that little breathy sigh you give when you stretch against me. So needy." He drew a trail with his fingers down her chest to her belly then made featherlight swirls on her thighs. Passion flowed and right that moment, it obliterated everything else in their lives.

He palmed her ass and lifted her onto him. Ruby peppered kisses along his neck. He stumbled on the stairs but caught her before they fell. They made each other dizzy and euphoric. He let her slide down his body, took her hand, and they tripped and kissed their way to the bedroom. "Gonna get lost in you. Gonna let you sooth away all my worries," he said.

"Come here, you beautiful man." Ruby pulled him down to her and enjoyed every bit of grumpiness he gave her.

* * * *

It was ridiculous how her body woke her up at three in the morning, or three sixteen to be exact, nightly. Even with the pure blissful exhaustion that came from Lachlan destroying her in bed at night, here she was awake and thirsty.

Ruby grabbed her pajama bottoms and Lachlan's sweatshirt, and after using the bathroom, tiptoed into the kitchen for a glass of water. *Old houses, creaky boards.* She loved every inch of character that came with her home, even the original floors that weren't subtle or quiet in their movement. But she was trying not to wake Lachlan, who was the lightest sleeper on the planet lately. Hopefully the naked workout they'd given each other earlier had lulled him into restful sleep. And after what they'd both been through in the last two months, after how much he'd taken on for her and her dad, he needed that. Dessert sat on the counter, forgotten about. They'd been too distracted, lost in each other. The magical powers of Lachlan MacGregory beat out chocolate any day.

She was reaching for the faucet when a black streak shot down the hall and slid to the front door. Ruby followed before the cat got into trouble in the pile of boxes in the front room. Sugar Baby's fur stood up like she'd been electrocuted. She paced back and forth, pausing to hiss at the door and paw at the air, fighting an imaginary battle. Ruby studied the cat in confusion. Sugar Baby, strange feline being she was.

But in between the cat's hisses, Ruby heard something else. The doorknob was shaking and there was shuffling movement on the other side. At almost three-thirty in the morning. *What the hell*? Ruby scooped Baby into her arms, ran upstairs and shook Lachlan awake. "Someone's breaking in."

"Ruby?" He was awake in an instant. Throwing on his jeans, he said, "What's wrong?"

She scrambled to her side of the bed and grabbed her phone. "Someone's trying to break in through the front door."

"Stay here," Lachlan yelled as he made his way quietly downstairs.

"Wait!" she whispered. She didn't want him facing the threat either. *Stupid man.*

Holding a shivering cat, Ruby called the police and tiptoed to the top of the stairs.

"What the hell are you doing here?" It was a good thing surprise was on his side. He pinned his dad against the door and grabbed the gun from his hand. He didn't think his dad would shoot him on purpose, but the old man was a loose cannon, and he appeared seriously unstable or high. Or scared out of his mind. Lachlan didn't give a fuck. What he did care about was why the hell he was breaking into Ruby's house. All the practice he'd had over the years in keeping his temper at bay, learning how to channel it into work and exercise, deserted him in an instant. Anger burned through his blood like acid. He was furious with his dad and himself. It was his duty to protect Ruby and this was the second time he'd put her at risk. Lachlan tightened the hold he had. "I asked you a question."

"Lachlan." Ruby's voice came from the stairs.

"Ruby," he said. "Go upstairs. Call the police."

"No way. I'm not leaving your side. The police are on their way." Graceful as always, she walked right up, took the gun from his hand and said to Denny, "It's you."

Denny looked from her to Lachlan. "You know him?" Lachlan asked, shock adding a sharpness to his anger.

"He's been lurking in the neighborhood. I think he followed me, Ford and Noah on our walk tonight," Ruby said. "I felt him... I... There was some prickle on my skin the last few days. I only saw him for sure this afternoon outside the pub watching us."

Lachlan planted his feet, torso rigid, trying with all his might not to unleash his fury onto this pathetic excuse for a man. "You've been stalking her?"

"I needed to get to you. You won't let me in your pub. I need help. I need to hide. You have to help me."

"That's rich," Lachlan said. "You destroyed my pub."

"I didn't. I swear." Denny held his hands up.

"Lured me away like a sucker then smashed the place to pieces. Low, even for you."

"No, no. You have to listen to me. I didn't do it. I was only supposed to get you away. Then I ran and hid. Wasn't getting caught up in all that." *Ran and hid, story of Dad's life.*

"Wasn't getting caught up in what, being a criminal?"

"The Luccianos. Their mind games. I owed them money, okay? Couldn't pay them back. They threatened to kill me."

"So, you what, offered to destroy my pub? How the hell does that pay your debt?"

"They don't appreciate you…you and all your high and mighty business owners, your super detectives shoving them out of the neighborhood. They're pissed. They used me for information…and they're going to kill me soon as I…they're done with me."

Lachlan felt Ruby leaning against him. Her heat seeped into his bones and stilled the rage. He took a good look at his father. Years of too much drinking and smoking, dangerous scams, running from some asshole or another—he was a washed-up shell of sallow skin and unrealized dreams. The man was finished. It was that knowledge that allowed the dark emotions to drain out of Lachlan completely.

"The only way I can help is if you go with the police and tell them what you know. All of it. They are the only ones who can protect you. You destroyed my business. You tried to destroy my life. You put Ruby in danger. For the love of God, what kind of man, what kind of *father*, does that?

"I never meant any—"

Lachlan cut him off. "I don't give a damn what you *meant* anymore. It's too late. The only way to salvage any of this is for you, for once in your life, to do the right thing. Give the police the information."

Denny glanced to the side and Lachlan followed his gaze. Four officers stood on the porch, guns in hand, pointed down. It was over. His father sank in on himself, defeat and exhaustion written all over his face. Lachlan handed Denny MacGregory over and turned into Ruby's arms. Unlike his father, he was determined to cherish his dreams.

* * * *

Together they sat next to each other in the backyard, watching the sunrise. Ruby held the baking dish with the chocolate orange pudding cake she'd made for him. "Thought you didn't cook?" he asked. He scooped another bite out and moaned at how good it was.

She licked her spoon. *Sexy as hell.* He nearly forgot his question. "Your mom came over after lunch yesterday and walked me through it, step by step. I wanted to surprise you."

"Wow." He took another huge bite, watched her smile go soft, and he fell in love with her all over again. "Sorry I missed out on it last night." He cupped her cheek and rubbed his thumb over the smooth skin. "Got distracted."

"Yeah," she said and sighed. She looked tired, but happy as the sky pinkened behind her. "How are you doing? That was a rough experience."

Lachlan tossed his spoon into the dish and sprawled onto the grass. "I don't know. Relieved is the best I've got when it comes to Denny. At least at the moment. Too exhausted to give him any more emotions right now. His problems put us, put *you* in danger and I can't comprehend that, a father doing that, to their child. *Any* person doing that to another."

"I know, honey."

"Glad it's over. Hope he can give the police some useful information, get rid of that shitty gang once and for all. And yet, still, I'm just fucking exhausted."

Ruby snuggled in next to him and rested her head on his chest. "I love you," she said. "I'm here for you, always. I promise."

They were the only words he needed, and he drank them in. "Best feeling in the world, Ruby. Wipes away all the bad to feel your love surround me." He snuggled her in his arms and together, tangled in the promise of each other, they watched the new day begin.

Chapter Thirty-Three

Lachlan grinned when he remembered the last wedding he'd attended. Tonight, he was perched against the wall watching Ruby dance again. She wore some shimmery dark green pant suit. The top was miniscule, leaving her shoulders bare, and the pants came to mid-calf, giving her strappy gold heels plenty of room to tease him. Up one arm she wore a gazillion gold bracelets, and she had matching gold clips in her hair. Dark, smoky-green makeup gave her eyes a sleek, jaguar-like gaze, seducing him from across the room. Her hands were in her pockets as she swayed gently to the music next to Ellie who held baby Alex in her arms.

How the hell does that outfit have pockets? I need to get my hands in those pockets.

"You going to ask her tonight?" Ford stood on his right, holding his drink.

"I don't know... Do you really think that's Ruby's style in front of all these people?" Noah asked. Lachlan was flanked by Ruby's best guy friends, who, not unlike the last wedding, were giving him advice again.

"What do you mean? Sparkly, flamboyant, spectacle?" Ford laughed. "That is pure Ruby."

"Yeah," Lachlan agreed. "And nope."

"Wait, what?" Ford said.

"She is all that, but her heart is tender and when I ask her to marry me, it's going to be the two of us, at least for a few moments before she calls all of you to show off her ring."

"That's so romantic." Ford sighed.

"You did pick a spectacular ring," Noah said.

They'd gone shopping with him. He'd thought it would be fun to ask for their input and he hadn't been disappointed. He'd gotten an entire day's worth of lessons on wedding rings and Ruby's taste. Lachlan had been surprised how much all Ruby's, all *their* friends, had swooped in to smother them with care and kindness after his dad had been arrested. Again, he shouldn't have, but it still didn't come easy to him, this belief that so many people supported him. He had picked a stunning ring, and he'd already planned how he was going to ask her. But he wasn't giving it away until after she said yes.

Three months had passed, since that night they'd caught his dad, and it felt as if they'd all come out from under an oppressive cloud of worry. Summer bloomed with bright days. More families were moving into the neighborhood. The music hall was about to have its grand reopening after being closed for thirty years. Businesses flourished. They were surrounded by babies and weddings and love. He swallowed pride at the knowledge that he'd had a hand in creating such a great neighborhood, or rather, reviving what it had always been meant to be.

Defeated was the reason Lachlan told himself for why Denny had given the police all the information he had on what was left of the Lucciano gang, including the names of the men who'd destroyed the pub and the location of the man who shot Detective Naylor. Ruby had said maybe Denny had had a bit of fathering left inside him, and maybe deep down he'd wanted Lachlan to have a good life. Lachlan let her believe that, although he wasn't convinced himself. But he'd decided moving forward, not to brood in the past, in regrets, in wishes for the kind of father he hadn't had.

Instead, he let Ruby soothe his wounds and he followed her into their wonderful new life together. Which included restoring their home to its original glory, falling into bed together every night to explore each other's bodies, lots of laughter and dancing. The music changed and Lachlan decided he'd had enough watching from his spot against the wall. He needed to get to his woman. The wedding might be nearly over, but their magical night was only just beginning.

"Gentlemen." He handed Ford his beer and headed toward the most beautiful woman in the room.

He walked up behind her, snaked a hand to her stomach and pulled her against his chest. "Mmm." He kissed her neck. "Pockets." Sliding his other hand into her pocket, he teased the crease of her thigh, that spot he loved. That they both loved.

"Hi," she breathed out.

"Dance with me?" He had to move. If they stayed like this, he'd lose control and make her come right here. He took her hand and rubbed his thumb over her soft palm.

Ruby stepped into his arms. "You are too dangerous for words, Mr. MacGregory. Lethal."

"Oh, yeah?" Lachlan pulled her close and chuckled. "And where did you learn to dance so well? I never did ask you that." He swung her out and twirled her in tight, exactly where he wanted her.

"When I was off exploring the country, trying to find my way, I learned how to box at a gym in Colorado. We sometimes took dancing lessons."

Ruby's mouth hung open. He took advantage and kissed her. When he was finished her eyes were lit up and that smile on her face, whew, it was his undoing. "You took dance lessons?"

"Yep. Ballet, some Irish step dancing."

She poked him in the side. "You're teasing."

He dodged her tickling fingers. "I swear." He tugged her closer her as the music changed to a slow song. "The lessons kicked my butt, but the teachers were pretty to look at."

"Mmm." Ruby snuggled in. "Pretty huh?"

"Not as pretty as you, though. Never seen someone as pretty as you, Ruby, not in my life."

"You're going to keep rocking my world, aren't you, my love?"

"I sure as hell hope so." He damn well intended to, tonight and every night after.

* * * *

Ruby and Lachlan walked hand in hand the two blocks from Katie and Leo's grand Victorian house where the Treversinis had held their evening wedding. The sky was clear, and she could see a few stars. Balmy air caressed her skin. She was a cat basking in the sun after a long cold winter. It *had* been a long winter for them. Thank goodness the drama was all over. She suspected they'd have more in their lives, but hopefully nothing like what they'd endured this past year. Tonight had been glorious, her friends getting married on their rooftop, surrounded by family and love, rich food and a party for the ages. She felt happy and lazy and in love herself. It was exhilarating.

"Hey," she said when Lachlan led her into the garden instead of up the front steps. "What's going on?"

Lachlan kissed her quick, let go of her hand and said, "Wait one minute." Then he flipped on a switch and the beautiful yard lit up. He'd strung her lights for her. Soft, round golden and rose-gold antique-style bulbs hung along the fence line and over the patio. Her roses and jasmine scented the night air with their perfume. On a small table, Lachlan lit a few candles, which circled a small red jewelry box.

"Oh!" She covered her face with her hands, then clasped them in front of her. She couldn't cry, not yet, not even happy tears. She wanted clear vision for this spectacular moment.

Lachlan took her hand in his and opened the tiny box to reveal a ring shimmering in rubies and diamonds. "Wow," she whispered.

"Noah and Ford helped me. It's a cushion-cut ruby with diamonds on the band."

His hand was shaking in hers and she squeezed it. "It's too pretty for words, Lachlan MacGregory."

"That's how I felt about you. When I first saw you. When I met you again as an adult. Your beauty stole my heart, from the first moment, left me speechless. I'm knocked breathless when you enter a room. Not simply because of your beauty, but because of the way you shine your delight and kindness onto the world. The way you love me."

She nodded and felt the tears fall anyway. In the wonderous garden, surrounded by lush plants and scented, seductive flowers, swirled in passion and love, she let herself experience all the emotions of the moment.

"You inspire me. You are my promise to a brilliant life. And I promise to cherish you, laugh with you, feed you and love you for the rest of our lives together, if you'll have me. Ruby Grace Naylor, I am so in love with you. Will you be my promise?"

"Oh, my love, yes!" she shouted and jumped into his arms. "You are mine, Lachlan MacGregory. And I promise to love you and care for you with all the wonder in the world."

Epilogue

The man was downright hot as he leaned against the railing, arms braced, waiting for her. *Jeesh!* All he had to do was put on his soft gray T-shirt and those jeans of his that molded his sexy butt and she was a goner, melted right there on the spot into a puddle of mush.

She loved a man who gave good date game, and Lachlan excelled at dates, ever since their first. Lachlan had told her to be ready by four. He was picking her up, which she found ridiculous but cute since they lived together. He'd said he also had a surprise for her and her excitement could not be contained. They were going for a walk downtown. He knew the way to her heart, holding hands, a beautiful stroll and food.

And this afternoon couldn't be more spectacular with its gorgeous dry sunny weather. Although she loved fashion and dressing up for her job, dates were entirely different things. She didn't just want to look pretty and professional and maybe show off a new haircut or color she'd been experimenting with—she wanted to feel and look special for her hottie.

Today she'd gone with casual chic. She'd paired her new black skinny jeans with a sexy but cute teal halter top and pretty wedge sandals to show off her sparkly pink toes. She'd kept her hair in a sleek bob for the summer and wore silver dangly earrings Lachlan had given her. When she stepped out on the porch and he turned to look at her, his intake of breath and smoldering look told her that her outfit was a win-win. She felt the same smolder toward him.

"Hi," she said, her voice squeaking as if she'd never seen such a hottie before. But that was how it was. Her heart sped up and she felt giddy every time she saw him. She always had, now she got to relish that feeling every moment. Not to mention she could still feel the soreness between her legs from their morning marathon sexcapades. From the dreamy look passing over his face, he was having similar delicious flashbacks. Mmm, she was living a fantasy right now and she never wanted it to end.

Lachlan let out a breath, stalked her and had his hands around her waist before she could blink. "Hi," he whispered against her lips. The tingles her man sent racing through her set her on fire. And glorious man that he was, he wasted no time in taking her mouth in a searing kiss that had the ground tilting beneath her. Mix that with his fingers playing along her bare back, she wanted to race him right back to bed. He trailed his lips along her jaw and up to her ear, where he stopped his kissing. *Bummer!* "You look fucking fabulous," he said, his voice as shaky as hers.

Ruby grinned at his words because she could be muddy and sweaty, wearing her gardening clothes and he'd say the same thing, like he'd done before he dragged her into the shower with him yesterday.

"Ready?" he asked and held out his hand. Ruby took his in response and let him pull her down the steps to the sidewalk.

"We haven't had a real date in a few weeks. I know it seems silly since we live together, but I'm excited. I love going on dates with my favorite man." They headed down the hill toward the downtown area. Even though they both worked in the neighborhood, it was still such a fun place to hang out when they weren't on the clock. There were two new restaurants she hadn't had a chance to try yet. One was a wine bar and the place looked stunning.

Lachlan squeezed her hand in his. "It's been a busy few weeks, hasn't it?"

August was almost over. The pub had been slammed all summer. She'd had to hire two more employees to keep up with the demand at her salon. Three new businesses in addition to the new restaurants had opened up in downtown.

Add that to working on their house, getting engaged and friends' weddings and they'd barely had time to catch their breaths. Ruby had loved every single, hot, sweaty, sensual minute of it. But she and Lachlan had been so overwhelmed the last two weeks that they'd really only seen each other in bed at night and during steamy goodbye kisses on the porch in the morning. There might have been one or two stolen quickies in his office and hers. *Mmm, I think I was meant to be in love.*

"Any hints on what we're doing?" she asked. "I... What... I..." They'd turned the corner onto Corvallis Street and her heart leapt in confusion.

"Surprise," Lachlan whispered. He'd moved and wrapped his arms around her from behind. The entire street was blocked off. Colorful booths and tents were lined up down the middle. At the far end, near the park, sat an enormous stage with what looked like a set-up for a band. Doors to most of the businesses were propped open and several food trucks parked near them had their windows open and picnic tables for diners, and there were people everywhere, laughing, talking, eating, strolling.

The wonderful hum of happy crowds stole around her. She barely had time to take it all in when her friend Ford grabbed the mic on stage and yelled, "She's here! Everyone, please welcome the guest of honor and the reason for this fabulous, fundraising shindig, the gorgeous and special Ruby Naylor!" For a few seconds, the noise stopped, then people turned and faced her, and the crowds broke out in applause.

"What the ever-loving heck is going on?" She was shaking, but Lachlan had her back. He always did.

"Look." He nudged her head toward the banner hung across the street. "Spa La La's Fifth Annual Breast Cancer Fundraiser."

"I can't breathe… You… What did you do?" Ruby turned in Lachlan's arms and smashed her face into his chest to try to stem the tears pouring from her eyes.

"Hey." He hugged her tightly. "I knew with the intense spring we had and moving and everything else going on, you were thinking of postponing your fundraiser till Christmas this year. And I didn't want you to have to do that. Or maybe we could do both, a smaller one inside in December, and an enormous one right now. I know how important it is to you."

This man, this man was everything to her. "*You* are important to me," she whispered. It might take her a few moments to recover her voice. Her heart raced in love, in excitement, in surprise.

He chuckled. "I know, beauty. I feel the same about you."

"I love you so damn much. You did all of this for me?"

"Yeah." Lachlan sounded as choked up as she felt. "So, is this okay for a date night?"

Ruby threw back her head and laughed. "This might be the best date ever." The smile he gave her lit her world into a million stars. She wiped the few tears that had escaped, took his hand and said, "You'd better tell me how you did all this, you sneak."

After she'd gotten hugs from her dad and many of their friends, Lachlan gave her a tour of the block party, explaining how much fun he'd had getting everyone on board and using all their neighborhood connections to make it a huge summer evening event. Her salon fundraisers had been fun, but they had truly outgrown her space and Lachlan had seen that.

There was food everywhere, fun carnival games to play, and several bands had also donated time to entertain. Flanked by his dogs Buffy and Chewie, Jackson Kincaid, adorned with a baby carrier and sleeping baby, sold raffle tickets, Natalie and her girls had set up a henna booth and their friend Shel had brought her bookstore on wheels and parked it near the food trucks. Clare, their new neighborhood florist, sold bouquets and gorgeous succulent wreaths. Connor was teaching kids how to make wooden boxcars and the firemen were there with one of their trucks, taking pictures of kids and families.

And everyone was donating their time and profits to the charity she'd established in her mom's name. It was amazing and almost too much to absorb. But she'd decided after her mom's death to live a brilliant life and so she calmed her racing heart and enjoyed the day with her beautiful fiancé and reminded herself how incredibly lucky she was.

As the evening sky started to darken, Ruby found herself at Ellie's booth with all the adoptable kittens and dogs. Katie was there with her sleepy youngest, while Leo and the two oldest girls spun themselves silly on the gravity-defying Starship ride. Sasha and her pup were taking a break from their pastry booth and Ellie and their friend Nate were down on the ground, surrounded by slobbering puppies.

Ruby had looked into the crate of kittens and fallen instantly in love, and she now cradled a tiny wisp of a thing to her chest. The runt of the litter was fluffy and white with a bit of gray and tan spots, and Ruby could feel the tiny bones through her fur. Her frantic heart beat against Ruby's hands. "Soft love, I've got you, baby," Ruby cooed to the warm kitten.

She felt Lachlan's presence before he spoke. "Are we talking babies this early in our relationship?" She turned and he was there, hands on his hips accentuating everything strong and glorious about his body. But it was his full smile that tilted to one side that had her grinning back. And there it was—her heart tipped right over again.

"She needs a home and I thought, we have a good home, and look, she's lonely." Ruby tucked her chin down and Lachlan fit himself against her, wrapping her up in his arms again so the kitten snuggled between them.

"Lonely, huh? We can't have that, can we."

"Sugar Baby needs a sister, and I think we're pretty good at taking care of kittens."

"So, a lifetime with you and a few fluff balls, huh?" He nudged his hips closer to hers. She was surrounded by strength and warmth, by a man showing her every day through tiny and sometimes grand actions how much he adored her.

Ruby smiled up at him. "Sounds pretty good, doesn't it?"

"Yeah, Ruby. It sounds fantastic."

And as twilight approached and the lights draped across the street kicked on, Lachlan kissed her. He was her stars and her moon, her beautiful promise of love.

Want to see more from this author? Here's a taster for you to enjoy!

Graciella: Handling the Rancher

Sara Ohlin

Excerpt

Cruz stood at the edge of the bluff above the Pacific. The ocean brooded, inky-dark and dangerous, while the wind whipped it onto the shore. He let the cadence of wild, crashing waves and gusting wind wash over him. He loved the water in its fierce and powerful nature as much as he loved it when it was calm and patient. Wide and open, the beach stretched on, completely untouched by footprints, secluded and vulnerable all at the same time.

He took one lasting breath of the misty sea air and headed towards his farm. *His farm.* He still had moments when he couldn't believe it.

Wispy slips of fog teased and lifted around Cruz, revealing the morning dew on the grass as he made his way up towards the main house of Brockman Farms. Mornings on the farm were his favorite, the way the new light barely stroked the land, how the hues of everything were rich in those few moments of soft sun and leftover darkness. The salty air mixed with the scent of damp earth as it rose up. Home—Cruz was finally home—a place most people took for granted.

He'd been back in Graciella for five weeks after more than a decade away. His relief on hearing that his father, T.D. Brockman, was finally dead had been such that he'd nearly wept like a baby when his brother Adam had called with the news.

Thank goodness no one had seen his near breakdown. And that it hadn't lasted long. He could finally breathe clear and easy here on this land he loved, knowing the monsters were gone. He aimed to do more than breathe easy, however. It was his time to take care of the farm and all the people who depended on it—and to put his stamp on something valuable.

As much as he liked helping out at the barns, this morning dictated that he make a dent on the estate paperwork and duties. That didn't mean he had to do it without a fresh cup of coffee. Cruz entered the main house through the back to grab a mug of their housekeeper Elena's rich espresso brew in the kitchen before he got to work.

Fueled by caffeine, he sat at T.D. Brockman's old desk, going through bank statements and employee schedules. Since he'd returned, the phone hadn't quit ringing with condolences for his father's death and calls from the press. He wasn't sure which group won the award for insincerity.

Who could blame them? T.D. Brockman had taken pleasure in his ruthless way of doing business. But he'd been a wealthy bastard, owning most of the commercial properties in downtown Graciella. And the farm was spread out over two hundred and fifty thousand acres, nestled between Oregon wine country and the prized breathtaking Pacific coast. Money was involved, and where money was involved, people were curious. What would happen now that he was dead? Everyone wanted to know.

The phone rang again. "Brockman Farms," Cruz answered, the words clipped at one more interruption.

"Mr. Brockman? This is Ms. Selby from the *Oregonian*."

Another reporter. "The family has no comment at this time."

"Please, Mr. Brockman—"

"No comment!" Cruz said through clenched teeth and slammed the receiver down. The only reason he'd left the damn thing plugged in was because there were legitimate calls from banks and people regarding T.D.'s investments that Cruz had to deal with as executor.

"You must be Cruz Brockman."

Cruz looked up at the musical voice. Normally he wouldn't have to force a smile for anyone, let alone for an elegant woman. "Hello," he said and tried to punch down his irritation. "Can I help you?"

"Do you ever wait to see who's on the other end or are you that rude to everyone on the phone?" she asked as she walked into the room. Her body language might have said cool and put-together, but the haughty tone in her voice gave away one serious, pissed-off attitude.

"Excuse me?" He pushed his chair back and stood. "This is my office and if I remember correctly, I smiled and said hello. Perhaps you'd like to start over—"

"Mr. Brockman," she snapped.

He locked his gaze with hers and came around from behind the desk. "I said, perhaps you'd like to start over." His tone was sharp, no longer concealing his frustration.

"I'm Miranda Jenks, the audit accountant. I've been trying to contact you for days to let you know when I'd be arriving, but your phone etiquette made that impossible. The times you actually picked up the phone, you hung up on me before I could say more than three words. I finally got hold of your lawyer. He should have mentioned I'd be here today."

Gorgeous and haughty, what a combination, like a goddess rising from the morning's crashing waves. The image, unbidden, teased through his temper. Cruz half-listened as he studied her. In her charcoal-gray suit and black high heels, with that tone of reprimand in her voice, she reminded him of his finance professor in college, who'd believed Cruz's choice of photojournalism a waste of time. That was where the similarities came to a screeching halt. His professor had been in her sixties, very short and very thick.

The woman in front of him certainly wasn't sixty, short or thick. In fact, she looked more like she could stand to eat a good meal or two. Contradictions surrounded her. Deep, confident and extremely sexy, her voice was like a rich port. It also vibrated with indignation. But the rest of her seemed guarded. Her long dark hair was pulled back and held in a simple ribbon at her neck. Tall and stiff, she did a good job of trying to pretend calm. Gaunt cheekbones shaped her face and dark circles rested under her eyes. Very green, very frustrated eyes. That expressive gaze and sultry voice were at odds with the rest of her controlled, veiled demeanor.

"Mr. Brockman?" Impatience sliced the woman's words.

"Accountant? Jake never mentioned you were coming today."

"Yes, I did, Cruz." Jake walked in. "Sorry I'm late, Ms. Jenks, I'm Jake Burns. We spoke on the phone."

"Nice to meet you, Mr. Burns."

Cruz watched her almost-smile at Jake and enjoyed the way her face warmed and softened a hint. *Wonder what she looks like when she really lets herself smile?*

"Cruz, good to see you." Jake smacked him on the shoulder. "Ms. Jenks, thanks for your patience. Cruz, Miranda Jenks—the accountant I told you would be auditing the books if we plan on settling this estate."

Cruz had a vague memory of the conversation. One of about five hundred he'd had about the estate since the funeral. "I apologize, Ms. Jenks," he said. "The phones have been on fire since T.D. died and I lost my patience with them days ago." He flashed her a grin in apology.

He held out his hand, and when she took it, his nerves sizzled. Every pulse point in his body awakened. He nearly tugged her closer so her entire body could touch his. She closed her eyes and quickly removed her hand, one that had trembled slightly in his and had such soft skin that he wanted to hold it again. She opened her briefcase to search through her paperwork.

"Excuse me, it seems my phone's busy today," Jake said. He took out his cell and walked into the hall.

"Ms. Jenks, thanks for coming all the way from...?" Cruz began.

"Houston."

"How was the trip?"

"The trip was fine. Shall we get to work? I'm certain none of us has any time to waste."

All business. Cruz sighed. From experience, he found accountants shallow and driven by money. But he needed one to handle the books. Cruz had lived most of his adult life traveling from one assignment to another, documenting the beauty and tragedy of the world, photographing and writing other people's stories. He had not been running a large company or settling estates, meaning he needed help to get things reconciled. Only then could he begin making lasting improvements and changes to Brockman Farms, fulfilling his dream of making this place something to be proud of.

"I'll need all the records your father kept. Bills paid, bills due, revenue, assets, expenses, wages, tax forms from the past few years, receipts, investments." She drew him out of his thoughts with her long list of demands.

Cruz looked around at the piles of paperwork covering the desk. "Most of it is here somewhere, but it's a mess at the moment, a mess I've been trying to sort through. Jake and I have some things to take care of. I know you've come a long way. How about if we begin in the morning? That will give me some time to get things more organized for you."

"Certainly."

Damn! The force of that word breathed at him like a dragon's fire. He could almost see the inner turmoil as she fought the need to roll her eyes at his incompetence. "But time isn't something you have a lot of, Mr. Brockman. I'm sure you're aware of that."

"I realize the importance of this, Ms. Jenks, but it's not exactly life or death now, is it?" He grinned at her again, trying to prod some emotion out of her. At the least he wished she'd relax. At the most he wanted to see her smile again. He liked the way it softened her face, gave her a bit of mystery, as though she was holding a special secret or two. He'd even take the fierce side of her—it showed her strength.

"That depends on how you feel about the IRS shutting you down for good."

"What the hell's that supposed to mean?" he demanded.

About the Author

Puget Sound based writer, Sara Ohlin is a mom, wannabe photographer, obsessive reader, ridiculous foodie, and the author of the contemporary romance novels, *Handling the Rancher, Salvaging Love, Seducing the Dragonfly, Igniting Love* and *Flirting with Forever.*

She has over sixteen years of creative non-fiction and memoir writing experience, and you can find her essays at Anderbo.com, Feminine Collective, Mothers Always Write, Her View from Home, and in anthologies such as Are We Feeling Better Yet? Women Speak about Healthcare in America, Take Care: Tales, Tips, & Love from Women Caregivers, and Chicken Soup for the Soul.

Sara loves creating imaginary worlds with tight-knit communities in her romance novels. She credits her mother, Mary, Nora Roberts and Rosamunde Pilcher for her love of romance.

If she's not reading or writing, you will most likely find her in the kitchen creating scrumptious meals with her kids and husband, or perhaps cooking up her next love story.

She once met a person who both "didn't read books" and wasn't "that into food" and it nearly broke her heart.

Sara loves to hear from readers. You can find her contact information, website details and author profile page at https://www.totallybound.com

TOTALLY
BOUND
Home of Erotic Romance

www.ingramcontent.com/pod-product-compliance
Lightning Source LLC
LaVergne TN
LVHW091031080826
845145LV00002B/441

* 9 7 8 1 8 3 9 4 3 7 5 3 3 *